Other Britt Montero Mysteries by
Edna Buchanan
from Avon Books

CONTENTS UNDER PRESSURE

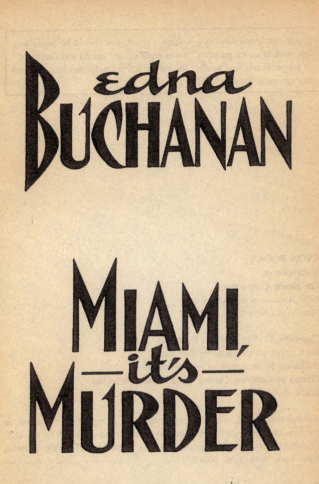

EDNA BUCHANAN

MIAMI, it's MURDER

AVON BOOKS ◆ NEW YORK

AVON BOOKS
A division of
The Hearst Corporation
1350 Avenue of the Americas
New York, New York 10019

First Avon Books Printing: February 1995

AVON TRADEMARK REG. U.S. PAT. OFF. AND IN OTHER COUNTRIES, MARCA REGISTRADA, HECHO EN CANADA

Printed in Canada

UNV 10 9 8 7 6 5

For Marilyn Lane, real friend, true sister

Acknowledgments

I am grateful to Dr. Charles Wetli, Dr. Steve Nelson, Dr. Roger Mittleman, Dr. Richard Souviron, Dr. Lee Hearn, and Dr. Joseph H. Davis, along with his colleagues Norman Kassoff and Veronica Melton; my creative and caring friends Marilyn and Ed Gadinsky, Ann and D. P. Hughes, Renee Turolla, Peggy Thornburgh, Pearl Thornburgh, Norma Thornburgh, and especially David M. Thornburgh. Thanks to Metro-Dade's best and brightest: Bud Stuver, Sergeant Christine Echroll, and Detective Rick Kology; and the city's finest: Major Mike Gonzalez, Sergeants Louise Vasquez and Jerry Green, Lieutenant Robert Murphy, and Officer Lori Nadelman. I am indebted to Dr. Bernard Elser, Rafael Martinez, M.A., M.S.Ed., and Dr. Julia Morton of the University of Miami for their expertise and their willingness to share it, and to Miami *Herald* star staffers Arnold Markowitz, Gene Miller, and Bill Rose and the *Herald* library crew, along with some of Miami's greatest natural resources: historian Dr. Paul George, photojournalist Bill Cooke, and Diane Montane of Exito. I also want to thank Mike Baxter, Otto Morales-Rubic, and the Rev. Dr. Garth Thompson, saviors of my hard drive and my sanity; my talented editor Leslie Wells of Hyperion; and Michael Congdon, my agent.

My life has such a wonderful cast of characters.

Nothing is covered up that will not be uncovered,
and nothing secret that will not become known.

—Luke 12:2, New Revised Standard Version

1

He was the man every woman dreams about—in her worst nightmares. By the first day of summer, he was stalking the city, a serial rapist attacking women in the rest rooms of downtown office buildings. He appeared and disappeared like a wraith, seen only by his terrified victims, six so far.

It was another crazy Miami summer. The B.O. Bandit, a bank robber with a distinctively bad body odor, was on a bank-a-day binge, apparently not even pausing long enough to shower. Police and frustrated FBI agents seemed unable to sniff him out. A city commissioner who solicited sex from an undercover policeman claimed to arresting officers that he was merely researching social problems. A ravenous forty-pound piranha was discovered circling expectantly in the pool of a beachfront hotel. Then snow fell from the sky (it plummets from airplanes in Miami)—half a ton of cocaine crashed through the roof of a Baptist church, jettisoned by the crew of a Cessna 310 under hot pursuit by U.S. Customs aircraft. And when Miami Beach bungee jumpers were buzzed by the crew of a police chopper, they filed complaints with internal affairs and the FAA.

Something about our sultry summers and their madness energizes me. I need less sleep, and I wake earlier from technicolor dreams to greet spectacular dawns with no need of an alarm clock. That's good, because summer accelerates the action on my beat, which is always busy.

I had nearly finished the story about the grounded copter crew when the newsroom police desk reported an apparent drowning on one of the Beach islands. I snatched up a notebook and my purse, eager for any excuse to escape the office. Gretchen Platt, the assistant city editor from hell, was in the slot today and had been hovering like a foreboding presence over my desk.

"I better get out there and find out what happened," I told Gretchen.

"A drowning, Britt?" She wrinkled her classic nose. Gretchen likes to avoid publishing negative news. Somebody might be offended. Somebody important. Like the Chamber of Commerce, the Downtown Development Association, or the Tourist Development Authority. Blond, beautiful, and dressed for the boardroom, she is the image of success, the hard-driving young executive plugged into the pipeline to power. The truth is she would not recognize a good story if it bit her on the ankle. Her idea of news is a puff piece promoting some local organization or cultural event.

"It's in an exclusive neighborhood," I offered, "on one of the residential islands. You never know who it might be, and it's just a few minutes away. It may be foul play. Doesn't hurt to check it out."

"Well, come right back," she said doubtfully. "I may have an assignment for you."

That worried me. Far better to plow my fertile beat and generate my own stories than leave myself open to Gretchen's whims and brainstorms.

I backed toward the elevator trying to tune out her

instructions and admonitions, nodding my head all the while like one of those little doggies in the back window of a car.

It was always a relief to break out of that huge building with its meat-locker temperatures and career into the afternoon air, even when the temperature was a muggy 96 degrees and the air conditioner in my six-year-old T-Bird was balky. The wet blanket of soft air warmed my chilled bones. I drove east across the Venetian Causeway, where purple bougainvillea and Mexican flame vines compete in a race to see which can be more spectacular. They hugged stone walls and railings beneath royal poinciana trees in brilliant scarlet bloom.

The narrow span linked a chain of man-made residential islands with romantic Italian names: San Marco, San Marino, Dilido, and Rivo Alto. Passing the sign that said Dilido I did a double take, winced, and shook my head. Some sicko with a can of spray paint had again blacked out the second *i*.

Red warning lights flashed and the alarm bell sounded as I approached the east drawbridge, so I floored it, roaring across with just a few feet to spare. I watched in my rearview mirror as narrow wooden barricades descended behind me and the bridge opened for a tall-masted schooner luffing between the channel markers on the south side of the bridge. These graceful sailboats skimming so silently across the water waste more gasoline than powerboats. Eight hundred cars are left to idle and overheat, waiting at a drawbridge opened to accommodate a single vessel.

The police scanner in my car spit out an exchange on the Beach frequency. The homicide detective at the scene changed the call from a drowning to a possible electrocution. He asked for the medical examiner's ETA (estimated time of arrival), and dispatch replied that the ME was en route. Interesting, I thought, turning left onto Sunset Island. My pulse quickened in recognition. I had chased a story here before. Could it be? Yes! The same house. Two blue-and-whites out front, one leaving. Rescue already gone. The electronically operated iron security gates stood open in a vacant yawn. No yellow rope, no crowd to be controlled. This was not that kind of neighborhood. Homes here are walled or fenced in by wrought iron. Most owners leave town for the summer. Those who do not would not step out into the afternoon heat to see World War III, much less a single dead body. A familiar Chrysler closed in behind me, driven by a woman with frizzy red hair. Lottie Dane had apparently overheard the radio report and had also swung by to check it out.

"You know who lives here?" I greeted her.

She shook her head. A Nikon 8008 with a long lens was slung over her right shoulder. The pockets of her loose khaki vest were stuffed with protruding orange and black film canisters.

"Dieter Steiner!" I said. "I came out here once to try to interview him before he got indicted for murdering his third wife. He wouldn't open the gate and threatened to call my editors—and the police," I said.

Bad things had happened to the brides of Dieter Steiner. Though not quite Bluebeard, the man was off to a good start. He had lost his first wife while scuba diving. He climbed into the boat, he said, turned, and she was gone. Her body surfaced later. No one suspected anything at the time. Accidents happen. Wife number two had apparently shifted her car into drive instead of reverse and accelerated while attempting to back out of a space on the sixth floor of a multistory downtown parking garage. Her Mercedes convertible shot forward, crashed the barrier, and plummeted to the pavement below, also killing an elderly pedestrian waiting for a bus. Another tragic accident.

"The self-made widower?" she said.

"Yup."

"I'll be go-to-helled." We stared at each other.

"Doesn't mean it's him," I said. "Could be a new gal pal, a workman, or his gardener, or his—"

A Miami Beach detective named Greg Wallace came strolling toward us from around the back of the house. He was hot, sweaty—and grinning.

"It *is* Steiner!" I said. "Look at that cop's face."

"Hell-all-Friday," Lottie said and checked her camera.

"Where is he?" I asked the detective.

"You already heard?" He jerked his head toward the back of the house and led us along a stamped concrete walkway that angled around the lushly landscaped side of the building.

Dieter Steiner lay on his back on the wooden dock, a quickly drying puddle surrounding his sodden sunbronzed body. His arrogance was gone. So was the shiny gleam of his single gold earring, clouded by salt water. Scattered nearby were rubber gloves and sticky peels off the backs of EKG pads, discarded by paramedics who had tried to revive him. He wore multicolor shorts and no shirt. His fists were clenched, his mouth foam-flecked. His fly was open.

We stood silent for a moment. The incoming tide made slapping, sucking sounds beneath the dock. "Hard to see what all those women saw in him," Lottie finally said.

Police had received the call via ship-to-shore radio telephone. A family on an outing aboard their twenty-four-foot Bertram had seen Steiner urinating off his dock into the bay. Moments later they heard him cry out, then plunge into the water.

"Neighbors say he made it a habit," Greg said.

"What?" I asked, taking notes.

"Exposing himself, using the bay for a bathroom. He usually did it in front of boaters. Especially if women were aboard. Maybe he was objecting to their wakes or trying to tell 'em they were coming too close."

"Or maybe he was just a jerk," I said.

"One less to worry about," he answered.

"What happened?" I asked the detective. "Was he under the influence? Or do you think he just got dizzy and fell?"

"That's what we thought at first," he said, mopping his brow with a handkerchief. "But the people on the boat saw him fall, circled, came back, fished him out, and tried CPR. No dice. I think I know why."

He looked significantly at a Budweiser Beer sign mounted on the dock.

"I think it was electricity. Ain't that something? The state didn't have to do it. He zapped himself."

"But how?"

"The ME will say for sure, but both the folks trying to revive him and one of the medics got zinged when they touched that pole." He indicated one of four supporting a striped canvas awning over the dock. The innocent-looking pole suddenly beckoned, as alluring as a wall wearing a wet paint sign. "Don't touch it," he warned.

"Why would it kill him and not them?"

"He was holding on to the pole that light's wired to—took a whiz in the water and got zapped."

I winced, wondering why men have the immediate urge to unzip and urinate whenever they see a large body of water. A surprising percentage of Miami's male drowning victims are fished out fully dressed, their pants open.

Lottie wondered the same thing. "Greg?" she asked. "Why do you guys always do that?"

"What?" Sweat banded his collar and ringed his armpits. He was printing carefully into the spaces on a report attached to his clipboard.

"You know, into the ocean and the bay, canals and pools?"

He looked irritated, stopped writing, and tugged at his collar with one finger. "Hell, I don't know." He shrugged. "Because it's there, I guess."

"They throw beer cans and pee into the water— 'cause it's there?" repeated Lottie.

"It must be territorial," I said, shaking my head. "Like dogs lifting their legs to mark trees and fire hydrants."

Greg looked exasperated. "Hey, it's just that most guys are beer drinkers and ready to take a leak anytime the opportunity presents itself."

"It's probably a latent desire to show their wienie anytime the opportunity presents itself," Lottie declared.

"Baloney! It's just one of those things." Greg's voice was rising. "God's will."

"Poetic justice, if nothing else," I said soothingly. "Especially if he was electrocuted. He was sentenced to the chair. The governor came this close to signing his death warrant before Steiner won his new trial. He's been living well." I turned, assessing the expansive pool patio area and the rambling two-story house, with big picture windows and a second-floor terrace bordered by ornate wrought-iron railings.

"Nice place," the detective agreed, "but he scrimped on the wiring. That was his mistake. Shoulda had it done right, by a pro. Don't touch a thing, okay?" He walked back out toward the front of the house to greet Dr. Vernon Duffy, one of Dade County's associate medical examiners.

Dr. Duffy, a New Hampshire transplant, looked wilted in the steamy heat. He carried his equipment in a foam-lined aluminum camera case. A voltmeter was tucked in an inside pocket, the electrodes dangling below the hem of his shapeless sports jacket. He reminded me of a nerdy high school friend of mine, now a NASA scientist. Slightly stooped and pale, Duffy spends too much time in the morgue. He nodded perfunctorily to me and Lottie, as though expecting us to be there, then glanced toward the body.

"Is that who I hear it is?"

"Was him," Greg said. "Guess his winning streak couldn't last forever."

"They never do," Duffy said, taking out the voltmeter.

"Won't be no tears shed over at City of Miami homicide," Greg said. "Or the state attorney's office. It really pissed them off when he walked."

Duffy stooped to touch the voltmeter's positive red probe to the base of the galvanized pole and dropped the negative black probe into the bay water. The needle swung to 120 volts. The beer sign, the type usually displayed in bars and cocktail lounges, was lit by a fluorescent bulb and hung from the metal support structure by two rusted metal brackets.

"Neither that light nor the box with the outlet is meant for outdoor use," he said, his eyes trailing the extension cord to a utility shed near the dock. "Didn't even have the wire grounded. Why would he use a sloppy hookup like that?"

"Lazy," Greg said. "Or just dumb. Look at that." There was a newer outlet, a three-prong that would have accommodated the ground wire, just a few feet away, near the davits for Steiner's boat, a high-powered blue-and-white eighteen-foot Custom Craft with PHOTOG painted on the prow. "He shoulda disconnected that old line."

"Looks like he touched the energized pole and grounded through the urine stream. The path of electricity went from his arm to his penis. I recall a similar case in Chicago," Duffy said, examining Steiner's feet, lifting one, then the other. He straightened up. "A man was electrocuted when he urinated onto the third rail in the subway system: knocked him right off the platform."

Greg nodded, his expression softened into one of fond reminiscence. "Yeah, when I was little, we talked another kid into peeing into a running lawn mower. The electricity went right up the stream of urine and knocked him on his ass."

I took a deep breath and stared at Lottie, who crossed her eyes.

As I turned to go back to the paper and write my story for the state edition, Lottie was shooting a picture of Steiner still flat on his back, gazing into the sun. "What's that for?" I muttered. "You know they'll never put a picture of an uncovered corpse in the morning paper."

She cut her eyes at me. "For your friend Danny Boy. Thought he'd like a last look at Steiner."

She was probably right. That's Lottie, always thoughtful.

Detective Daniel P. Flood had arrested Steiner and proved the man had murdered his wife. I covered the story from start to finish. Dan's strong case convicted Steiner and sent him to Death Row—but could not keep him there. The defense had won a new trial based on the judge's flawed charges to the jury, and the second time around was a no-go: witnesses had died, disappeared, become amnesiacs or oddly reticent. The defendant had walked away a free man.

It was unusual to leave a sudden death scene where there were no tears. Everybody seemed almost cheerful, I thought, unlocking the T-Bird. Then another player arrived, parking her open green Jaguar convertible on the swale. The young woman adjusted her sunglasses and frowned at the patrol car, the detective's unmarked, and the medical examiner's vehicle blocking the driveway. She wore white tennis shorts with a matching pullover. Her legs were long and tanned.

She paused, staring at me, her expression puzzled, and glanced toward the back of the house where slanted sunlight shimmered off the glowing green foliage.

"Where's Dieter?" She studied me curiously.

"Are you a friend?" I asked quietly. "Something's happened."

Her eyes strayed over my shoulder.

"Don't go back there," I warned.

"Why, what's going on?" She turned to look at me for a moment and didn't like what she saw. A shadow crept into her widening eyes.

I stepped in front of her, reaching for her arm. "An accident. You mustn't go . . ."

She eluded me and broke into a run, loping around the shaded side of the house.

"Wait!" But she didn't hear me. She had already rounded the corner, was in sight of the dock, and had begun a high-pitched cry that rose and fell with her footfalls.

"No-o-o-o!"

I followed. The detective caught her wrists, speaking in a low voice, trying to step between her and the body, but her knees buckled and she was falling.

"We're getting married!" she screamed, struggling. "He can't be dead. What are you saying? What do you mean?" As I left she was sobbing, fists clenched and begging. "Why is he lying there? Don't let him just lie there!"

When brokenhearted people weep, I am often moved to join them. I fought the urge as I drove back to the office, telling myself that this young woman was actually lucky. She would always remember Steiner as a tragic lost love, never knowing that in this case having what she wanted would probably have been far more tragic for her.

I had been brand new on the beat when Eloise Steiner was found in a wooded glade just outside a city park. The cops had not yet taken me seriously, and the favorite sport of some was trying to gross out the new female police reporter. Instead of shunning me as usual, Dan and his partner had invited me to view the body. Surprised at my good fortune—reporters hate being restrained behind yellow crime-scene tape—I dutifully followed them down a brushy path overrun by brambles and weeds. The sight in that dark place in the woods was one I will never forget. The cops expected weakness. They saw none. I remained coolly professional, or at least generated that impression, exhibiting only a clinical curiosity. The pretense was not easy. The corpse had been there for three days, in midsummer, and Eloise Steiner had been nine months pregnant.

When the news broke, Steiner called the cops to report that the still unidentified body could be his wife of less than a year. He had last seen her at about 10 A.M. the prior Saturday, when she drove off to shop a garage sale. She had promised to return by 2 P.M., he said, but she did not come home, then or ever.

Detectives never got to ask why he had neglected to report her missing. By the time they arrived at his big bayfront home, Steiner's attorney was at his side. He had declined to speak to police or submit to a polygraph.

Back at my desk, I called the library for the clips on Steiner. Onnie didn't wait for a copyboy to deliver them, she brought them out herself. "So the good Lord caught up with him," she said.

"Sure looks like it. How's Darryl?"

"Excited about first grade." A wide smile creased her face, the color of burnt toast. "He can't wait to go."

"Give him a hug," I said, and punched the password into my computer terminal. I watched Onnie hurry back to the library. A former battered wife who had escaped the situation, she was now a single mother on her own. The job I had recommended her for was working out, she had put on some weight and a little makeup, and looked good. It never hurts a reporter to have a good friend in the library, especially on deadline.

I reached for the phone and dialed Dan Flood at home. He answered on the second ring.

"Hi, Danny, it's Britt. You won't believe the story I'm working on. Guess who got killed this afternoon?"

"Well, let's see, I hear Dieter Steiner got pissed off."

"Who told you?" I yelped, annoyed. "How come you always know everything first?"

"Your friend and mine, Ken McDonald, our favorite lieutenant, called to break the news that Steiner is off the map." At McDonald's name my stomach spasmed, as usual. Would that ache ever go away? I wondered.

"Looks like there's some justice after all," I said.

"Maybe there is," Dan replied.

"Now I need a quote from the veteran homicide detective who sent Steiner to Death Row. What's your comment?"

"It was quite a shock," he said, chuckling.

"Seriously."

"Okay, okay." I could hear Dan breathing for several moments as he paused to think. "He faces a higher court now," he said solemnly. "Sometimes justice triumphs after all."

The first two Mrs. Steiners had died three years apart. Both were young, attractive, and well insured. Both had been cremated. No chance for second looks in their cases, but Dan had done a superb investigation into the death of Eloise, wife number three.

"Good," I said, tapping Dan's words onto the screen in front of me. "Anything else?"

"Off the record? He got what he deserved. He shoulda fried a long time ago. Nobody will miss that son of a bitch."

"One person will. Everybody's got somebody, even Steiner. His fiancée showed up. A pretty girl in a

Jaguar. They were planning the wedding. She's taking it hard."

He sniffed. "Fate did her a favor, probably saved her life."

"She'll never believe it." I sipped from the Styrofoam cup of *café con leche* I had brought back to my desk. "You know how love is."

"Yeah." His tone changed to a more familiar one. "You know, I was expecting your call, kid. After all these years, I know exactly how you operate."

"You should know my MO by now, Pops. How are you anyway?"

"Lousy. When I roll out of bed in the morning it sounds like somebody making popcorn. Everything's breaking down. I'm dying, but we all are, every day."

"Quit complaining, you sound good to me," I said fondly. "You have to listen to your doctors, do what they tell you, and take care of yourself."

"Sure. Let's have coffee, Britt, or lunch sometime next week."

"You bet," I said, working on my lead.

It read:

A man who escaped death in Florida's electric chair due to a legal technicality was apparently electrocuted in a freak accident at his luxurious Miami Beach home Wednesday.

I sat next to Bobby Tubbs, the assistant city editor in the slot, while he edited the story. Then I hovered around the city desk until the copy editor wrote the headline. I like to make sure there are no slipups and the head actually has something to do with the story. It did.

MURDER SUSPECT ELECTROCUTED AT HIS BEACH

HOME, in 55-point Bodoni. By Britt Montero, *Miami Daily News Staff Writer*. That's me.

I returned to my desk, picked up the sheaf of telephone messages, and riffled through them. Two were from my mother.

As I reached for the phone, I became suddenly aware of a figure looming behind me. Eduardo de la Torre, the tall elegantly garbed society editor, stood poised at my elbow as though posing for *GQ*. I knew what he wanted. Despite his breeding and genteel manners, he is always voraciously eager for all the details of death, disaster, scandal, and crime in the elite circle he writes about. The more lurid the better.

"Like to join me for a cup of coffee?"

"I've got some." I lifted my cup. "You never told me you and Dieter Steiner were friends."

He shifted his shoulders uneasily and showed me his aristocratic profile. His family tree boasts Spanish nobility, and he never lets anyone forget it. "Why do you say that? He's no friend. It's just that you and I haven't traded stories in a while."

"Come on, Eduardo, the only time you invite me for coffee is when one of your social register people is in trouble—robbed, indicted, or dead."

"Then it's true?" he breathed, raising an arched eyebrow.

The story would appear in half a million newspapers in the morning, but his almost prurient interest always makes me perversely reluctant to share details. He just seems to enjoy them too much. However, Eduardo can often be a good source for information and unlisted home telephone numbers when his socialites forget their manners and come to the attention of the police reporter.

"Is what true?"

"Steiner. Is he dead?"

"I didn't know he was in the Black Book."

"You mean the Social Register. Muffy, his fiancée, is in: one of the Palm Beach Benedicts," Eduardo said chattily, ticking off names on his immaculately manicured fingers. "And Eloise was. And so was he, during the year or so they were married. He was out, of course, once they arrested him for her murder."

"Naturally. Well, he's out for good this time. He's dead."

"Who?" chimed in Ryan Battle, the general assignment reporter who sits behind me. "Who's dead, the B.O. Bandit? Did you hear that local banks are buying canaries? When the canary dies they know the bandit is in the neighborhood."

I stared at him balefully. The frustrated cops hunting the bandit weren't laughing.

"No, not him," Eduardo said eagerly. "It's Dieter Steiner, the German photographer, the one whose wives kept dying."

"What happened?" Ryan got up from his desk and drifted over to mine.

"Yes, what happened?" Eduardo echoed.

I told them, briefly.

"Did you actually see the body?" Eduardo's eyes gleamed like black marbles. "What was he wearing?"

"Not much," I said truthfully, then told them Lottie had pictures. They trotted off to the darkroom together to peer over her shoulder. It was a dirty trick and I knew Lottie would hate me for it, but it gave me my chance to escape.

I punched the elevator button and rode alone to the lobby, neither sad nor glad that Dieter Steiner was dead. Mostly I felt a sense of closure, as if fate had somehow taken its natural course.

That is what I love most about this job—it is a front-row seat on life. The law could not touch Steiner, but something beyond it did. I thought of Eloise, the two women before her, and Daniel Flood at home. He would probably sleep better. The best revenge, I thought, is just living.

Lottie met me downstairs in the parking lot ten minutes later and we drove over to La Esquina de Tejas for *media noches*—midnight sandwiches—with ham, pork, Swiss cheese, mustard, and pickles stacked on sweet rolls. We ate them at a table covered by a plastic tablecloth and paper place mats bearing the map of Florida.

"Thank you very much for sending the Bobbsey Twins back to the darkroom," Lottie griped, dousing her side of black beans and rice with hot pepper sauce. A Texan, she is addicted to liberal doses of Tabasco on everything, including her breakfast oatmeal.

"Knew you'd appreciate them," I said. "Sorry."

"Think Steiner woulda married that poor new woman?"

"If he did, Dan's sure she would have been found downside up in a ditch."

"What did he say about Steiner finally getting what he deserved?"

I mimicked Dan's low-pitched growl. "He said, 'Hell, Steiner was just a blade of grass in the whole yard. He ain't the only one. His ain't the worst case by far.' "

"What is the worst?" Lottie patted her lips primly with a napkin and leaned across the table, dark eyes intent.

I thought about it for a moment. We both knew how Dan obsessed about old cases, the "unsolved" murders in which he knew the killer but could never build a prosecutable case. Justice gone awry was his favorite topic of conversation.

"Mary Beth Rafferty, I guess."

Lottie watched expectantly as I stirred the Cuban coffee that would probably keep me wired till dawn.

"Mary Beth Rafferty is an old case, a big one," I explained. "From long before you came to Miami. I was just a kid, ten or eleven when it happened. But I remember it." I sipped the coffee, then rested the cup on its tiny saucer. "My mother would not let me out of her sight for months. That murder struck fear into the entire city. You have to remember, Miami was like a small town at the time. Mary Beth was a little girl, abducted, sexually molested, and murdered."

Lottie did an exaggerated shiver. "Unsolved?"

"Technically. Nobody was ever charged, but the police always had a suspect, and you will never guess who."

Lottie's eyes widened. "Somebody I would know?"

I nodded. "Eric Fielding."

"You're kidding. The politician? Our wanna-be governor? I've made the man's picture a half dozen times." She put down her fork. "Tell me."

I began the story. "This was twenty-two years ago. Little girl named Mary Beth, eight years old, out playing three o'clock in the afternoon, just down the street from her house, in the Roads section. Guy snatches her and drags her off into the woods. Her little playmate runs home, too scared to tell anybody for a while. Not long after the alarm goes out, a seventeen-year-old kid on a bike finds her nude body on a canal bank. The seventeen-year-old kid? Eric Fielding."

"And you think he did it?"

"Dan's convinced he's the doer. For sure. Never was another suspect, from what I understand. The kid had a history of window peeping, and he came along just too conveniently."

Lottie looked solemn. "The person who reports finding a body often turns out to be the person who put it there."

"You've got it," I said. "They like the recognition, being the center of attention. Some even think it ensures that they won't become a suspect, as if the cops were that stupid."

"Why didn't they arrest him?"

"Wanted to but never had enough."

"No witnesses?"

"Only the playmate, a little boy who'd been hit and nearly killed by a car once, left with a bad limp. He was with her when she was snatched by the killer, but his mother freaked and wouldn't let cops near him. She was overprotective to begin with, I guess, and scared as hell. Not surprising. The Fielding family was loaded, big bucks and political clout even then. When Dan and his partners pushed, they got cease-and-desist calls from the city manager and the mayor, suggesting they look someplace else for the killer." I leaned forward. "Dan says our would-be gov did that little girl as sure as the sun will rise tomorrow. I've never known him to be wrong."

Lottie absently chewed her sandwich. "If they were so sure the little boy could have identified Fielding as the one who snatched Mary Beth, couldn't Dan have forced his mother into letting the boy talk to them and have a look at a lineup?"

"She was a working woman, a single mother bringing up her only child alone. He would have pointed a finger at the son of a rich influential family. What would you do? It must have scared the bejesus out of her. And look at Fielding since, graduated from Harvard Law School, elected to the city commission twice, and now front-runner for governor."

"Knowing Dan, it must make him as mad as a red-assed dog," Lottie said. "Something ought to be done. I can't believe we may elect a governor who got away with murder."

"He'll fit right in with all our other elected public officials," I said glumly.

"I'm serious. Somebody, maybe a good reporter," she said, cutting her eyes at me, "oughta take another shot at it."

"Oh, sure," I said. "The cops can't nail it down for twenty-two years, and you think a reporter is gonna prove he's a killer now, before election day?"

"Wouldn't hurt none to try," she said. "Sometimes old secrets tend to ripen, and all you have to do to have 'em fall into your lap is shake the tree one more time."

Maybe it wouldn't hurt to shake the tree, I thought. That's the wonderful thing about Lottie. She believes nothing is impossible.

"Dan was one of the best detectives the city had," I said mournfully, as we drove back to her car, still parked at the paper. "And they forced him out."

"How can they do that?"

"Legally, they can't force a terminally ill cop to re-tire. But they do it anyway. The brass said it was too risky for him to keep working homicide. They said it could be hazardous to his health, because of his heart."

"The job's probably all that's been keeping him alive."

"Exactly." Dan's wife of thirty-four years had died suddenly, collapsing on the street, of an aneurysm. Six months earlier their only daughter, a Marine, had been among those killed by a direct SCUD missile hit on a barracks in Saudi Arabia during the Gulf War. The run of bad luck came full circle when Dan's previously undetected heart condition flared. "It was all he had left. We can relate to that."

"Tell me about it," she said. "When's the last time I had a date that didn't get screwed up by the job? When's the last time you had any kind of date?"

Kendall McDonald, Dan's former partner, and I had been romantically entangled for a short sweet time, until ethics and our jobs conflicted and he succumbed to ambition. The breakup had worked for him; he made lieutenant. I ignored Lottie's comments on my love life, or lack of same.

"It was a real bummer," I said. "They transferred Dan to a desk job, processing reports, shuffling papers. When that didn't work, they assigned him to the front desk, in the lobby, in uniform." We stopped at a light and I turned to her. "Can you believe that? Here is a guy who hadn't worn a uniform in decades, a detective proud of his homicide closure rate, reduced to the job they usually give to screwups or handicapped cops."

"Riding a desk."

"Right, meeting and greeting every irate citizen, mental case, and weirdo who wandered in off the street. That did it. After two days he put in his papers and retired."

"He survives the war on crime and gets stabbed in the back by his own." Lottie sighed and shook her head. "If not for bad luck, he'd have no luck at all."

"I know." I sighed too. "I even had fantasies about adopting him."

"What?"

"I conveniently managed to cross his path when I was out with my mother—and introduced them, hoping they would hit it off."

"What happened?"

"Nothing. So I asked him to lecture the residents at her condo about security; they'd had some burglaries. Nothing. I guess my matchmaking for her is about as successful as hers is for me."

"Poor baby," said Lottie. "You want a daddy."

I grew up without a father. Mine died trying to free his native Cuba. I was three when he was executed by a Castro firing squad. "You could have worse people than Dan in the family," I said.

My dashboard police scanner crackled with routine calls as we rode through the silent streets, me thinking about Dan. In a career that spanned thirty-five years of Miami's evolution from quaint southern resort to Miami, the exotic international capital as well known for violence as for its palm trees and beaches, it was only natural for some cases to go unsolved. But homicide detectives always hope. First-degree murder has no statute of limitations.

Dan's career was longer than most cops'. But now it had ended, and he was leaving behind cases that no other Miami homicide detective would even remember, much less pursue. The victims were forgotten, except by a few loved ones—and Daniel P. Flood. Dan was the last link to these murder victims, and unless his doctors were mistaken, he would soon join them.

2

I woke up earlier than usual, thinking about the Mary Beth Rafferty case and what Lottie had said. I spooned cat food into Billy Boots's dish, ignored Bitsy's wagging tail, and popped her into the tub. Soaked and soaped up, she looked more like an oversized rat than a toy poodle. But she endured the shower spray and the brushing and combing with patient good humor. I never wanted a yappy little dog, but I had inherited Bitsy after the sudden death of her owner, who was killed in the line of duty. Ducking the dog's vigorous shaking, I wrapped her in a bath towel, carried her to the kitchen, and fed her breakfast. When she finished I got the leash and took her for a run to dry off.

Carefully skirting puddles and dirty gutters, we jogged slowly to the boardwalk and back. Very slowly. Bitsy's legs are short. By the time I picked her up to carry her the last block, she was all fluffy white and panting for a drink.

After I showered, slipped on a subdued dress, and fortified myself with strong Cuban coffee, I tied a red ribbon in her topknot the way Francie always did and drove her to Miami police headquarters. This was Bitsy's first trip back to the station, but she remembered, growing eager as we climbed out of the T-Bird. She even tried to scamper into the front seat of the first patrol car we passed. I tugged at her leash as the officer quickly closed his door.

"Sorry," I said. "She thinks she's still a police dog."

The ceremony hadn't started yet, and people were still milling about the cavernous lobby. I worried that someone might object to my bringing Bitsy to this solemn occasion, but instead I got several sad nods from patrolmen. We stood off to one side, watching. The chief and his staff appeared in full dress uniform with gold braid. I spotted Dan then, caught his eye, and smiled. He made his way across the lobby and stood next to me.

"Hey, there, you look great, kid."

"So do you, Dan." We both knew that was a lie. The man had changed so much that seeing him was almost painful. He looked shrunken and suddenly aged. In twelve months, thirty pounds had melted from a frame that had been strong, beefy, and vital.

There were other officers and detectives and a number of civilians, some I knew from covering too many police funerals. This time I took no notes. We were there to pay our respects.

An honor guard marched in smartly, carrying the stars and stripes and the flags of Florida and Miami. The chief stepped to the microphone.

"We have gathered here on this police memorial day to honor fallen heroes, men—and women—who made the supreme sacrifice to protect and preserve the lives and well-being of the citizens of this city." The feedback from the mike made his voice echo in the huge lobby. "Especially the new names engraved on this memorial since we last met here."

I studied Dan's creased face as he stared straight ahead. He closed his eyes, head down, lips moving silently. His name was not among those we honored, but he had given his life as well. The job has killed him too, I thought.

The chief strode forward and placed a wreath of spring flowers, carnations, lilies, and daisies, in front of the memorial, a huge twenty-by-twelve-foot stainless steel plaque. Thirty-two names, officers who died in the line of duty, and the dates of their deaths were engraved in the shining reflective surface.

On cue, a dispatcher began the roll call of dead heroes. Each name was broadcast as if in Surround Sound via the police radios worn by all the officers present.

A small boy wearing a tiny police uniform snapped to a salute. The elderly couple with him wiped away tears. The faded-looking man rested one arthritic hand on the little boy's shoulder and reached his other arm around the woman to comfort her. I remembered their handsome, husky son, the little boy's dad, a motorcycle patrolman. I tried not to look at the child.

When the dispatcher called Francie's name, Bitsy's ears perked. She strained at her leash, prancing in place, and began to bark excitedly. When I picked her up, she uttered a high-pitched whine as if in pain. I hid my face in her soft fur and carried her outside.

We waited until the seven-man honor guard marched out to the front of the station. The sergeant ordered them to present arms. The trumpeter played taps and the honor guard fired three volleys, a twenty-one-gun salute. Bitsy never flinched, but I did.

Dan came up beside me. "I knew so many of them." He shook his head. "All those good cops, gone. For what? Murderers laugh at the system. They get away with it. You know the one who killed Foster in that

Overtown ambush has already been paroled?"

I didn't know.

"And the scum who shot Francie during the riot has never been caught," he muttered. He patted Bitsy's head awkwardly, like a man unaccustomed to touching such a small dog.

"You're a survivor too, little one."

I shifted Bitsy to my left arm, dug in my pocket for a Kleenex, and blew my nose.

We made a date for lunch on my next day off and I drove Bitsy home. She crouched as usual on the passenger-side floorboard. Poor Bitsy, I thought. She and Billy Boots tolerated one another, but her new lifestyle must seem dull. Our only drama and excitement came at mealtimes, as I tried to keep the cat away from the dog food and restrain the dog from diving into the cat's dinner.

My wonderful landlady, Helen Goldstein, takes Bitsy out frequently and fusses over her until I come home. The dog does not lack attention, but no way could her current life compare to the excitement of being smuggled into a patrol car at midnight with her policewoman owner and being involved in high-speed chases and transporting prisoners to jail until dawn. No wonder Bitsy yawned and looked bored. We both missed Francie. Dan was right. There is no justice, I thought. I dropped the dog off at home and went to work.

On the way to the office I thought about what Dan had said, and Lottie the night before. I thought about Mary Beth Rafferty. I made some telephone checks. My beat seemed quiet, and I told the city desk I was working on a weekender about the Downtown Rapist.

Then I sent to the library for the clips on the Rafferty case.

The newspaper library was still called the morgue when Mary Beth Rafferty was killed. Every story was clipped and filed by hand, hard copies with the headlines and photos still attached. Yellowed but intact, they are neatly folded into bulging pastel-colored envelopes. Sometimes other reporters neglect to refile them properly and they are difficult to find, but the old clippings are easier to read than today's endless gray computer printouts. Those were simpler times at the newspaper, before computerization, and simpler times for Miami. Murder was not yet common, and a case like Mary Beth Rafferty's commanded front-page coverage for weeks.

The same photo accompanied most of the stories. Mary Beth was dressed as if for Easter Sunday. Her nose was small and turned up, and she had Shirley Temple curls under a narrow brimmed bonnet that tied in a bow beneath her chin. She was eight years old.

She was naked when found, a cloth stuffed in her mouth. Some stories said she had been sexually molested, others implied she had been sexually mutilated. Her body bore signs of a struggle with her killer. Stories by two long-gone reporters disclosed that police had immediately rounded up more than two dozen known "sex perverts and suspicious characters." Within days they had questioned two hundred men.

There was minor mention of the playmate with her that afternoon. Frightened, he had gone home after Mary Beth was snatched. When the girl's mother began looking for her, he said a stranger had taken her.

The stories reported that the body had been discovered by a teenage boy, Eric Fielding, son of a prominent family and a student at prestigious Bayside Academy.

Months after the murder, Mary Beth's father, an insurance salesman, had offered a $10,000 reward for the arrest and conviction of his little girl's killer. "Nothing has happened on the case in three months," William Rafferty was quoted as saying. "The police claim they're still working on it, but I think they've dumped it into their dead files. The monster who did this terrible thing has got to be caught."

Detective Daniel P. Flood had responded to the father's allegation of inaction. "We are actively investigating," he was quoted as saying. "This case is not forgotten, and it won't be until it's solved."

He meant it, I thought, feeling a rush of affection for the man and wondering if anybody else on the department still remembered little Mary Beth.

William and Judith Rafferty were not in the current telephone book. Their address at the time of the murder was now given in the city directory as that of a Ronald DeAngelo, phone unlisted.

I knew I should be working on the rape story for the weekend, but I decided to drive over there and see what I could find out before other news stories broke and I missed my chance.

The Roads section was a graceful neighborhood of ancient trees and sprawling houses. A shaded flagstone walk led up to an old-fashioned screened porch.

An attractive dark-haired woman answered the door. Fashionably dressed and made up, she was one of those women of indeterminable age, anywhere from thirty-five to fifty-five. She wore a linen dress in cool pastel blue and was fastening a single strand of pearls.

I introduced myself, apologizing for troubling her. "I'm looking for some people who used to live here, the Raffertys."

"I'm just on my way out." Her voice was soft and cultured.

"Do you remember them?"

Her smile was hesitant. "Yes, I do."

"Any idea how I can reach them?"

"They were divorced many years ago," she said quietly.

"I didn't know that," I said, frowning, wondering if we were talking about the same people. "The couple that lost their little girl?"

The woman shook her head. "They didn't lose her," she corrected. "She was taken, murdered."

Something about her voice told me whom I was talking to. "Are you a relative?"

"I'm Judith Rafferty DeAngelo," she said. "What do you want?"

"I had some questions about Mary Beth."

Families are usually thrilled when a reporter delves into the unsolved murder of a loved one. They want justice and are relieved that someone else cares. But of course most such cases are not more than two decades old.

"Why now?" She looked puzzled. "Is there a new development in the case?"

"Not really," I said, fumbling. "But it was very newsworthy, and sometimes we go back and follow up old stories."

"There have been thousands of murders in Miami since my little girl—" She checked her gold watch. "You can come in for a few minutes."

I followed her into a well-furnished parlor with heavily draped windows, a shiny hardwood floor, and oriental rugs. A family portrait hung over the fireplace. Apparently she and her new husband had two more daughters.

"They're eleven and twelve now," she said, following my eyes to the portrait. "Wonderful girls."

"They're lovely," I murmured, then plowed on to the reason for my visit. "What did you think then? Did you and your husband ever have any gut feelings, any real suspects in the murder?"

She hesitated, then glanced again at my card. "Miss Montero, I don't know if you have children—"

"No, I don't, but I can imagine how terrible—"

"No, you can't," she said. "No one can who hasn't lived through it. It destroyed us. Our marriage. My former husband's life. It nearly ruined mine.

"You have to realize that none of the victims' advocate or support groups like Parents of Murdered Children existed then. We had to get through it alone. My husband could not handle it. They even questioned his whereabouts at the time our daughter was taken. It was apparently routine police procedure, but he couldn't forget or forgive that he could even be suspected of such a horrible crime against his own child. The detective was very kind and tried to help, but when no one was arrested William became disappointed with the police and obsessed by the case."

"I saw his reward offer in the clips."

She nodded. "When it amounted to nothing, he hired private investigators. They did nothing but take our money. He went to psychics who took what was left. He drank." Her brisk, busy demeanor had slowed and softened to an attitude of hurtful remembrance, as though a past not easily forgotten had overtaken her.

"Is Mary Beth's father still in Miami?"

"He's dead," she said simply, eyes never wavering. "I didn't know that," I said. "I didn't see it reported."

"He relocated to Atlanta after our divorce. A heart attack, six years after the murder. He was thirty-nine."

"I'm sorry."

"It nearly destroyed me, too, but I refused to let it happen. The detective . . ."

"Dan Flood?"

"That's right, Detective Flood. He kept coming back, to say he hadn't forgotten. But there was never anything new, and all it did was reopen old wounds. I was finally forced to tell him not to contact me again unless it was to report the arrest of the person responsible."

I swallowed and nodded. Putting the past behind her had been a matter of survival, but it seemed sad for Mary Beth.

"Our old neighbors have all either died or moved away. My daughters know very little about all this." She leaned forward, the light in her eyes slightly hostile. "Do you realize how difficult it is not to be an overprotective parent after such a tragedy? Especially when they were Mary Beth's age." She smiled and closed her eyes for a moment. "That's the first time in years I've spoken her name. Do you realize that Mary Beth would be almost thirty by now?" Her voice was low. "She'd have children of her own." She stood abruptly and checked her watch again. "We don't want publicity. To what end? We certainly don't want to invite any more tragedy into our lives."

"It had to be a very difficult time to endure," I murmured.

"It was. I never would have survived without the help of Sylvia and Matthew Fielding," she said, as we walked to the door.

My spine began to tingle. "Oh? The candidate's parents?"

"A wonderful family. And a wonderful man. I hope he wins."

"He was the one who found your daughter that day."

"Yes." Her eyes clouded. "We knew them only slightly then, as neighbors, but as parents they reached out to us in every way. They even made it possible for me to remain in this house after the divorce, and when I remarried they helped Ronald launch his business."

"They invested?"

She nodded. "Matthew Fielding is my husband's partner in the business. Fluorescent light bulbs. The factory is in Hialeah."

My mind raced. "What about the little boy, Mary Beth's playmate that day?"

She paused and tilted her head as she held the door open for me. "I'm not sure what became of them," she said as I stepped outside. "I can't recall the woman's name. She worked as a domestic at a home here in the neighborhood. Her poor child was traumatized, and she was terribly upset. It was all so long ago." And she closed the door behind me.

I detoured, on the way back to the paper, to drive by the murder scene. The spot where Mary Beth Rafferty's body was found on that long-ago afternoon was gone. No mangroves, no sandy filled-in lot. The Sea Breeze, a fourteen-story condominium with a pool and covered parking, now occupied the site.

At the office, I spent some time in the library reading about Eric Fielding. He was well known, but unlike many of my colleagues, I have never been thrilled by the power and glory of politics and rarely riveted by its coverage. He liked to describe himself as a law-and-order candidate and was a strong supporter of capital punishment.

That was interesting, but I felt inclined to drop the whole thing at that point, until I read more about the candidate's private life. The details sounded harmless but made the hairs prickle on the back of my neck.

Fielding had married late, just a few years ago, and when he did, he married a widow with a little girl. His stepdaughter was now eight years old.

3

I wanted to talk to Fred Douglas, the city editor, but he was not in his office. Gretchen caught me as I left to go home.

"How's the rapist piece coming?"

My expression must have looked blank, because her eyes grew suspicious.

"Your weekender on the Downtown Rapist," she said accusingly. "It's on the budget."

"No problem," I said. "You'll have it."

Back to the present, I thought, pushing the past out of my mind and heading home to work in peace.

I opened a bottle of Iron Beer and sat down at my kitchen table to study my notes on the Downtown Rapist.

He was a predator who stalked working women. Six so far—that were known. Cops suspect that for every reported rape, as many as ten go unreported. Nobody knows for sure.

This attacker was in his thirties, spoke with a Spanish accent, and ambushed his victims in the brightly lit office towers that spike the downtown skyline. He selected the one location where finding women was guaranteed: the women's rest room. When his victim entered, he was waiting.

My concentration was broken by the telephone on

the counter behind me. Startled, I snatched it up, forgetting I was not at the office.

"Britt Montero."

"Hello, dear," my mother said. "Where were you?"

"Just got home." I tucked the mouthpiece under my chin.

"You work too hard."

"So do you, Mom." In retail fashion for years, she now managed the main downtown office for a growing chain of boutiques.

I wound a strand of hair around and around my index finger, my eyes compelled to return to the words in the open notebook in front of me.

The rapist would press a hunting knife to his victim's throat and warn her not to look at him. When she was overpowered, blindfolded, and gagged, he would take a paper towel from the dispenser, print OUT OF ORDER on it, and tape it to the rest-room door.

The familiar rhythm of my mother's voice was a surrealistic accompaniment to the chilling image of the rapist at work.

"Some of the girls from my building, and of course everyone from work is going." I tried to focus on what she was saying. Something about a luncheon and fashion show at the Falls. "All the guests get favors, little goody bags, you know, full of cosmetics and perfume samples from the participating stores at the center."

My unwilling eyes were irresistibly drawn back to my notes. Her wrists were bound to her ankles, convenient for what he did next.

"Some of the fall lines are simply divine," my mother said. "The colors and the adorable knits are to die for."

Downtown rest rooms were now dangerous places for grown women. Police were advising them to go only in pairs—impossible, of course, for the employees of many small offices. Half a dozen attacks in four buildings.

My weakness for Cuban coffee dispatches me on endless quests for rest rooms. Such places had never struck me as unsafe. Until now.

"Britt? Britt! Are you there?"

I tore my eyes from the pages. "Mom," I blurted, "have you been reading about the rapist? Do you know he attacks women in rest rooms?"

"Ours are locked," she said after a pause, sounding slightly puzzled at the sudden change of subject.

"Mom, he gets into them anyway." My eyes drifted back to my notes. "I'm working on a project about the Downtown Rapist."

"The what . . . ! Oh, good Lord, Britt!"

"Don't fret, Mom. You're in more danger than I am."

"Don't you tell me not to worry, Britt. I read in *Newsweek* just the other day that at least sixty journalists were killed or reported missing last year."

"Mostly in Yugoslavia or El Salvador. I promise not to go there." These were tough times in the newsroom. With the budget crunch I was lucky to receive twenty-two cents a mile for driving to a shooting in Opa-Locka, much less airfare to a war.

Reporting can be risky business in Miami, though I would never admit it to my mother. One journalist lost both legs to a car bomb, and some of us have been shot at, beaten, threatened, and stabbed, to say nothing of rocked, bottled, and mugged. But all in all the profession has a lower casualty rate than more death-defying occupations, such as all-night service station attendant and convenience store clerk.

"A lot of reporters also go to prison." Her tone seemed to imply that that was where I was headed.

"That's Cuba, Mom, not here."

A beat passed, then two. "You know I'm not comfortable discussing that."

I wondered where that line came from and whether she was seeing a therapist. "Look," I said, suddenly contrite. "Where is this thing you want me to go to?"

She told me.

"Okay, if things stay slow on the beat Saturday, I'll try to take a break and come by to say hello. If not, let's have dinner on Monday, my day off," I said.

"Fine," she trilled. "But let's make it this Friday, instead. The Fine Arts Center is opening a wonderful new show, the Headache Art Exhibit."

"The what?"

She laughed. "It was written up in your own paper. It's the work of artists with headaches, exposing their pain."

"You're kidding."

"You've heard of suffering artists? This gives new meaning to the phrase. Your art critic said it's wonderful. The self-portrait by one artist shows his skull exploding; another depicts a hand yanking a fistful of brains like taffy from the head of a screaming man. There might be some interesting people there," she said meaningfully.

Exactly what I need after a hard week's work, I thought. My lower right eyelid had begun twitching almost imperceptibly. It does that occasionally. I pressed my fingers against it, squinting. How did this happen? Dinner on Monday had evolved into some sort of extravaganza on Friday, with the specter of matchmaking lurking behind the scene. My mother picked up on my silence.

"What's wrong?"

"Nothing. My eyelid is twitching."

"Lack of potassium. Eat a banana, dear. Or bake a nice sweet potato. You don't eat or sleep right."

"I don't know about Friday."

"He's an ophthalmologist, Britt."

"Who?" I knew it, I thought.

"My friend Emma's son. She can't wait for you to meet him," she gushed. "He'll only be in town for a few days."

I sighed, holding my eyelid tight as something inside it did the polka. With the other, I saw Billy Boots boldly force his whiskery face into Bitsy's dish. The dainty little dog stopped eating and politely sat down, watching the cat devour her beefy food.

"Britt, I hope they find the rapist, but why are you always so fascinated by the dark side, engrossed in contemptible things that shouldn't involve you?"

"Contemptible?"

"Yes," she snapped. "You're just like . . . like . . ."

"Say it," I said wearily. "Like my father."

Stretching the phone cord and my right leg to the max, I tried to move Bitsy's dish to safety with my foot, but the greedy cat moved with it, picking up speed, wolfing the dog food with amazing speed.

"None of us is young forever," my mother said. My attention wandered back to my notebook. "Opportunities don't always come again," she warned.

They come far too often for the Downtown Rapist, I thought.

"Uh-oh, something is boiling over in the kitchen," I said. "Have to go now. Call you tomorrow. 'Bye."

Burdened by guilt, I glared at poor Bitsy, who was sniffing at her empty dish. "What's wrong with you?" I scolded. "Why don't you ever stick up for yourself?"

I opened another can for her and warmed up a slab of leftover *pulpeta* for me. My Aunt Odalys's homemade meat loaf is a winner, concocted with ham, beef, hard-cooked eggs, and stuffed olives. She had delivered it in a Care package the day before. My father's youngest sister and my mother have not been on friendly terms since my fifteenth birthday. I made a note to buy some bananas, tossed a light *ensalada* with an oil and vinegar dressing, poured a glass of red wine, and cut a slice of crusty Cuban bread.

Feeling better after dinner, I clipped my beeper to the waistband of my running shorts and took Bitsy for a stroll around the block. The night was beautiful, with pale trailing clouds strewn like fishermen's nets across the sky. A few neighbors waved, stopping to chat along the way.

The rapist stalked the forest of my mind, casting his shadow across every man we passed, particularly those young and dark-haired and his height. Strangely, no one but his victims had ever seen him. No strangers had been reported wandering the corridors of the buildings.

I checked the time, displayed in lights high atop the landmark 407 Lincoln Road Building, and wondered if Harry Arroyo, the lead detective on the case, would be working late. This might be a good time to call him. I didn't look forward to it; I would win no popularity contests at the Sexual Battery office right now. But I'm used to rejection, I thought glumly. The rape squad lieutenant had already hung up on me twice today, but Arroyo was usually less testy. Anybody was usually less testy than the lieutenant.

Years ago the then all-male members of the rape squad liked to refer to themselves as the Pussy Posse. The department had come a long way since those days, but rape investigators could still be difficult and sometimes insensitive. Detectives had tried to keep the lid on this case, hoping to apprehend the rapist in the act. I heard about him after the third attack, but the lieutenant had warned that publicity would tip off the suspect. "The rapist will become more cautious, change his turf, alter his MO, making it tougher to catch him," the lieutenant had insisted.

That thinking always confounded me. A man out there raping and robbing must assume that the cops want a word with him. Besides, they had been unable to stop him. How many big-city bathrooms could a handful of cops keep under surveillance? How many other women would fall victim? News coverage might flush him out or provide valuable new information. The rapist's wife, mother, or lover, a neighbor, co-worker, or employer might grow suspicious, I argued, and turn him in. If nothing else, it would at least alert potential victims to better protect themselves.

The first story dubbed him the Downtown Rapist. He was not scared off. The man either didn't read the newspaper or didn't give a damn. He either had chutzpah or was powerless to control the demons that drove him.

I fumbled with the key, suddenly aware of the darkness around my front door. Unsnapping Bitsy's leash, I walked into the kitchen and found that Billy Boots had upchucked on the floor.

"What did you expect after pigging out on that dog

food? I told you it wasn't good for you." I mopped up the mess with a paper towel, then picked up my notebook and settled back into my favorite stuffed chair next to the telephone.

What I needed was a news peg. I pushed number five on the automatic dialer. I listened to it ring, wondering if perhaps my mother was right. Normal people program the numbers of best friends, lovers, close relatives, and maybe their favorite boutiques or pizza delivery chains into their telephones. Mine connects me to the homicide bureaus of two police departments, the morgue, the fire alarm office, the rape squad, the police public information office, the County Hospital emergency room, the city desk, and Lottie.

Harry Arroyo answered. "Hey, Harry, this is Britt Montero, from the *News*."

"No shit. I know who you are and where you're from." He sounded sullen, as I had expected.

"Anything new on the Downtown Rapist?"

"Not for publication."

I pretended not to hear. "Do you have a composite yet? What about a psychological profile?"

He answered with a question. "Any idea how much grief you've caused us?"

I hate that. "What do you mean, Harry?"

"TV is busting our balls! The Downtown Development Association is mad as hell."

Each of the three new rapes since the original story had been reported in increasingly hysterical tones on TV.

"The Chamber of Commerce is calling the chief, he's busting the lieutenant's chops, and the lieutenant is busting ours. Feminist groups are hassling the mayor—and now you call, all sweet and innocent, and ask what's going on. You *know* what's going on, for Christ's sake; you started it!"

"Harry, nobody wants to see you catch this guy more than I do."

"Oh, sure. Bet you'd love to see him locked up. How would you sell papers then?"

"This isn't about selling newspapers, Harry. You know that." I tried to sound sincere and helpful. "Have you checked to see if maybe the same guy worked in more than one of those buildings?"

He sighed and replied grudgingly. "We're going through the personnel records now."

"Anything?"

"It's not easy. Each building has a maintenance staff or a hired cleaning crew. Office cleaners come and go; records on those kinds of low-paying jobs aren't kept so good. Then each office has its own employees. They've got runners, messengers, delivery men, Fed Ex, UPS, all kinds of people coming and going." The anger had faded from his voice, replaced by the weariness of a frustrated cop at a dead end.

"Odd that nobody but the victims has seen him. Must mean he blends into the woodwork. He either belongs there or looks like he belongs there."

"Maybe he does."

"Like a security guard?"

"We've looked at some of them."

"What about recently paroled sex offenders? Or maybe one of the service companies hires prisoners on work release."

"We're checking; no lack of them either."

"What about the composite? The victims agree it looks like him?"

"Pretty much."

I scribbled furiously in my notebook. This was the first official confirmation that a police artist drawing had been done.

"What about the psychological profile?"

"Not for release to the media."

Yes! I thought. They've got one! "Why not?" I complained. "Half a million readers. Somebody out there might recognize him and drop a dime."

"Don't ask me, ask the lieutenant."

"Where does he carry the knife? Is it in a sheath?"

"Some kind of bag—like a gym bag or carryon."

"That must be where he puts the money and jewelry he takes from his victims." We had reported that the women were also robbed. "You think he's a rapist who robs, or a robber who rapes when he has the chance?"

"A rapist. A lot of guys take jewelry to convince themselves they're really robbers, not rapists, but the loot is strictly secondary with this guy. And that fits in with the other stuff he takes."

"What other stuff?"

"We ain't saying."

"What do you mean? What other stuff? What else does he take?" No answer. I would have to coax the information out of him, bit by bit. "Harry?"

His chair creaked as he changed position. "Yeah?"

"He takes their underwear?"

"Ummm, not exactly."

"Shoe fetish?"

"Nah. Let's just say he takes selected items of their clothing."

"What for? Think he masturbates on them later, while he relives the rapes?"

"Won't know till we can ask him. Let's just say the man likes souvenirs. But don't you print that,

Britt! You hear?" His stress level rose, infusing his weary voice with new energy. "He reads that, he'll dump the evidence, and we need to catch him with it."

"He knows what he took, Harry. Reading it would be no surprise to him."

"Yeah, but he don't know for sure that we know."

I sighed. My neck felt stiff and my head began to ache again. "What about his accent?"

"The two Spanish-speaking victims say he sounds Cuban."

"Is he circumcised?" American-born Cubans usually are, those born in Cuba are not.

"Nope."

"Think he's a Marielito?"

"Possible. Won't know till we catch him."

"Tattoos?"

"Maybe."

"Where are they? What are they?"

"Britt." His tone was exasperated. "The lieutenant finds out I'm talking to you, I'll wind up on the Squat Team for sure."

"SWAT?" I said hopefully.

"Nope, you heard me. Squat!"

Mules arrived in Miami from Colombia, Bolivia, or Peru, their intestines and stomachs packed with cocaine-filled condoms. If they fit a certain profile— one clue was a Colombian peasant in a three-piece suit—Customs pulled them out of line to be X-rayed at County Hospital. Smugglers had a choice: immediate surgery or a powerful laxative. Most elected the latter. Their bodily functions were monitored by cops assigned to recover the drugs—the Squat Team. Police work is not all guns and glory.

"They wouldn't do that to you, Harry." I hoped

he could not sense my grin. "You're too good a detective."

"Yeah, catch me talking to you? The lieutenant would freak, go on another goddamn rampage, and I wind up watching some—"

"What about the lab work on the rapist?"

"He's a secretor."

A secretor's sweat, saliva, and other body fluids, including semen, reveal his blood type. "Good, what type is he?"

"I can't say."

"What about the psychological profile? What do they think?"

"He's got no respect for women."

"Come on, Harry. We knew that." Brutalized and humiliated, the women were left bound and positioned for maximum shock effect. Whoever opened the door found them naked and exposed. A young CPA trainee working late when attacked was not discovered until the next morning. She was still under sedation, weeks later.

"You got to get all this from the lieutenant. Nothing came from me, right?"

"Right."

"Probably has a history of arrests, not necessarily for rape, has trouble with male-female relationships, comes from a dysfunctional family, was abused psychologically and maybe sexually as a child. Had temper tantrums as a kid and has a love-hate relationship with an older, dominant female relative. May even live with her."

The usual. "Anything else?"

"Above-average intelligence, holds a job, and lives or works in the downtown area, not far from the crime scenes."

"That's interesting."

"One other thing. He's got gonorrhea, the penicillin-resistant strain."

"Oh, no! Are the victims infected?"

"Two, so far."

"God, Harry, stop this guy!"

"Tell me about it. I'm doing everything but putting on makeup, wearing a wig, and sitting on the potty in the little girls' room. Now do us a favor, will you, Britt? Put our phone number in your story." His voice was raspy with fatigue. "Ask anybody with information to give us a call."

"Sure. Now you do me a favor."

He groaned. "What, Britt?"

I couldn't help thinking about my mother. "Catch him, Harry," I said.

I reread my notes, then carried Billy Boots into the kitchen. Delighted at the attention, he suddenly stopped purring when he recognized the hairball medication. Dark and sticky stuff in a toothpastelike tube, it looks and smells like molasses. The blurb on the box assures pet owners that cats will lick it eagerly straight from the tube. I read this aloud to Billy Boots. Unimpressed, he tried to escape. I was too fast and forced it between his clenched teeth, telling him he'd thank me later. I held his jaws together as he struggled, then finally swallowed, a resigned expression on his face.

I washed my hands, brushed my teeth, undressed, and turned out the lights. Usually my sleep is untroubled, but as I slipped into that void just before slumber, I wondered if at this moment out there in the darkness, somewhere in a gleaming downtown tower, a woman lay undiscovered, tied and terrified. Her sobs haunted my dreams.

4

In the morning I drove to the rape squad office hoping to corner the lieutenant and push for release of the rapist's composite and psychological profile.

The office was nearly empty, desks and phones unmanned. The lieutenant was out. Not a detective in sight. "Everybody went to a scene," said the secretary. A small prim woman with a tiny scarlet mouth, she was dressed in a straight skirt, a tailored white shirt with a little tie, and comfortable shoes. Wary eyes peered out of a worn face, as though she had heard it all on this job but would never repeat a word.

"The Downtown Rapist again?" I asked.

She shook her head. "You know I can't give out information."

I took a deep breath. "I'm not asking anything about the case," I said sweetly, pissed as hell that I didn't know what was going on. "All I need is the location. That's surely no secret."

She shook her head again, peered through her half glasses at the sheet of paper in her IBM Selectric, and dropped a tantalizing tidbit. "Homicide is out there too."

What had I missed? Damn, I thought, I hadn't heard a clue on the scanner.

"What's the address?"

She was unmoved. "You know the lieutenant"—
her eyes darted around the room as if to be sure the
lieutenant wasn't lurking and listening—"and what
would happen to me if I start talking to the press."

Rather than waste time trying to finesse her, I
stormed out in a huff and punched the medical examiner's number into the lobby pay phone. The clerk at
the front desk answered.

"Hi," I said, identifying myself and trying to sound
casual. "Which doctor is going out to that scene in the
city, the one that homicide and sexual battery are at?"

"They already left," she said cheerily. "Dr. Duffy
and the chief are both out there."

"The chief? Both of them? That's unusual."

"Yep, they left a while ago."

"Sure we're talking about the same scene?"

"The one at 176 Southwest Fourteenth Street?"

"That's it."

I would have to scramble now. Homicide detectives often didn't call the medical examiner for hours,
waiting for the lab to finish before even touching the
body. Whatever happened was hours old. How did
I screw up? How did our police desk miss it? The
address was a rundown residential neighborhood on
the fringe of Little Havana. Sounded as if it was
inside a house. Probably an older woman, I thought,
mind racing as I piled into the car. Young rape-
murder victims are usually abducted to remote woods.
Older women are more likely to be attacked by intrud-
ers in their own homes.

It was unusual for sexual battery to respond to a
homicide scene.

Maybe there was more than one victim, I thought,
one murdered, one raped. I was probably the only

reporter in Miami to miss it. The city desk obviously had not heard about it or I would have been paged. Damn. I floored the T-Bird through an intersection on the amber light, praying not to be stopped. Traffic was heavy, and I usually got lost in that aging neighborhood, full of narrow one-ways and dead-end streets. None of the transmissions on my dashboard scanner indicated crowd control or a manhunt in progress.

I hate waiting with a media mob for a two-paragraph press release written in police jargon saying next to nada. The T-Bird's air conditioner industriously pumped out hot air, adding to my discomfort and irritation. Outside temperatures had climbed into the mid-90s, and it felt hotter in the car. If the problem was a Freon leak I had yet another reason to feel guilty. In addition to blowing a story on my beat, I was polluting the atmosphere and enlarging the ozone hole. As I neared the neighborhood I watched traffic but saw no other news media or TV eyes-in-the-sky. The pack had to be there already, maybe even there and gone. I hate to arrive after TV crews have already stampeded through neighborhoods, alienating witnesses and infuriating residents. The whole damn block would probably be roped off. No chance for me to get anywhere near this scene.

I was wrong.

The house was CBS construction with peeling paint, a closed garage, and gritty pavement right up to the front porch. Official cars lined the street: several cruisers, a number of unmarked, a county car from the ME office, but no flashing lights, no PIO officer, no other reporters. No yellow rope.

At all.

It was eerie.

Instead of being last, was I first? Not sure what to make of it, I found a space for the T-Bird halfway down the block and walked up to number 176. The drapes were drawn and the jalousies opaque. A leaky air conditioner wheezed in a front window.

After two minutes or so, a woman answered the doorbell. A civilian. I had expected a cop.

From behind her came murmured voices, movement, and activity. She looked in her late forties, with lank hair dyed mousy brown but growing in gray at the roots. Her face was ruddy, her eyes red-rimmed, and her bony chin stubborn. She wore a rumpled T-shirt and black stretch pants with rubber thongs.

"What is it?" she said in a whiskey voice.

I didn't have the faintest idea what was going on and didn't know what to ask, so I introduced myself.

"A reporter?" She turned to someone behind her and raised her voice. "This isn't gonna be in the paper, is it?"

"I tend to doubt it," the chief medical examiner replied. He had discarded his jacket and his tie was loose.

A paunchy homicide detective wearing a semiautomatic pistol in a Velcro holster on his hip came up behind the woman and peered over her shoulder. "Britt, how'd you hear about this?" His tone was blustery but his expression bright, with an amused edge.

The woman stepped back passively as both the doctor and the detective came to the doorway. "What happened?" I asked them.

"Nothing you can put in the newspaper." The detective smirked.

"It's a homicide, isn't it?"

"Nope. Just an accidental death." The chief looked serious.

"Then why do you have so many people out here?"

"Because we don't get to see cases like this one too often," Dr. Duffy said, emerging from another room.

"Shut the door." The woman sat down at a kitchen table, her voice cross. "You're air-conditioning the whole goddamn neighborhood."

I stepped inside, across the scarred wooden doorsill.

The detective turned to the woman. "You mind?"

She shrugged, planted a sharp elbow on the table, and rested her forehead in her palm.

"It's an unusual scene, an educational experience," Duffy said quietly.

"Damn straight," said the detective. "I heard of 'em, but this is the first one I seen." His expression was close to a leer.

"What happened?" I asked, baffled.

"The husband of the lady in there died accidentally," the chief said. "You've heard of sexual asphyxia?"

"Sex—I don't think so."

I glanced back at the woman, her face buried in both stringy hands. The doctors and I moved in the other direction, into the living room, trailed by the detective. Other cops were departing, shaking their heads. The rape squad lieutenant had already gone.

"Solitary sexual activity, essentially narcissistic, practiced by men who simultaneously induce mechanical or chemical asphyxia," the chief said. The halo of fine white hair around his smooth pink face made him look almost cherubic.

"Masturbating?"

"With a twist," Duffy said. "They cut off the blood supply to the brain in order to enhance orgasm."

Good grief, I thought. He saw my bewildered expression.

"They accomplish that by tightening a ligature, or by hanging, or by inhaling hydrocarbons. Their carbon dioxide level rises, which supposedly heightens orgasm. But sometimes they go too far."

"Terminal sex." The detective grinned.

"What did this one do?" My voice was barely audible.

"Hanging. His wife goes out this morning, comes home a couple hours later, and there he is," the detective said.

"Where?"

"The bedroom. The scene is pretty bizarre," the chief warned. "They always are. There isn't all that much literature on this type of case. Many are mistaken for homicide or suicide."

He stepped toward what appeared to be the bedroom. "The wife thought he had committed suicide, but clearly that's not the case." I followed him.

The house was warm, but gooseflesh crawled up my back and down my arms. The rescue squad, summoned by the widow, had cut him down. The dead man wore a sheer red teddy. Dark body hair bristled through the garment's lacy openwork. Almost fifty, he was grizzled and out of shape and looked hideously obscene, but his appearance had apparently fascinated him. A large mirror had been moved from the dresser to the floor so he could watch himself.

Except for a sheer black stocking on his right leg, he was naked from the waist down. His penis had been adorned with a purple ribbon, which was tied around it. His hands were bound with a stained silk scarf.

We stood in utter silence for moment. Most of the cops had satisfied their curiosity and left. "How can you be sure this isn't a murder or a suicide?" I whispered.

"That, for one thing." Dr. Duffy pointed to something that lay on the floor in front of the dead man.

A *Playboy* magazine, opened to the centerfold.

"He didn't intend to die. He miscalculated." The chief spoke in his usual scholarly manner. "Note that the scarf binding his hands is loosely knotted and that he padded his neck with a towel, to cushion the noose."

"They don't want rope marks," Duffy pointed out.

"Exactly," said the chief.

I suddenly felt a headache coming on.

"They skate on thin ice," the chief said, "but elude death. They always have an escape mechanism. But sometimes they err."

"Or just get carried away," the detective said, his eyes knowing. "These guys are into fantasy, big time."

"True. He is relatively old for this," the chief said thoughtfully, zipping his Minolta into a leather case. "We see some victims as young as twelve. Guess he was lucky, had been doing it longer."

I swallowed and remembered to take notes. "You said some use an inhalant? Like what?" I tried to avoid the dead man's eyes. It was difficult. There is something terribly sad about dying during solo sex, leaving your deepest secrets exposed to complete strangers who invade your bedroom.

"Instead of compressing their necks," the chief said, "some achieve the desired effect by inhaling adhesive solvent, Freon, nitrous oxide, deodorant, various gases and solvents, even typewriter correction fluid."

"Right," Duffy added. "Remember the dentist who used nitrous oxide and an anesthetic mask? Usually they just wear plastic bags over their heads."

The chief nodded.

Plastic bags over their heads? "Typewriter correction fluid?" I mumbled.

"Contains one-one-one trichloroethane," Duffy said, nodding grimly.

No wonder the managing editor's executive assistant, in her small windowless office, looks goofy by five o'clock, I thought.

"The line that separates a little bit from too much is a fine one," the chief pointed out, peeling off his surgical gloves. "Some people don't know the difference. Unlike many other deviations, these people don't have their own publication—like those who are into bondage, SM, and fist fucking and compare notes on their types of aberration."

Publications. Fist fucking. I was beginning to feel a bit goofy myself.

"Takes all kinds," the detective drawled. "You know," he said casually, "like the people who enjoy loaded guns pointed at them during sex."

Shit, I didn't even know about them. We all turned to look at him.

"You know," he said, conscious of our reaction. He gestured weakly, grin shrinking as color climbed his cheeks. "The element of danger." From the way the two doctors eyeballed the detective, they were not totally familiar with that one either, but he obviously was. Thirty-two, I thought, and still surprised by what my mama never told me.

"You think many people are into this kind of stuff?" I asked quietly.

"No way to tell." The chief tugged at his earlobe. "We only see the ones who slip up. This may be more common than we think."

"Mr. Creech obviously crossed the line." Duffy was still scrutinizing the detective, who had suddenly become very busy with his paperwork.

"Creech?" I said, startled. "His first name isn't Emerson, is it?"

"Sure is," said the cop, consulting his clipboard.

"I know him!" I said, glancing back at the bedroom. "Uncle Dirty. I didn't recognize him."

"Not surprising," the chief said wryly.

The widow still oblivious, her back to us, mechanically made coffee in the kitchen. Her name was Ruby, I remembered now.

I lowered my voice. "This will really interest some people at city homicide."

The detective perked up at the new direction of our conversation.

"How long have you been in the unit?" I asked him.

" 'Bout a year and a half."

"You won't remember the case. He was a prime homicide suspect years ago, my first year at the paper. The murder victim was Darlene Fiskus, his niece. She was fourteen, in junior high school."

"I think I remember that one," the chief said, nodding. "The cheerleader."

"Right. He went to pick her up after a football game one night. People saw her get into a car the same color as his, but nobody could ever positively identify it or the driver. He claimed it wasn't him, said he'd had car trouble and when he arrived late she was gone. She was found the next morning, raped and face down in a garbage dump."

"They could never make a case," the chief said.

"Uh-huh. They found her prints and a few hairs that matched hers in his car—but he was her uncle and often drove her to school. I tried talking to him once, outside the station after he was brought in for questioning. He wouldn't talk to me, or the police. Had served time for the attempted rape of a thirteen-year-old neighbor a decade earlier. And Darlene had confided to her best friend that her uncle had tried to 'bother' her just a week before she was killed." I shook my head in disbelief. "The investigators always referred to him as Uncle Dirty."

The detective made a face toward the bedroom.

"Interesting," the chief said thoughtfully, rubbing his chin. "I don't know any other case of a subject involved in this sort of aberrant behavior also being involved in sex crimes against other individuals. But in this business there is always a first."

"Maybe he swore off little girls and turned to this," the detective said. "May have thought it safer."

"Definitely wasn't—for him." Duffy took his radio from his pocket and notified dispatch to send the body snatchers to remove the deceased.

I ventured into the kitchen to express my sympathies. The scratched countertops and aging appliances were a shade of avocado popular twenty years ago. The widow was staring into the depths of a coffee mug clutched in both hands. "Did you know he did this sort of thing?" I asked.

"I knew he liked the young ones," she mumbled, "but I never knew about none of this." Her weathered face looked hard.

"Were those your things he was . . . wearing?"

"Never saw those frillies before." Her eyes darted around the room, then locked on mine. "I look like the type to wear that stuff?" She glanced down at her faded T-shirt and threadbare stretch pants.

"I wrote about his niece, Darlene . . . when she was killed."

Her head jerked up, an indefinable flicker in her flat and hostile gray eyes. "That all happened a long time ago."

"It's never been solved."

She managed a half-hearted shrug.

"The police suspected your husband. . . ."

"They weren't the only ones," she said bleakly. "They weren't the only ones. I loved that little girl like she was my own, never had any children myself. My husband's family . . ." Her voice trailed off as she rubbed her upper arms with both hands as though a chill had come over her. "If you don't mind, I don't want to talk anymore." Summoning up her tattered dignity, she pushed back her chair and carried her cup to the sink, chin up, shoulders square.

Under some circumstances, I would have tried to push further, but I was uninvited in her home and her husband lay dead in the next room. I walked toward the front door. The medical examiners' wagon had just arrived and the doctors were outside. The detective was in the bedroom finishing his paperwork, probably gloating that some men were weirder than he was.

As I left the house, I wondered if she might have killed him to avenge her niece. Given the family history, this was no marriage made in heaven. But how could she hang a man his size? No, I am too suspicious, I told myself, rolling down all the car windows in a futile attempt to cool the interior before driving off. That happens in this business, I thought. When your mother declares that the sun will rise tomorrow, you call the weather bureau first. Then you check out your mother.

"Terminal sex," I told Lottie later in the photo lab, describing the hangman's noose, the mirror, the lace teddy, the silk scarf, and the open *Playboy.*

"Were the pages stuck together?" she asked eagerly.

"I didn't check," I said, wrinkling my nose. "That never even *occurred* to me."

She leaned back in her desk chair, rested one hand-tooled leather cowboy boot on her knee, reached inside, and scratched her ankle. "Hell-all-Friday," she mused aloud, "how do these horny bad boys even think these things up? That's worse than the ones who like guns pointed at them while they're doing it."

"You know about them!"

"Not from personal experience, a-course." She winked and looked sly. "If I did, I sure wouldn't admit it."

5

The story of Emerson Creech's demise was not reported in the newspaper. Many of the most fascinating never are. Since we had never identified Uncle Dirty as the prime suspect in the murder of his niece, his death was not deemed newsworthy by my bosses. I proposed a feature on autoerotic deaths. "Not in this newspaper, not ever," said Fred Douglas, the city editor.

As I read Creech's routine obit published in agate type in the DEATHS column the next day, I wondered about the others listed last name first in precise alphabetical order, and if any of them had gone to meet their maker in such bizarre fashion.

I still needed to connect with Riley, the rape squad lieutenant who had been off duty by the time I departed the Creech house. This time I called first. The lieutenant was in, terse as usual, and reluctantly agreed to spare me a few minutes if I got there fast. When I arrived, everybody in the outer offices was focused diligently on work, none of that relaxed atmosphere or camaraderie that permeates most detective bureaus. The lieutenant, I thought, must be in one of those infamous bad moods. Again.

When I breezed by, saying I was expected, the secretary lifted her eyes with a warning look that said, Lots of luck.

Taking a deep breath, hoping not to catch one of Lt.

Riley's notorious temper tantrums, I tapped first, then walked in. The lieutenant slammed down the phone and brusquely motioned me into a chair.

"What's on your mind, Montero?"

"The Downtown Rapist," I said.

Pale eyes guarded beneath colorless lashes, she scrutinized me carefully. "Had any calls with information on him?"

"No." I could see my window of opportunity close as she dismissed me as useless. "But I was hoping we might get some, if I did a story about him for the Sunday newspaper."

"Nobody's stopping you," she said, pointedly consulting her watch. Why is it, I wondered, that everywhere I go, people begin checking their watches and steering me toward the door? "You already made our investigation public, destroying whatever advantage we had in that respect." The coldness in her eyes told me she was not the person to turn to for sympathy should I ever be raped.

"I need your help on the story."

She leaned back in her chair, wearing an amused expression. Her dark-blond hair was almost straight, shoulder length, with a slight natural wave. Her leathery skin reflected too much time spent in the sun.

Women cops must be tough and ambitious to achieve promotion. She was both. Even to the extent of using only her first two initials, K.C. Kathleen Constance Riley was a perfectly good name, which I had once used in print when she shot the right kneecap off a deranged gunman who was determinedly battering her wounded partner. The story made her look professional, even heroic. Yet her anger at me was wild enough to make my own kneecaps tingle. She had warned me never, ever, to use her full name in a story again.

Women have made more progress in police work than in any other formerly exclusive male profession. They stand shoulder to shoulder with men in uniform—and, like Francie, share space on the memorial plaque in the lobby.

K.C. Riley had fought for rank and respect and won both. I appreciated the obstacles she had overcome but was fed up with her Dirty Harry imitation. Acting *muy macho* doesn't prove you are as good as a man.

"My help?" She exuded sarcasm, sucking in her cheeks and pursing her lips. "My help? After you've turned this investigation into a three-ring circus, putting the mayor, the chief, and all of us on the hot seat?"

I refrained from announcing that I was just doing my job. I love saying that to cops, because that is what they always claim while doing unpleasant things to you. But this was not the moment.

"You have a limited number of detectives, lieutenant. If half a million people learn more about the rapist on Sunday, we have a good chance of coming up with something."

"Yeah." She leaned forward, eyes pitiless. "Dozens of crank callers, spiteful women turning in ex-husbands and boyfriends, and hundreds of false leads for my overburdened detectives to check out. This investigation is already like a string tied to an elephant. The more we follow it, the bigger it looks."

"But the right lead might be among them. We both want the same thing, lieutenant."

"No, we don't," she said heatedly. "I want to catch

me a rapist; you want to sell newspapers and make a name for yourself."

"This story won't affect the paper's circulation or my job, one way or the other. Nobody reads bylines. Don't forget, lieutenant, I'm a woman too. I love Miami. I was born here. The people I care about live here. I want justice in this city as much as you do." I paused. "Maybe even more."

Her head jerked up at that.

I'd heard the lieutenant had bought a house in Hollywood, just north of the county line. Cops used to move up to Broward when housing costs, property taxes, and the crime rate were all lower. That's no longer true, but Dade cops still tend to settle on the far side of the county line. Beats me; maybe they like to distance themselves from their work.

"I live in Dade County," I said. "A whole lot of police officers go home to Broward. They don't even live here." I was pushing the envelope now and knew it.

Her tongue touched her upper lip as she sat studying me, probably wondering how, or if, I knew where she lived. I had landed a low blow, I knew. Why, I asked myself, did this woman and I always butt heads when we should be on the same side? I took a deep breath and made my move. "I understand you have a composite drawing of the rapist and a psychological profile. I'd like to use them in my story."

"Who told you we had them?" Suspicion edged her voice, but I sensed less hostility.

"I guessed," I lied, protecting my source. "It's only logical that you would have them by now."

"Then guess the rest. If I cut that information loose, it would compromise the integrity of our investigation. Everybody would know, including the bad guy.

He'd change his habits, his appearance, he might move—"

"Even if he tries, he can't change who and what he is. He's been hitting every two weeks." I lowered my voice. "How many more women will you let this happen to, to preserve the integrity of your investigation?" Leaning forward, I met her steely gaze. "Is it more important to stop him or to hope for an arrest, someday, on your terms?"

She tossed her head back and stared at me, chewing her upper lip and fiddling with a metal paperweight in the shape of a hand grenade.

I flipped open my notebook, took out my pen, and looked up expectantly.

She sighed, placing both hands on the desk blotter in front of her. She considered her fingernails, short and unpolished, without adornment. "We believe he's Cuban," she said. "He may have served time in prison there." Her expression remained unchanged as she removed a file from the squat metal cabinet behind her chair and opened it. The face in a composite drawing stared up at her.

She slid it across the desk. High cheekbones, clean-shaven, wavy hair, prominent nose, eyes close together.

"Lean and muscular build, a skinny little son of a bitch, but he's strong. Mid to late thirties, five-eight or five-nine, approximately a hundred and sixty-five pounds, nice even teeth, hairless chest. Probably started stealing panties from clotheslines or laundry rooms and worked his way up. Probably has a record for minor sex crimes, like wienie waving. He's still escalating. He didn't hurt anybody more than he had to, at the beginning. Now he's deliberately frightening his victims more. He's pricking them with the knife. Their fear and humiliation excites him. He's becoming more dangerous. He could be working up to murder."

She paused, as though lost in thought. "All but one has happened before four in the afternoon. He may be fitting this in with his own schedule. He could be a maintenance man who starts somewhere at four and likes to go to work happy.

"The first was only an attempt, because he couldn't get an erection. Now he makes the victims perform oral sex so he can. Then he does it from the back, seems to have trouble having sex from the front. Can't maintain his erection."

"Why do you think that is?" I asked, scribbling furiously.

She paused, toying again with the paperweight. "I don't know how much of this you can put in the newspaper. He probably does it from the rear because he won't see the victim as a person if he's not looking at her face. When he tries from the front, nothing."

"He's got problems."

"Tell me about it."

"What about lab work on him?"

"He's a secretor."

Eighty percent of us secrete our blood type into our body fluids, our tears, sweat, mucus, semen, vaginal secretions, and saliva. Sometimes a suspect can be typed off a cigarette butt. The best legal proof of sex between two people is a used condom with the man's semen inside and the woman's vaginal secretions on the outside. "Good, what type is he?"

"O positive, the universal donor." She smiled sardonically. "You wouldn't want to get too close to this guy."

I put on my curious face, not wanting to let on that Harry had told me. "Does he have AIDS?"

"Nope, gonorrhea, the bad one, penicillin resistant."

"Think he knows it?"

She shrugged. "Do me a favor. If you do mention that, don't be specific. Just say that he has something wrong with him. That he's diseased and dysfunctional. Maybe he'll see a doctor or go to a clinic and we can get a line on him."

"Does he ever wear condoms?"

She shook her head. "These guys are smarter than they used to be, they know all about the serology work, but we still don't see condoms much with serial-type rapists. We *are* seeing them more with gang bangs." She looked quizzical.

"Maybe it's all the safe sex warnings they get in the public schools now." I was thinking out loud. "Be nice if they warned them against committing rape too. So you've got DNA?"

"It's being run." Her pale eyes brightened at the prospect. "Eventually, every sex offender will have to provide blood for a Florida bank of DNA prints. We'll have them on file, like fingerprints."

"Will it be national? So if we get some serial rapist from Seattle you can identify him?"

"You've got it. The FBI developed the software that runs the program, and it's being shared with police crime labs."

"Can't be soon enough," I said.

"Just pray we get the funding."

"How has this guy been able to stalk women in these buildings without being seen by anyone else?"

"We're still trying to figure that one out, checking personnel records, cabbies who work the area." She ran her hand through her straw-colored hair. "We did a grid run of other crimes in the vicinity, in case he was exposing himself or pulling robberies before he turned to rape."

"Hear anything from informants?"

"Rape is not the kind of crime guys brag about in bars," she said, her voice sharp. "Usually if you get information from somebody, it's not because they were told, it's because they noticed something."

"Think he's married?"

She sighed. "Some of these guys are. They have a wife, kids, a sex life—the marriage may not be the best but the spouse doesn't notice anything."

"What does he wear?"

"T-shirt and blue jeans, nothing distinctive, except—" She caught herself and stopped. Apparently she had decided to hold something back.

"What?"

She shook her head. "At last, Britt, something my detectives haven't already whispered in your ear."

The woman is good, I thought, and wondered how far she would have gone in the department had she been a man. "Excuse me?" I said, in what I hoped was a tone of bewildered innocence.

The lieutenant smiled, showing her teeth. There was no humor in it. If I worked for her I would not want her to smile like that at me. I tried to guess what curious fact she might be withholding.

"Anything printed on his T-shirts?"

"Like his name and the firm he works for? We wish. We had one like that once. Wore a shirt with his name sewn over the pocket. The name of the plumbing company he worked for on the back." She smiled bitterly. "A brain the size of a ball bearing and a penis to match."

"Does he bring anything with him besides the knife?"

"A couple of victims saw something like a duffel bag before he blindfolded them. He may carry the knife in that."

"What does he use to tie them up and blindfold them with?"

"Duct tape."

"Have you been able to get prints off it?"

Her eyes dropped again to her own hands. "The man wears latex surgical gloves, the ones with talcum inside to make them more comfortable, easier to slip on and off."

Somehow that detail chilled me more than all the rest. A rapist cold and calculating enough to don rubber gloves before touching his victims, like a dentist or a brain surgeon.

"Where do you think he gets them?"

She shrugged. "He could buy or steal them from any one of a thousand places."

"Does he say anything unusual or have any distinctive body odor? Remember the one who smelled like the fast food restaurant where he worked?"

"Like greasy French fries, onions, and hamburgers?" She nodded. "No odor on this guy—and he says the usual. 'Don't scream, I will kill you. Keep quiet. Open your legs. Oh, baby, oh,' the usual shit."

We exchanged a wary handshake. My cautious little dance with the lieutenant had worked—this time.

"By the way, how's Dan Flood doing?"

I must have looked startled.

"Saw you with him at the memorial ceremony."

"He's okay, under the circumstances. I know he misses the job."

"Tough, he was a good man. But when you can't

hack it physically anymore, it's time to turn in the badge before you endanger yourself or somebody else." Her words echoed the department line. "Don't screw us on this one, Britt. It's too important," she said in parting. "Make sure you put our number in there. We'll set up a hot line, manned by a detective. Recorded, of course."

I nodded, wondering if she was alone when she got home to her new house in Broward County.

I knew how I felt. I wanted to go home and soak in a hot bath. After the last three days, I didn't care if I ever fell in love again. Memories of Kendall McDonald and his warm body next to mine were fading fast. Was he the last of an endangered species? Doesn't anybody do normal sex anymore?

6

It was nearly midnight Friday when I finished the Downtown Rapist story. I drove home through the mother of all thunderstorms. Whirling wind and rain, whipped almost horizontally, beat against my windshield. Lightning spiraled across the sky, cosmic-sized sparks, setting off high-voltage pyrotechnic fireworks followed by violent cracks of thunder. Sporadic flashes illuminated palm trees bent and twisted by the storm's ferocity and deserted streets flooded by the deluge. The good news was that my late night at the office saved the ophthalmologist and me from each other and our mothers' good intentions.

To make amends, I made an appearance at the fashion show Saturday. My mother seemed pleased, and it made me giddy to mingle even briefly in a world of music, pink linen tablecloths, and lavish centerpieces surrounded by happy, well-dressed people whose chief concerns revolved around the length of fall hemlines. My mother looked ultra chic in soft flowered silk, exquisitely cut. She beamed, whispering eagerly in my ear as we ogled the fall line of evening wear, gorgeous glittery satins and shimmery silks. Unfortunately, my nights out in Miami are usually spent at shootings, fires, or other disasters. Sequins are out. Rubber boots and hard hats are in. I slipped away from the luncheon to make my routine checks at

Miami police headquarters, which lacked the same ambience.

The young cop on duty did a double-take and raised an approving eyebrow. My luncheon garb, a bright yellow blazer over a black silk shell and matching slacks, was the best dressed he'd ever seen me. A persistent signal from my beeper, clipped to my purse, interrupted my check of the overnight log and reports. The city desk was calling. Six inches had to be trimmed from my weekender on the Downtown Rapist in time for the street edition. I went back to the office, eager to do the cutting myself rather than have an editor hack at my story.

I took a look when the first copies of the early edition came up to the newsroom. The story ran out front, though the composite did not appear until the jump, on page 12 A. As I scanned the copy, my heart skidded downhill. The last graf, with the police hot-line number for readers to call with information about the rapist, was missing. Obviously it had not been dropped due to a lack of space, because there was a short, a tiny one-paragraph story, in its place.

HAVANA—Tunnels dug beneath Havana to provide shelter in the event of an enemy attack are also being used to grow edible mushrooms, the Communist Youth Weekly Juventud Rebelde reported Saturday.

Mushrooms?

I charged the city desk like a maddened animal.

"I removed it," Gretchen acknowledged placidly. She pursed her lips, looking righteous. "We don't work for the police. Why should we publish their number? They just want to use us."

No wonder people hate the press. Nobody wins an argument with Gretchen unless they outrank her on the corporate chart, so I didn't argue.

"By the way," she called, as I stalked away. "It is important to remember that when you are out in public you represent this newspaper."

"Excuse me?"

"I'm glad to see you taking more pains with your appearance." She eyed my outfit and nodded smugly. "Very nice."

Jesus! I thought.

I immediately went over her head, knowing she'd hate me for it and I'd pay later. Fred Douglas happened to be in his office, unusual for a Saturday.

"She's got a point," he said without conviction, evading my eyes. Loyal to the core, he backs up his people. But he is also fair and reasonable.

"Not in this instance," I said coolly. "Of course we're not working for them. But catching this rapist is a community effort, and part of the story is that the police have installed a special hot line." I avoided mentioning that it had been set up solely in anticipation of the story.

Fred busily rearranged the papers on his desk. He looked noncommittal.

"The story says help is needed to identify the rapist, then describes him," I went on. "Without the number, how on earth will a reader with a tip find the right cop to give it to? There are twenty-seven police departments and six thousand cops in Dade County. You know what will happen. All the readers who want to help will call us instead of them." I turned to gaze meaningfully at Gloria, the city-desk clerk, talking innocently on the telephone, two lines blinking on hold. "We'll need a few other people to help Gloria answer phones. Hundreds of calls will come in for days. A lot of them will write, we may need to add somebody in the mail room—"

"Okay, okay, Britt," he said, trying to sound impatient as he raised both hands in surrender. "I get the point. No need for overkill." I returned to my desk and acted busy, pretending not to notice as he went to the city desk and told them the number should go back into the story for the final.

I couldn't wait to get to the office Sunday. The cops had more than eighty calls by 11 A.M. We would get the spillover, people who don't talk to the police, who prefer a reporter, or who found the hot line busy. I already had a stack of messages, and my phone was ringing when I arrived. I crossed my fingers and snatched it up.

The caller sounded middle-aged and dead serious. She was sure she had seen the rapist. I opened a fresh notebook, pencil poised.

"A month ago," she said breathlessly, her voice dropping. "I don't want you to use my name, of course."

"Where was this, what happened?" I asked, taking notes.

"On I-Ninety-Five. I was driving north, to the Sawgrass Mills Mall. His car pulled up in the lane next to me. The way he looked at me, I'll never forget it. When I read the story this morning I knew it had to be the same man."

"What else did he do?"

"Uh, nothing. I took the exit and he kept going."

"All right. What kind of car was he driving?"

"It wasn't new, it wasn't old. It could have been Japanese or German, but I'm not sure."

"Did you get a tag number?"

"No." She sounded slightly irritated at my foolish question. "I was busy driving. I called you instead of that police number. I didn't want them coming out to my house for my neighbors to see or anything, but I'm sure it was him. I'll never forget the look on his face."

"Thanks for calling."

"I thought it was the right thing to do," she said.

At least she wasn't tying up the hot line and making the police hate me, I thought. I shuffled hopefully through the messages, skipping optimistically to one that read *Woman says she knows how to catch the Downtown Rapist.*

The elderly voice who answered quavered slightly but sounded sincere. "I'm so glad you returned my call," she said eagerly. "There was a case just like this one a few years ago, on *Columbo,* or maybe it was *Kojak.* They solved it and caught the man, I just don't remember exactly how. But if you contact the network and get them to show you a copy of that episode, the police could see how they did it."

"*Columbo,* or maybe *Kojak,*" I repeated, eyes closed.

"Or was it *Perry Mason?*" she said slowly. "Wait, no, I think it was probably *Kojak,* on CBS, or maybe it was NBC. I remember it distinctly. Did you get that?"

"Yes, thank you very much."

"Glad to help."

The next woman divulged the name of the man she said was the rapist and the address where police could pick him up at that very moment if they hurried. He was her former son-in-law, who incidentally had not made his court-ordered child support payments since the fall of 1991, though he had money enough to buy a new red TransAm and live in a fancy apartment. He was of Polish extraction, born in Detroit, and looked nothing like the composite.

I didn't know whether to put down my pencil or jam the point into my jugular. I hoped the readers calling the cops had more substantial clues.

To my relief, a story tore me from the telephone. The police had found something in the water off the Venetian Causeway.

Police divers often plumb the waters around bridges for weapons deep-sixed by fleeing felons. They find lots of tin cans, junk, and old tools. This was something bigger, spotted with the naked eye by the captain of a passing tour boat: a car submerged in forty feet of water just off the causeway.

A broad-shouldered blond man in an immaculate white uniform stood apart from the tight circle of cops, firemen, and divers. He was impossible not to notice.

"You Coast Guard?" I asked, picking my way over coral rock and brushy outgrowths.

He shook his head, flashing a killer smile. "I'm Curt Norske, captain of the *Sea Dancer*."

"I remember your dad," I said, with a surge of memory. His father, a Miami pioneer, was city manager years ago. Well respected and forward-thinking, he had retired before I joined the paper and died several years later. The *Sea Dancer*, berthed at Bayside, cruised Biscayne Bay and the residential islands on sightseeing tours several times a day. I introduced myself.

"So you're the one who writes those stories. I read all your stuff. You're good. Had no idea you were so young and photogenic. Why aren't you on TV?"

"Because I write for the newspaper." Was he putting me on? He sounded serious and had a gorgeous smile. Of course, this man was trained to charm tourists.

"Captain Norske—"

"Call me Curt." His hazel eyes, flecked with gold, remained focused on me, despite the sounds of passing traffic and the shouts of the cops, the divers, and the wrecker driver, who was backing his truck up to the water's edge.

The connection and the energy it generated between us stirred something so basic that I automatically reminded myself to stay professional. "Curt, did *you* spot the car, or was it a passenger?"

"It was me," he said. "I take her through the drawbridge here at least twice a day. Never noticed a thing. Today, the light was just right, the water super clear— and the wreck may have moved, shifted on the bottom, probably during that bad thunderstorm Friday night."

I remembered it. Bitsy and Billy Boots had been huddled together under the bed when I burst in, drenched and windblown after the short dash from the car.

"Had a Japanese tour group aboard, so I dropped a buoy to mark the spot, took the tourists back to the dock, reported it, and drove back over here to show the cops the right place."

A diver in a wet suit emerged, saying that the car was overturned, its roof crushed. There didn't seem to be anyone inside.

This car, savaged by saltwater corrosion, had obviously been there for a long time. Scores of stolen and abandoned automobiles are reclaimed from the depths of greater Miami's hundreds of miles of waterways every year. Divers had attached a line to this one and were ready to bring it out.

"Better move back a little," Curt warned. "You don't want to be too close in case that cable snaps." He touched my back, guiding me to a safer vantage point, an odd sensation. The most attention I usually get at a scene is cops and firemen cursing and yelling at me to move back.

Yanked by the wrecker from the floor of Biscayne Bay, the rusted hulk emerged, oozing mud and water. It came to rest on dry land for the first time since being abandoned by some thief or insurance-hungry owner. "Looks like a Chevy Malibu!" a policeman yelled.

The tag was bent, oxidized, and coated with silt. The diver bent to study the plate, rubbing off some gunk with his hand. An older, heavyset cop in uniform yanked open the driver's door to look for identification. "It's an 'eighty-seven Florida tag," the diver said.

"Christ!" The cop jumped back from the car as though startled by something terrible. He had been. What looked like a piece of cloth was still tangled in the fastened seat belt. The driver. He had obviously been there for years.

The older cop stepped our way. He had his hand on his chest. "Jesus," he said, "I didn't expect that. Looks like somebody's been missing a long time."

Curt and I watched solemnly. Covered with barnacles and sea growth, the still-dripping hulk sat on the bank of the bay surrounded by uniforms and detectives. The missing man's wallet was still inside what remained of his trousers. "We're gonna have to let it dry out before we try to find any ID in it," the cop said. No sign of foul play. A simple accident. The car had been buffeted about on the bottom by storms and strong tides. They were lucky to have found it.

A family is spending this Sunday afternoon somewhere, I thought, unaware that a missing loved one is about to come home.

I asked the cop handling the report where he'd be and arranged to call him later.

"You're not leaving?" Curt said.

I nodded. "Back to the office."

"I was hoping you'd come over to Bayside for the afternoon tour on the *Dancer*. No charge. You ever take one of our cruises?"

I smiled. "No, that's something the tourists do. Just like native New Yorkers never visit the Statue of Liberty. Only newcomers take the tours, the rest of us are too busy making a living."

He stared down at me. "Did you say you're a native, Britt?"

"Born here." I nodded. "So was my mom."

"Mine too. Wonder why it took so long for us to meet? It's about time. Realize how rare we are? Nobody was born in Miami, at least almost nobody. Come aboard the *Dancer* this afternoon. I'll show you our home town like you've never seen it."

I smiled. "I can't today, but maybe another time—"

"You'll love it; it's relaxing away from the murder and mayhem. You can have a drink. We have a bar aboard."

The man was persuasive. I considered his motives.

"I won't write a story about it," I warned. "No free publicity. Unless, of course, the boat sinks and dumps a load of screaming tourists in the bay, or the passengers riot and start throwing each other over the side, or they all evacuate except the captain, who goes down with the—"

"I catch your drift." He grinned. "I know the stories you write. Think I'd invite somebody like you for publicity? I don't ever want you to write about me or my business."

We both laughed, our eyes connecting again with a certain sizzle.

"I just want to see you," he said.

I didn't notice the Jeep Cherokee pull up and stop on the bridge. Great timing for Kendall McDonald to walk back into my life.

"Britt!" The familiar voice took me by surprise.

"I didn't think lieutenants worked on weekends," I said inanely, struggling with the sense of confusion his presence always elicited.

"I'm off, but I was in the area, heard it on the air, and came by." Lean, long-legged, and as attractive as ever, he wore an open-necked shirt and chinos. *Buenísimo*. He studied Curt curiously.

"They found the remains of the driver," I babbled. "It's apparently been there for years."

"That's what I hear. You the one who spotted it?" he said to Curt.

They exchanged names and shook hands like old friends. As Curt explained again how he had sighted the car, another police cruiser wheeled off the road to join the scene. "Careful," he murmured, taking my arm as if I was some breakable china doll. McDonald's eyes flickered, noting the gesture.

"We were just leaving," Curt told him.

McDonald turned and barked irritably at the heavyset cop who was trying to read the vehicle identification number off the rusted car.

"Valenti, why isn't this scene roped off?"

"Well—uh, we just recovered the vehicle," the startled cop said. "Appears to be an accident."

"Cordon it off," McDonald said brusquely, his electric blue eyes snapping, as though irate at the hopeless incompetence surrounding him. Why this sudden fixation with yellow crime-scene tape? I wondered.

His attention returned to us.

"We appreciate it if witnesses speak to a detective before talking to the press," he said coolly. He motioned with his hand-held radio, directing Curt over to the marked patrol car.

"What?" I yelped indignantly. "All he did was spot the shadow of a car underwater. He's no witness. It's an old accident."

"You know better, Britt," he said, turning to me, "than to talk to the witnesses before we do."

"No, I don't," I muttered. I was surprised by his attitude. Our encounters at the station and at crime scenes since our breakup had been all business, but civil and polite.

"We were having a private conversation here," Curt said. His friendly demeanor was fading. "Come on, Britt, I'll walk you to your car. Then I have to get back to Bayside."

"I asked you to wait over there," McDonald said.

Both men seemed to swell, sizing each other up as if in some primal testosterone-fueled territorial dispute.

The tension was obvious and the cops, firemen, divers, and wrecker crew all paused to watch.

"I have all the respect in the world for the police," Curt said pleasantly. "Help 'em out every chance I get. But I'm due back to work right now. Officer Valenti there has my name and all the information he needs. Call me if you need me, detective."

"That's lieutenant," McDonald corrected, whipping out his business card.

Curt studied it blandly. "Here, have one of mine." He smiled and presented a gold-embossed card to McDonald. "That's captain. Captain Curt Norske." I bit my lip, admiring the gleam in his eye.

We strolled toward my T-Bird, leaving McDonald scowling at Curt's card. Then he wheeled and began berating Officer Valenti, who didn't deserve it.

We said nothing until I unlocked my car.

"What's wrong with that guy?" Curt muttered under his breath. "Did he forget that cops are supposed to protect and serve, not hassle and pester?"

I laughed. "He's not always that bad."

"Now, about your phone number. . . ." He paused, expectantly.

I hesitated. I *am* a professional, and I *was* on the job. "You can always reach me at the paper," I said, digging in my pocket for *my* card.

"Here's my number, any time."

Taking a gold pen from his breast pocket, he scrawled across his card and watched me read it.

"Sure you can't come cruising this afternoon?"

"I have to go back to the office." I slid into the car and started the engine. "But I really would like to, one of these days, captain. It's something I've always wanted to do."

"Deal. I'll be waiting." He turned and strode back to his car, a white Eldorado convertible.

Kendall McDonald looked my way as I pulled out. I hit the gas a shade too hard, and my tires spit up a cloud of dust and gravel along the side of the road.

For the first time I felt more anger than sense of loss after seeing him. He had dumped me in order to make lieutenant. How dare he act so snotty and officious? I liked the cool way Curt had handled him. I smiled to myself, then settled back into reality: the Downtown

Rapist, messages stacking up on my desk, and a long-dead driver in a rusted waterlogged car.

Less than an hour later, one mystery was solved by a phone call from my favorite tipster. "Had a hell of a time getting through, Britt," Dan said. "Got a hot story for you."

I love it when somebody says that to me. I know it's crazy, but nothing turns me on more than stories. No wonder my mother despairs of having grandchildren.

"Hear about the car they fished outa the water off the Venetian today?"

"Yes, I already know about it." I riffled through a stack of messages. "I was there."

"Yeah, but do you know who that was behind the wheel?"

"Who?" I put down the messages and picked up a pen. "You know who it was?"

"The news on the radio said the driver was still strapped into a Chevy Malibu with 'eighty-seven tags."

"That's right."

"Paul Eldridge, an old missing persons case of mine. Disappeared in the spring of 'eighty-seven, driving his '85 blue Malibu from Miami Beach to Miami."

"Wow!" I said. "Right time, right place. Sure sounds like 'im."

"There are dental records they can match up, if there's enough left," he said.

"The entire jaw was there," I told him.

Eldridge, Dan said, had attended a bachelor party for a buddy that night, a co-worker about to be married. A dozen friends did a little drinking and a lot of joking as they watched a strip show at a club on the Beach. At 2 A.M. Eldridge climbed into his car and drove off into a light rain, evaporating like the mists rising off the city's wet and steamy pavement.

His family—wife, parents, and in-laws—had reported him missing at once. They had hired private detectives, passed out flyers, offered rewards, and called the police every day for months. He reappeared in their fantasies, suffering from amnesia. In reality, he missed his friend's wedding, his baby girl's first tooth, Christmas, his own wedding anniversary. In their hearts his loved ones had come to know they would never see him again. They always insisted that he must have met with an accident or foul play. After years passed without a trace, when his bank accounts and credit cards remained unused, Dan, a bit dubious at first, had tended to agree.

Though police had done a cursory check, the family's private detective had hired divers to search the bay and waterways along the missing man's logical route home. They found nothing.

Sometimes drivers who have been drinking fail to take the logical route home. Sometimes they become confused. Everyone had checked along the MacArthur Causeway, a mile and a half south of the Venetian, Dan said. Now we knew that for some reason that night he had driven the narrower, less-used toll road. A violent thunderstorm six years later and the sharp eyes of a stranger had solved the mystery, forcing the bay waters to yield their well-kept secret. Dan said the distraught wife had never believed her husband would deliberately disappear, abandoning her and their baby daughter. She was right.

"The widow won't be shocked that he's dead," Dan said. "She's known since day one. Gotta give her credit. Now everybody will see she was right all along. She can bury him now and get on with her life. That little baby must be in school by now."

I thanked Dan for calling. "Like old times," I said. "Leave it to you, you never forget a case."

I told him about my visit to Mary Beth Rafferty's mother, the incriminating fact that the Fieldings had provided her with financial aid, and the little girl who was now Fielding's stepdaughter.

"You oughta write about it," he urged.

"I don't know," I said doubtfully, "it would be hard to get it into the newspaper without some concrete proof."

I was delighted, however, to have the story on Eldridge a full four hours before police released his identity.

A new unsolved mystery had made headlines and an old one had been resolved. That's another thing I love about this job: it's never boring. Stories begin and stories end. Stay long enough and you see the cycles.

7

I stopped by the office on the way to meet Dan for lunch. It was my day off but I wanted to scan my messages, hoping for news on the Downtown Rapist.

I had a stack of mail as well as phone messages. None from Kendall McDonald, not that I had any reason to expect one. I returned a few calls, but they were long on chitchat and short on substance. I called Harry at the rape squad, opening mail as we talked.

"Nothing concrete, Britt. We've logged upwards of seven hundred calls since your story appeared. People are working overtime checking them out. So far most of it's crap."

"Like what?" I wanted to know, though I had a pretty good idea from my own experience.

"Oh, shit, Britt, there's so many. One woman was sure the rapist was a guy who sits in a car outside her daughter's school every afternoon eyeballing the young girls. Had school security check him out. He's there every day—picking up his own kid. 'Nother woman said she's sure the guy followed her through every aisle in her neighborhood drugstore, watching her every move. Said she was terrified and convinced that the only reason he didn't attack her was because too many were people around."

"Could he be inept store security?"

"You got it. You ever wanna join the department,

Britt, you can work with me. Apparently he thought she looked suspicious."

"That's funny," I said. "He thought she was a shoplifter, she thought he was the rapist."

"Welcome to Miami," he said, "home of the handgun and paranoia."

"What else?"

"The usual cranks. Women trying to throw in their ex-husbands and boyfriends, neighbors with feuds trying to pin it on each other, guys trying to cast suspicion on a boss who fired them or their ex's new flame, and one phony confession."

"Oh?" I tore open a letter. Handwritten on lined paper:

Dear Madam,
Your poetic license has expired. You'll have to
pay more dues.

It was unsigned.

"Yeah." Harry went on. "Guy had everybody excited for a while. Called the hot-line number from jail, where he was locked up on a burglary charge, says he's who we're looking for. Gave accurate information, details not in your story, stuff that only we and the victims know. He almost had us."

Damn, I wondered, how much are they holding back?

"How could he know those things? Maybe he *is* the guy."

"Nope. We backtracked him. Found out he'd been picked up in the county and was cuffed to a chair outside the burglary office waiting to be interviewed. They share space with the sexual battery unit on the other side of a wall divider. So while he's sitting on one side, a detective on the phone is on the other, talking to a city rape squad detective who is filling him in on the case. The county detective had it on speaker phone for the benefit of the two other investigators in his office. Unaware, of course, that this scumbag on the other side of the divider is taking it all in.

"So later, sitting in jail, a two-bit burglar, busted again and facing career criminal prosecution and hard time, decides his life lacks excitement and attention. He'd rather be the guy sought in a major front-page case than a petty thief."

"You're sure?"

"This guy was in jail in Palm Beach when one of them happened."

"Sorry." I sighed.

"Goes to show," he grumbled, "the fewer people, even cops, who know anything, the better off we are."

This was not the moment, I thought, to press him for more details. "Most people who call want to help—"

"Sure, but the sincere ones know nothing, leaving us with crazies, scumbags, and liars."

"And maybe just one with the real thing." I ripped open another envelope. This one looked grungy, as though it had fallen on the floor in the mailroom and been stepped on a few times.

"Let's hope so, and let's hope we recognize it, if it comes."

I said goodbye to Harry as I scanned the letter. Another weirdo.

Say Britt Montero,
Hello, I did got from your newspaper a sto-

*ry. You put a lots of words. You write a good
English language but who are you to say? Take
good advice. Write about Haitians. Don't make
me angry.*

The signature was either a scrawled bow and arrows
or unintelligible initials.

I crumpled the letter and tossed it, with the others. Then I snatched up my purse and smoothed my
navy blue slacks, leaving a powdery smudge on the
front. "Don't they ever dust around here?" I muttered, glaring up at the air-conditioning vents, which
continually spew out fine black particles of dirt, bac-
teria, and germs that I was convinced were killing us
all. No wonder poor Ryan was always sick.

I stopped in the rest room to wash my hands, then
went to meet Dan for lunch at Clifford's, a family
restaurant on the Boulevard just north of the city
limits. Other establishments come with new styles
and trends and go, but Clifford's has been there forever: a large and bustling family dining room out
of sight of the bar, which is dimly lit with quiet
booths and tables. I stood blinking just inside the
door, waiting for my eyes to adjust to the sudden
darkness. Dan rose, hailing me from a booth in the
bar.

His voice, so strong and positive on the telephone,
had been that of the old Dan, but his clothes hung
loosely and his face looked puffy. His skin looked
ashen in the poor light. I kissed his cheek, then slid
into the booth across from him. He had a lit cigarette in one hand and a glass of something resembling
scotch in the other. There were already two butts
in the ashtray, and he couldn't have been waiting
long.

"Hey," I said lightly. "Thought you quit smoking last year. And isn't it a little early for that?" I gestured at his drink.

"Who said you were my mother?" His grin was the old Dan.

"Sorry," I said. "Been waiting long?"

"Got here a little early," he said. "Got me a head start." He raised his glass and I shook my head and clucked in mock disapproval.

He was eager to chat, full of animated small talk about the department, about old cases. Nothing, I noted, about his new life in retirement. We talked about Eldridge and other stories that had been in the news, and we ordered.

I opted for the seafood salad, Dan ordered the prime rib, rare, with French fried onion rings.

"Are you crazy?" I whispered as the waitress left. "You sure that's what you want?" He looked sheepish, called the waitress back—and stubbornly ordered another Johnnie Walker Black. He watched slyly to see my reaction.

"Okay, okay." I pouted. "I won't say a word, but I thought you were listening to your doctor, who definitely wouldn't approve—"

"I thought you weren't gonna say a word."

I gave up and unwrapped my silverware.

"Britt, it's all right," he said gruffly. "Don't worry about me. I handled DOAs every day in homicide. I saw enough to know exactly what's going on inside me." He jerked a thumb toward his left chest. "Bad habits aren't gonna shorten my life now."

I smiled into his eyes, wondering how it feels to know you have more yesterdays than tomorrows. It must be terrible, I thought. Get hit by a bus or caught in a crossfire between strangers and there is little time to consider your fate. Knowing you will soon die is something else.

"I just want to keep you around," I said lightly. "I don't have many real friends. I can't afford to lose any."

"I'll be around, I promise." He patted my hand. "Looky here." He held open his jacket, displaying an array of vials and bottles in his shirt pocket. "I could open a pharmacy."

A small brown bottle stood out, with a strip of red tape across the twist-off lid. "What's that one?"

"Nitro," he said, "for chest pains. The tape is my own idea. Makes it easier to spot and hold on to in case I need it in a hurry. The bottle is so damn small." He held it up, frowning at the fragile bottle dwarfed between his thick fingers. "The doctor said to stash 'em everywhere so they're in easy reach. Keep one in here," he said, patting his pocket, "one in the car, in the kitchen, in the bathroom. Never know when you might need it in an emergency. See? I'm prepared for anything." He slipped the bottle back into his shirt pocket with the others. "Now tell me all about this Downtown Rapist."

I did. "Cranks galore are calling the hot line. I'm getting some of the slopover: calls, letters."

He looked up from his salad. "Anything?"

"Naw." I shook my head, laughing self-consciously. "One wacko wrote that my poetic license has been revoked; another told me take his advice and start writing about Haitians instead of Cubans before I make him mad."

"They sign them?"

"I don't think the first one did. The second one, some scribble. You know how they do."

"Latino?"

"Seemed to be."

"Pass them on to the squad, Britt. Let the lab take a look at them." He launched a new assault on his salad.

"There's enough on their plate already. They hate me for breaking the story, and they'll hate me even more if the publicity doesn't bring in something useful."

"Yeah, but you can't take chances, Britt. The guy is dangerous."

"Who said you were my father?"

He laughed. "Okay, okay, you got me. But I know how you work, Britt, and sometimes you navigate a little bit too close to the edge. You always were a wing walker. Remember, I'm not there anymore to watch out for you or catch you if you take a tumble."

I smiled. Dan gave no impression of impending doom or helpless resignation; in fact, his speech and even his controlled movements exuded a crisper, harder-edged vitality. "You know the secret of being a successful wing walker?" I asked. "I interviewed one once."

"Don't look down?"

"Nope, the secret is you never let go of anything until you have a firm grip on something else."

"Always sound advice," he said.

"You know, you never told me why you became a cop way back a hundred years ago."

"Same reason you're a reporter. Too lazy to work and too chicken-hearted to steal." He grinned, baiting me.

"No, seriously."

"Okay. I couldn't sing, I couldn't dance—"

"Come on," I coaxed. I parked my chin in my palm and my elbow on the table. "You were the little boy who always wanted to grow up to be a policeman, right? Is that what made you do it?"

"The truth is that in those days they brought truck-loads of country boys down from Georgia. They'd throw 'em all into a rock pit and then lower a ladder. The ones who climbed out became firemen, the rest, cops."

"I always thought the ones who broke up the ladder and started clubbing each other over the head became cops."

We were still laughing when the waitress brought our meals. "Looks good enough to eat," Dan told her.

To me, he said, "You see the candidate's litera-ture and all his commercials?" His eyes burned with old outrage. "They're everywhere: newspapers, radio, TV." He stared into his glass and shook his head. "Too much."

He ordered another drink and raised speculative eyes to me. "Think he'll make it?"

"More astute observers of the political scene than I am seem to think so. Chances are the paper will endorse him."

"How the hell could they?" His voice was sharp.

"He did all right, never stole a freight train or stepped into big trouble on the city commission. The editorial board feels he did a fine job."

"Christ. That man just can't be governor of this state."

"You and I are not gonna vote for him. But that probably won't stop him."

Dan put down his fork and toyed with his drink. "I'll never forget the day we found Mary Beth Rafferty."

He was slightly slurring his words. I wished he hadn't ordered that other drink and was vaguely concerned about his mixing scotch with all his medication.

"We were searching the whole south end for her, about to call in firemen to help. Then the Fielding kid shows up on his bike, all sweaty and nervous. Says he found a body." He paused. "It was at what they now call Kennedy Park, at the foot of Kirk where it goes into the water."

I nodded. "It's a high rise now. The Sea Breeze."

"It was all landfill then, logs, dirt, the crap you fill a lot with. Near the water the fill was mighty thin. Mangroves all over the place. We found her draped upside down, her back over a mangrove. Her head and her feet were hanging. No clothes on, a rag hanging out of her mouth. She was dead. Eight years old. I felt bad." He lit another cigarette, taking a deep drag. "I had a daughter." He looked out across the darkened room. "Mary Beth Rafferty was a very pretty little girl."

"I know," I said gently. "The ones involving children are always the hardest."

He picked up his knife as though it were a weapon. "What really pisses me off is that when he first started into politics, I personally"—he sliced savagely into his prime rib, pink juice oozing—"went to his backers and warned them they would be supporting a homicide suspect as a candidate for public office. You know the only question they asked?"

I shook my head and swallowed a piece of shrimp.

"Not 'Did he do it?' Not 'Is he guilty?' No, all they wanted to know was: 'Think you'll ever have enough to charge him?' I told 'em the truth: 'Not unless we get real lucky or he has a change of heart and confesses.' They never withdrew their support. Never considered dropping him. The power brokers, the movers and shakers, they didn't give a shit about what the man did, what he's capable of, or that little girl."

"You know how politicians are."

"Yeah," he said, resting the knife on his plate, "full of lust for power, money, sex, ego. I've *arrested* people I could trust more."

"It *is* hard to believe," I said. "Anyone looking at the man now would wonder how he possibly could have done it."

He leaned back and looked at me wisely. "I'm surprised at you, Britt. You know better." He lowered his voice. "That's what makes them so dangerous. That's how they get away with it. They look like everybody else, like you and me.

"Sure," he whispered. "Look at them." He regarded the half dozen people sitting at the bar, their backs to us.

"Your rapist could be the guy sitting, second from the end, on your left." He gestured with his knife. "The one at this end could be a serial killer just passing through." He stared at each one, a dangerous light growing in his eyes. "The guy with the sideburns sitting next to him might be the one who killed the North Miami cop in that bank robbery last month. He fits the general description. He might be the one."

I looked at the man in scruffy work pants, his hand in a dish of pretzels. I didn't think so.

I lowered my voice too. "Really, Dan. You're becoming paranoid," I whispered, then laughed. "This is a nice place. I bring my mother here for dinner." I stopped when I saw he wasn't laughing. The drinks, I thought, wondering where our conversation had taken a wrong turn.

I could think of better ways to spend my day off. "Dan," I complained. "I may smack you upside the head if you don't order some coffee. I'm gonna have to drive you home."

"No, you won't." His mood suddenly flashed from dark to light. He smiled, shaking his head, straightened up, and pushed away his glass. "I'm fine, just talking."

We ordered coffee and he tried the bread pudding. Then we wrestled over the check. He won, so now I owed him lunch.

We hugged and promised to do it again soon. My promise was heartfelt. He obviously needed to be out among friends as much as possible so he did not brood about past injustices and the sinister side of human nature.

"You know," he said, in parting, his arm around me. "Nothing would make me happier than if things worked out between you and my old partner Ken McDonald. I'm still hoping. We'd sort of be related."

"It would be easier," I said, deadpan, "if you just adopted me."

Despite his smoking, drinking, and eating habits and the jacket that was now two sizes too big, Dan's body language belied his physical condition. He still looked sound as I watched him cross the parking lot to his car, his tread steady and determined.

He waved and I felt comforted. His spirit was still strong.

It had been a long week. After leaving Dan, I went to the Spa, worked out on the Nautilus machines, and repeated body sculpture exercises with five-pound hand weights until I ached. Then I took to the beach and swam, arching my back, floating face up, cooling off, drifting and drinking in the pink skyline, the art deco hotels in ice-cream colors with their rounded corners, spires, parapets, and porthole windows, framed by sparkling shades of turquoise and green. No sharp edges are visible from out beyond the breakers, surrounded only by clouds and water. The city glowed softly, like a magic place in a fairy tale.

My plan was to stay home, read, and retire early. Instead, edgy and restless, I called Lottie, who was still at work. She would be home by seven, she said, early for her. Taking Bitsy with me, I stopped at La Esquina for takeout, then drove to Lottie's place. I left the food in the car and we walked, exploring the neighborhood while waiting. Lottie showed up only twenty-five minutes late, surprisingly prompt for a newspaper employee. It's impossible to escape a newsroom on time. I met her there in the lavender twilight with the package of savory-smelling warm food.

"Hey, girl, whatcha doing here?" she asked as she hauled her gear out of the car. "Ain't this your night off? Where are all the men in your life?"

"Same place as yours, I guess."

She let us in the front door. Lottie's house is an experience, furnished and decorated with mementos collected during two decades of world travel as she captured dramatic and historic events on film, living on the road, out of a camera bag. She was always thinking ahead to the day she would decide to settle in one place and sink roots. I'm grateful that she chose Miami.

She switched on the lights. She looked grimy and weary, and her freckled face was smudged.

"You look like you had a hard day."

She put her things down and gave me a baleful look.

"I'm fine," she reassured me. "But you won't believe what happened to me. I feel like I been shot at and missed, shit at and hit. Promise to post my bond? It will be necessary if I ever get my hands on that slimy little turd, Eduardo."

Her clothes looked like she'd been mud wrestling. "You got all messed up like this on one of his society shoots?"

She shot me a steamy glare, still too irate to speak. Without comment I carried the food into her bright and cozy kitchen, opened the refrigerator, perused the contents, and poured her a glass of cold white wine.

"Here," I said. "Why don't you drink this and take a shower while I warm up the food?"

"Wow," she said gratefully, "this must be what it's like to have a house husband. That's what we need, guys to pamper us and our stuff." She sipped gratefully, closed her eyes for a long moment, then disappeared into the bathroom.

I transferred the *arroz con pollo* and plantains to her cookware, then zapped them in the microwave. By the time I set out her Wonder Woman place mats and her Fiesta dishes, she had emerged wearing a thin robe of Haitian cotton, barefoot, pink-faced, her copper-colored hair wet and a soft tawny towel draped over her shoulders.

"Now," I said, refilling her wineglass. "What did Eduardo do?"

"It all started—" Her mouth was full of chicken. "Ummm, this is heaven." The chicken oozed flavor, mingled with caramelized onions, roasted sweet peppers, and occasional green peas nestled in yellow saffron rice kissed by garlic and a taste of sherry. "Where'd you get this, La Esquina?"

I nodded as she continued.

"It all started with me shooting the ground-breaking of the Cleveland Indians' new spring training stadium down in Homestead this morning."

"What was Eduardo doing—"

"Wait." She held up her hand and swallowed a sip of wine. "I was just getting started. Coming back I hear an emergency call, a possible suicide, on the scanner. Guess who?"

"Dunno, I've been out of the loop today." I bit into a crunchy circle of plantain and nearly swooned. I had no idea how hungry I was. "Who?"

"Little Muffy, Dieter Steiner's fiancée."

"Is she okay?"

Lottie looked disgusted. "She's about the only one. Despondent little rich girl says nobody loves her, she wants to die, and roars off in her expensive sports car. Her parents panic and call the cops, who spot and chase the car, trying to save her. She runs that gorgeous Jag into a ficus tree just off San Souci Boulevard. Two police cars, sirens whooping and wailing, speed to her rescue and collide with each other. The sight of two wrecked squad cars causes a chain reaction involving six other cars and a beer truck. Traffic jams both ways, for miles. When I leave my car on the shoulder to go shoot pictures, some French Canadian in a rental car, busy gawking at the mess, rear-ends it."

"Oh, no! I didn't see any damage when you pulled up."

"It ain't bad," she said, with a dismissive gesture. "Just the rear bumper."

"Is Muffy all right?"

"Good as ever. Got out of the car under her own power, complaining that the sirens startled her into hitting the tree."

"Bet they charged her, didn't they?"

"Buncha traffics, then took her off to County for a psychiatric evaluation. Probably sitting in some posh psychiatric hospital by now." Lottie leaned back in her chair and reached again for her wineglass. "Then I get sent out to the Haitian demonstration."

"Didn't know one was scheduled."

"Wasn't, it was impromptu. Didn't even have a permit. They was marching to protest the batch of boat people the government sent back this morning. Had to be ninety-eight degrees out there. I had to run to keep up with them for four or five blocks, lugging that forty-pound camera bag."

She squeezed her eyes shut, massaging her temples. "Got the damnedest headache."

"Stress," I commiserated.

"No, the smoke."

"What smoke?"

"Didn't get to that part yet. The Reverend Julian St. Pierre and his followers decided to burn the President in effigy at the new Haitian Refugee Center."

"Oh, no."

"Yep, but the thang wouldn't burn until one of 'em tossed gasoline on it."

"Oh, no." I guessed what happened next.

She nodded. "It got away from 'em. Two of 'em went to the burn center, and about a dozen went to jail. The fire trucks had trouble getting through because police had closed off the street to contain the demonstrators. By the time they arrived the roof was already involved and we had ourselves a three-alarmer. Lordy," she said, rubbing the bridge of her nose. "Burning buildings always do something bad to my sinuses; my head's been aching ever since.

"I was filthy, sweaty and smelly, smoky and sooty.

I walked in water. My feet and my good boots got soaked—"

"Why didn't you wear your fire boots? You had all your gear in the car, didn't you?"

"A-course, but it was five blocks away. I never expected them Haitians to set themselves and their own center afire. It all happened so fast, who the hell had time to run back to the car, for Jesus' sake?"

"But Eduardo?"

"I'm getting to him," she said peevishly. "I'm getting to that slick bastard. Had to lay the groundwork first. I'm back at the paper, busy as hell, my darkroom as backed up as a cheap toilet, when Gretchen calls." We exchanged a meaningful glance at the dreaded name. "Eduardo needs me right away to shoot pictures at some society cocktail party for visiting Latin American dignitaries to kick off Hispanic Heritage Week."

"Why you?"

"Villanueva was assigned but got stuck in traffic somewhere on another job. I got elected because I was dumb enough to pick up the phone in the darkroom. Gretchen and me, we get into it pretty good over the phone, but Eduardo is bitching and moaning on the other line that he needs a photographer right away."

"Did she see you?"

"No." Lottie looked puzzled at my question. "I was back in the darkroom."

"Good."

"This was a private cocktail party before a big black-tie event. And Britt, I don't have to tell you how those people overdress. The women are all gussied up in long gowns. And there I am in the Embassy Room at the InterContinental, dirty and sweaty, ashes and smoke in my hair, my feet soaking wet and sooty."

"*Caramba*. Oh, Lottie!"

"I felt like Little Orphan Annie."

I couldn't picture Lottie, five feet eight inches tall with unruly red hair, as Little Orphan Annie, but I nodded, making sympathetic noises.

"What did you do?"

"I sneaked in a side door and hid behind the areca palms, miserable, lurking back there trying to signal Eduardo, who's all duded up in black tie, to steer the ambassador and the other fat cats whose pictures he wants in my direction so I can shoot them from behind there without showing myself."

I nodded, made sense.

"But did Eduardo cooperate? Did he give me a break? Oh, no. He makes a big deal, giganto fuss, gets everybody's attention, announces my presence, ignores the fact that I'm trying to whisper and hush him up. Then when he drags me out, insisting that I mingle and shoot candids, he suddenly sees—or smells—my clothes, backs off, and pretends not to know me, like I'm some homeless person. It was humiliating, Britt. I mean, I'm no complainer. I never mention that my arm has been numb for two years and that my neck is permanently stiff from lugging heavy camera equipment. He didn't have to do that."

"I know, I know," I soothed. "Women in this business have to be tougher. Eduardo could never handle the things you do."

"Damn straight. Look at you, Britt. You almost got killed in the last riot. A friend dies in your goddamn arms, and what did you do? Went back to the paper. Look at us. Cramps, PMS, whatever, we're out there. We don't blow deadlines, we don't complain or ask for special treatment."

True. No excuses for a woman struggling to make it in a male-dominated profession.

"Eduardo will pay," I promised. "He'll get his. Meanwhile, guess who I ran into?"

She scrutinized me for a long moment through sly half-closed eyes. She reads me like a book. "Some man," she said. "That cop. McDonald. He's back!" She perked up, instantly interested.

"Not exactly." I told her what a jerk McDonald had made of himself.

"So who was this new fella?"

"The captain of the *Sea Dancer*."

"Curt Norske? Hot! Hot! Hot! That man is so hot, you have to stop, drop, and roll!"

"You know him?"

"Sure, shot his picture once, on some story. Nearly melted my camera lens. Some charity party on his boat. Big blond hunka burning love. Gorgeous smile."

"That's him. Did he make a pass?"

"Polite and friendly, but he sure didn't invite me on no private cruise or ask for my number."

"It's not a private cruise, just a free one. I couldn't believe how McDonald acted."

"Sure showed his ass, didn't he? He don't want anybody else honeyfuggling around you. I knew it. I told you. He sees you with somebody else and gets as red hot as the doorknob to hell. Sure, he landed the job he wants, but it cost him. That badge ain't gonna keep him warm on a cold night. Bet he's on your answering machine already." Her expression was hopeful.

"Not too many cold nights in Miami." I sighed, picking at my yellow rice. I shook my head. "It didn't work then, Lottie. It wouldn't work now."

We settled in her comfortable living room, feet up, drinking wine, the TV on, volume low, Bitsy in my lap. Lottie's dog, Pulitzer, a sleek greyhound that she saved from being destroyed after he could no longer race, curled up in front of her chair.

"What's this?" I said, studying a tiny replica of a 1940s jukebox that sat on her coffee table.

"A radio," she said. "Lights up when the batteries are good. Got it from a mail order catalog."

She looked embarrassed, gesturing toward a stack of colorful catalogs in a magazine rack next to the couch.

"I never get a chance to shop," she said, as I picked one up. "So after a tough day like today, I sit here alone with my credit card, thumbing through those catalogs. Lordy, you order once and they send you a buncha new ones every day. Anyhow, I have a glass of wine or two and the next thing I know I'm dialing some eight-hundred number, ordering some doodad or another. You can call 'em twenty-four hours a day," she said brightly. "It don't matter how late. Then, a-course, by the time it comes in the mail I cain't even remember what I ordered. It's a surprise package waiting when I get home. Like Christmas. Though some of it is pretty weird"—she frowned— "and when I open the package I wonder why in hell I sent for it."

She looked a bit miffed at my expression.

"We all have our little weaknesses and idiosyncrasies," she said, shrugging. "We all get lonesome."

"Look at this," I said. "These don't look half bad." I showed her some of the silk flower arrangements in the catalog I was leafing through.

She looked over my shoulder. "Funny, with all the tropical flowers here, I still miss the evening primrose, the tufted Indian paint, the bluebonnets and bluebells from back home," she said wistfully. "And look at you, you've been hung up on that blue-eyed devil for too long. You've got to get out, Britt, take this boat captain up on his offer. See more men."

"I had lunch today with Dan Flood," I offered.

"Nice." She rolled her eyes. "But I mean somebody who's more than an old friend, somebody your age, with a life expectancy of more than six months. How is Dan doing, by the way?"

"He's depressed, living in the past. He's on a lot of medication. I'm worried about him. I just hope he's not suicidal."

"Poor Dan. Who wouldn't be, facing a death sentence?"

"You never know, Lottie. A doctor sent my great-granddad to Miami to die of TB when he was twenty-six—and the man lived to be ninety-two. Dan Flood may fool the doctors and outlive us all."

Lottie looked doubtful but raised her glass. "To Danny's health," she said. "You catch the Downtown Rapist yet?"

"Hey, look at that," I interrupted. The handsome face of Eric Fielding had flashed on the screen. "Turn up the sound."

A paid political commercial. We watched in silence as he spoke sincerely into the camera. The perfect politician: perfect haircut, perfect profile, perfect jacket slung over his shoulder, the state capitol behind him.

"Think he really did it?" Lottie said, her glass in her hand. "The little girl's murder, I mean. Mary Beth . . . what was her name?"

"Rafferty. Mary Beth Rafferty." I nodded. "I sure do."

"Too bad," she said quietly. " 'Cause I think he's gonna make it. He's got a lot more money, political support, and charisma than the other guy."

I shuddered involuntarily at the thought as we watched the unfolding images on the screen, Fielding smoothly addressing a classroom full of eager children about their future and that of our state. These children never heard about Mary Beth, who lost her future twenty-two years ago when this man was a teenager.

"The cops were convinced he got away with murder. The fact that he then had the chutzpah to go into law and politics made it even harder for them to swallow."

"What is it with this state?" Lottie said, the wine slowing her words and thickening her drawl. "Since I've been here we've had the governor they called the Prince of Darkness 'cause he looked like Dracula, then the country bumpkin—and now it looks like we're gonna have a man who committed murder. I kinda miss Dracula."

"He wasn't that bad," I agreed. I checked the time on Lottie's wall clock, a grinning ceramic cat with big eyes that rolled back and forth with each movement of its pendulum tail, proof of another catalog shopping spree, no doubt. "I'm keeping you up," I said. "You've had a long day." I put down my wineglass. "I better head home while I can still drive. They're cracking down, and I'd sure hate to get picked up DUI."

"The cop who busted you would probably be named officer of the month. You can stay in the guest room if you like."

"No, thanks."

"Let Bitsy drive."

"I'm fine." I really was. She had consumed most of the wine.

She leaned back, closing her eyes wearily. "Thanks for coming, Britt. Go ahead, just leave me for dead. I'll be okay."

8

Awash in a flood of dead-end calls and letters about the Downtown Rapist, I welcomed my turn at Take Two, a regular Friday feature. T2 is an update on a story or newsmaker now faded from the headlines. Sort of a "Did you ever wonder whatever happened to . . . ?" Some reporters gripe when assigned to do a T2, but not me. Like real life, journalism is full of unfinished stories. I am always curious about the people whose names and faces are splashed across newspaper pages, and T2 is a handy excuse to look them up and see what their post-headline lives are like.

My topic of choice, of course, was an update on the Mary Beth Rafferty case. I bounced it off Fred Douglas.

"You want to identify a rising political star, a candidate for our state's highest office, as a suspect in an ancient murder that happened when he was a child?" His voice climbed to a crescendo.

"A teenager," I said quickly, sitting on the edge of a chair in his office. "He was a teenager."

"Number one, the case is too old. Most of our readers don't even know it happened. Two, Fielding has an unblemished record and was never publicly linked to the murder."

"It was reported that he found the body."

"People find bodies in Miami every day," he scoffed. "That doesn't make them killers."

"What about the financial links between his parents and those of the murdered girl?"

He sighed. "What about them? It could mean the people are civic-minded saints, concerned and caring neighbors. Maybe they see the new husband as a savvy businessman who will return big bucks on their investment. Nothing against investing. Christ, Britt." He looked irked. "Maybe you've been on the police beat too long. The man is running hard in the most important campaign of his life. The word is he's set his sights on the White House and may have a shot at it. Nobody's ever accused him of anything in this case, and there's no new information. No way this newspaper would publish tenuous allegations that would smear him."

"But it looks like he really did it."

"If you can prove it, it's a helluva story, a lot bigger than a T-Two. But you yourself said the mother of the murdered girl isn't even interested in reopening the case. It's a dead issue, Britt. Don't waste any time on it. Drop it."

"But—"

"Drop it!"

I backed off and returned to my desk, cheeks burning. I sure didn't want to be reassigned to cover politics in Homestead or the county sewer-bond issue. The mere thought made my eye twitch. Now I knew how Dan felt when his superiors told him to lay off Fielding as a suspect twenty-two years ago.

My first idea for a T2 torpedoed, I decided to track down a paroled gunman named Applewaite who had shot down a Miami policeman named Foster six years earlier. Dan had griped about it at the police memorial service. Applewaite, a little man who used guns to make himself taller, had been sentenced to twenty years. He had done only five before the prison system's good time, gain time, credit for time served, and early release policy combined with the parole commission's benevolent wisdom to spring him back out onto the street.

It took several calls to track down Applewaite's parole officer, who made the usual speech: the man had paid his debt to society, was doing extremely well in his new life, and should be left alone by the jackals of the press. After consulting his records he proclaimed Applewaite a real success story, excelling in his employment at a Hialeah paint and body shop.

I called six Hialeah paint and body shops before I found the right one. The owner said Applewaite never showed up again after day three on the job, and he had heard the man was in jail in Monroe County. That was exactly where he was, on an armed robbery charge. I loved this T2.

And it was a good excuse to call and shoot the breeze with Dan. I told him how my editor had vetoed my initial idea and we vented our mutual outrage against newspaper management and Fielding's White House aspirations. He was pleased that Applewaite was back behind bars.

"Thanks for letting me know. That's the safest place for him," he said cryptically.

Talking to him cheered me up. More genial than he had been at lunch, he even made me laugh.

"Nothing should surprise us anymore, Britt. Let me tell ya, if there was any justice, Elvis would still be alive and his impersonators would be dead." We promised we would have lunch again soon.

* * *

Half believing Lottie's prediction that jealousy would reawaken McDonald's romantic attentions, I checked my messages with an anticipation I tried to deny.

He didn't call, but lots of other people did.

The next afternoon I began returning calls and opening mail simultaneously, phone tucked beneath my chin. One message intrigued me. Somebody named Jeff had left word that he was "Not the Downtown Rapist."

He sounded relieved that I had returned his call.

"Listen," he said urgently, speaking softly as though afraid of being overheard. "I'm in a bind here." His voice had a side-of-the-mouth quality, the slick oily pitch of a guilty motorist trying to con a cop out of issuing a traffic ticket. "The law has been out to talk to me on this Downtown Rapist thing."

"You're a suspect?"

He made an exasperated sound. "No. Well, I don't know if they believe me. I might, I might look, ya know, suspicious. I admit I sorta sneak around, ya know. I park the car a couple blocks away, circle around on foot, I might duck in and out of a building, but it ain't what it looks like."

"What is it, then?"

He hesitated.

"If the police were interested in you, they must have a good reason." Curious now, I was prodding.

"Things are not always what they seem."

"Most of the time they are," I said flatly.

"Look," he whined. "I admit that I walk around a lot near the Universal building—"

"Where the rapist has struck. Twice."

He took a deep breath and let it out noisily. "I just cut through it, through the lobby. You know those apartment houses across the street, facing the block directly behind that building?"

"Yeah."

"Well, I go by there maybe a couple a times a week, ya know, to see somebody."

"A supplier?"

"Nah, a broad. You know."

"So what's the big deal?"

"The big deal"—he lowered his voice—"is that I'm a married man with a family."

"And . . ."

"I don't need my wife getting wind of this whole thing. I wanna make sure you don't put nothing in the paper."

"So did you give the police the name of your . . . friend, and are they going to go talk to her?"

"That's another thing," he said. "It's a very sensitive situation, ya know."

"She's married too."

"You catch on fast."

His guilty conscience combined with a lack of knowledge about how cops and newspapers operate had the man envisioning his name in headlines. Little did he know that no one cared, except those immediately involved in his little soap opera. I didn't feel sorry for him, though he and his lover were probably only doing what lots of married folk do. No matter what care cheaters take, there is no way to foresee being entangled in a net tossed out by police in a manhunt.

"There's kids involved on both sides," the man on the line was saying. "This could hurt a lotta people, you know?"

"You should have thought of that," I said, sounding pious.

"Nothing's gonna make the paper, is it?" His voice quavered with concern.

"No." I sighed and reassured him. "Don't worry. If you're not the rapist and you don't get charged with anything, the police and the newspaper don't care about your private life."

There was a pause. "You're saying I should."

"I didn't say that, but it doesn't sound like such a bad idea," I said, tearing open a letter scrawled in thick black marker on lined, yellow paper:

The jump out boys are ruining Miami. I don't get
high anymore—I just get cross-eyed and sleepy.
I demand better drugs!

I smiled, setting the unsigned letter to one side. It would give a grin to members of the VIN (Vice, Intelligence, and Narcotics) Squad, better known on the street as the jump-out boys for their speed and agility when jumping out of their undercover cars and trucks to seize stunned suspects and their drugs.

"You're so right," the man on the phone was saying with an almost religious fervor. "I'm gonna give this whole thing some serious thought."

I tore open the next letter.

The grungy envelope looked familiar. Another regular pen pal.

Say Britt Montero,
Why do you not listen. You have offended me.

A scrawled bow with arrows.

I crumpled and tossed it. A tiny dust trail leaked from the envelope as I did. My hands felt powdery. I squinted up at the air vent, then down at the tiny drift of powder on my desk. Yuck, I thought, touching my fingers to my nose. The stuff was sweet smelling and came off the letter.

My heart skipped a beat. I almost fished the crumpled thing out of the waste bin, but turned instead to the medical writer, who sat behind me to Ryan's right. "Miriam?"

She looked up, squinting behind the ultraviolet protective lenses of her glasses, which reflected a greenish glow from her computer screen.

"Those surgical gloves with talc inside. Is there enough of it to leave noticeable traces on a paper the wearer handled? And does it smell like dusting powder?"

"How the hell would I know?" she said impatiently and went back to work.

I thanked her profusely for her courtesy and then called Rico, an emergency room nurse and sometime source. His answer to both questions was no. Now I was becoming paranoid, I thought. Just another weirdo who writes letters.

A sudden flurry of activity stirred the newsroom and I looked up. My heart lurched and I was sure I was hallucinating. Eric Fielding stood six feet from my desk.

He was real. Tall, trim, and tanned, wearing a navy pinstripe suit, a white-on-white silk shirt, and a power tie, he was vital and youthful looking, despite the shock of prematurely silver hair. His wife was with him, an athletic-looking blonde who would have looked at home on a tennis court. Tall and rangy like her husband, she was the perfect image of a politician's wife, smiling easily, carefully and casually dressed in a Laura Ashley cotton print. A child in a pink sundress tagged along after them. She wasn't wearing a little hat, but she made me think of Mary Beth Rafferty.

Fielding was pressing flesh, shaking hands, high-fiving the political reporter, smiling down at Gretchen, who gushed all over him.

I bid a hasty goodbye to my caller.

"What's he doing here?" I asked Janowitz, a veteran general assignment reporter who had wandered up from his desk at the back of the newsroom.

"Came in for his editorial board meeting," he said.

Candidates seeking endorsement by the *News* are routinely interviewed by the board. They rarely sweep though the newsroom shaking hands, but being the hometown candidate, Fielding was already on friendly terms with most of the editors and reporters.

"Come, Kimberly," I heard Mrs. Fielding say. She took the child's hand and led her to one side, so she would not be lost in the newsroom crowd clustering around her husband.

"Just spent a couple of days down in the Keys," Fielding said heartily. "A little golf, some fishing, a family break from the campaign, resting up for the homestretch."

"The polls are looking good," someone told him.

I joined the crowd. "Britt Montero," I said when my turn came.

He nodded; his handshake was firm. "Saw your piece on Applewaite this morning; it was right on target. That is exactly what we need to prevent in this state. Intolerable," he said, eyes flashing with righteous indignation. The man is good, I thought, really good.

I opened my mouth and saw Fred Douglas in the

group surrounding us. His eyes narrowed, and he gave a slight shake of his head.

"Good luck," I mumbled, not believing the words that came out of my mouth.

The smiling candidate turned to pump someone else's hand.

He walked back to the executive offices, trailed by the political writer and Gretchen. His wife and her little girl stopped at the Style section, where Eduardo and several other writers appeared overjoyed to see them. Fred instructed Ryan to escort Mrs. Fielding and Kimberly down to the third-floor cafeteria, where they could enjoy refreshments while waiting for the candidate.

"Should I buy?" he asked anxiously. "Can I put it on my expense account?"

I sat at my desk pretending to work, watching the hallway between the editorial offices and the elevator. Something inside me could not pass up this chance. I checked the time. Endorsement interviews are usually forty-five minutes to an hour long.

Sure enough, he reappeared an hour later, beaming and jubilant, still trailed by fans and glad-handers. I left my desk, carrying a notebook and pen. "Mr. Fielding," I said, "your wife and daughter are in the cafeteria. I'll show you where it is."

As the elevator doors opened the hand-shakers backed off and went back to work. We stepped inside, alone together.

My questions should have been worked up to subtly but there was no time for small talk.

"Mr. Fielding, do you remember Mary Beth Rafferty?"

He reacted like he had heard a shot, smile fading.

"I certainly do," he said, following a pause. "That was something no one could ever forget."

"The case is still unsolved."

"I'm aware of that." His color suddenly didn't look as healthy or vibrant. Perhaps it was the lighting.

"I guess you are aware," I said softly, "that the police considered you a suspect?"

His eyes assessed me coldly. No speech writers to help him here, I thought. "At the time," he said carefully, "everyone was considered a suspect."

"But to the detective who investigated the case, you still are. Why—"

The sluggish elevator I always complain about now seemed to move with lightning speed and the doors opened onto the lobby.

"Sorry," I said, as he moved to step out. "I forgot to hit the button for the third floor. We have to go back up."

People who were waiting came aboard and recognized Fielding. "Good to see you," he murmured, shaking hands with a business writer and a columnist for the Spanish-language edition.

Fielding stared stonily at my profile for the rest of the ride.

"Here we are," I said brightly. "Third floor."

The cafeteria was a long trek through winding halls to the left. I stepped to the right, into a small alcove near the personnel office, and he followed.

"What is this?" he said. "Did someone suggest you bring this up?"

"No," I said. "I just wanted to ask a few questions. Why do you think the police still suspect you?"

His jaw tensed. "I was not aware that they did. I have not spoken to them about it in years. During campaigns like this people like to repeat ugly rumors and innuendo and half-truths. Listen, Ms. . . ."

"Montero," I said.

He nodded. "I'm on a tight schedule. I'm sorry we don't have more time, but I want you to understand that that terrible day years ago changed my life forever."

"In what way?"

"I was a young man, a teenager, who discovered the body of a horribly violated little girl. That child is one of the reasons I stand here today, as a law-and-order candidate, one of the reasons I have pursued a life of public service." The politician picked up momentum and was on a roll.

"Didn't you have a history of window peeping prior to the murder?"

"Who has been feeding you these things? Who have you been talking to?" he demanded, voice tightly controlled. His eyes no longer projected self-assurance and confidence. They were those of a man confronted suddenly by his past. "I was your typically curious teenage boy. Whatever mistakes I may have made then were no more serious than most, and far less serious than those of today's troubled young men."

"Then you *were* a troubled young man. Have you ever undergone psychiatric care?"

"What are you trying to do?" He stared at me with undisguised contempt.

"I'm just trying to piece together what happened," I said reasonably. "I'm curious about the financial arrangements between your parents and Mary Beth Rafferty's mother."

"You have no right, you have no right—" His face had reddened, a pulse throbbing in his temple. "This has gone far enough. I won't dignify your inferences with any answers. I don't know what you think you're doing. But there's a great deal at stake here, and I will not be blackmailed or intimidated!" His voice rose. The anger in his face was frightening.

"I'm only a reporter," I said. "I'm supposed to ask questions."

"Watch your step, Ms. Montero," he said slowly. "You watch your step."

He wheeled blindly away from me.

"The cafeteria is to your left," I said weakly. "Straight down the hall. Just follow it around and you can't miss it."

He spun around for a last malevolent look and stared, as though memorizing my face.

Swell, I thought, watching him stride quickly down the hall. I love Florida, I was born here. Now if this guy gets elected, I'll have to move.

I returned to my desk, trying to act innocent. It wasn't easy. Especially after Ryan came back. "Guess what, Britt? Maybe we're not gonna endorse Fielding after all."

"What makes you say that?"

"You should have seen him after his interview with the board. They must have hammered him. He was upset, mad as hell."

"Really?"

"Snapped at the wife and kid. All he wanted was out of here."

"Not a good sign," I agreed.

I had trouble getting to sleep that night, and shortly after I succeeded, the telephone woke me. It was Harry Arroyo.

"What happened?" I said, sitting up in bed, suddenly wide awake again. "Did you catch the rapist?"

"No," he said bleakly. "He just hit again."

"Oh, no," I said. "And he got away?"

"Yeah."

"What happened?"

"This was different from the others. He's changing his MO on us."

"How?"

"This one wasn't in an office building rest room. It was in the parking garage. And he cut her. He's getting more violent."

"You sure it was him?"

"Without a doubt."

"How bad is she hurt?"

"She'll be okay," he said. Easy for you to say, I thought. But I knew what he meant. Her physical injuries were not life threatening.

"I'm glad you called, Harry. Thanks." He had never done that before, and I was appreciative.

"It wasn't my idea, Britt. The victim wants to talk to you."

"What?" Fear constricted my heart. "Is she someone I know?"

"No. But she said she has to talk to you. Can you come down?"

"Sure," I said. "Give me twenty minutes. Where are you?"

"At the station," he said. "We just brought her in from the rape center."

The time on my bedside clock was 2:15 A.M. I pulled a comb through my hair and dove into my navy jumpsuit, kept ready and waiting, hanging on the back of my closet door to slip into fast when called out on middle-of-the-night stories. Bitsy trotted right at my heels, expecting to depart with me. She yelped and whimpered as I left without her.

Normally I love late night driving, minus the traffic, heat, and hectic pace of daylight hours. A sudden summer rain had fallen earlier, and the streets were wet and empty. He was out there somewhere. Why couldn't they nail him?

I locked in the city frequency on my scanner and heard the crime scene being worked at the Eastcoast Bank Building. They had waited until the rain stopped to tow the victim's car in for processing under bright lights.

The sleepy officer manning the front desk used his key card to give me access to the lobby elevator. It was quarter to three. The station was deserted. Most members of the midnight shift were out on the street.

Harry met me outside the rape squad office.

"She's a troubleshooter on the bank's computer systems," he said. "Didn't plan to work late tonight, but they had some trouble on the mainframe. Name is Marianne Rhodes, white female, thirty-one. Engaged to a stockbroker who's on the way. She was aware of the rapes, carried Mace in her purse, and called for a security-guard escort when she had to use the rest room.

"She logged out of the building at 11:21 P.M. Security guard walked her to the third level of the parking garage. He watched her unlock her car and open the door, then turned back inside to go on clocking his rounds."

"What happened then?"

"She gets into the car, and before she can close the door he's out of the shadows and right on top of her, with the knife."

I felt a sickening chill.

"This is the most violent he's been with a victim. He smacked her around pretty good, cut her, and left her tied up," he said. "She probably would have been there all night except that the same guard, on rounds an hour later, noticed her car still there. He walked over to take a look and found her inside, bound and taped across the mouth."

"He didn't see anybody else?"

"Nope, just cleaning women and employees working late. The guy's like a ghost."

"Why does she want to talk to me?"

"Because the rapist is mad as hell. At you." He smiled as he turned and opened the door to his office.

"Me?" I asked, following him numbly.

The woman sat on a wooden chair clutching her elbows as if she was cold, head down, her knees together. She wore what was once a nice suit. The fabric was torn, cut, and bloodied. The right side of her face was bruised and swollen, her eye blackened. On the left side, a bloodied bandage didn't quite cover the sutures.

Her dark glossy hair was matted on the side with the sutures and coated with a powdery substance. There was a cut under her chin, and the front of her white blouse was bloodstained. Her stockings were torn and her skirt stained and dusty.

"Are you all right?" I said, knowing that she was not.

"You're her?" Her eyes were red and watery.

"Britt Montero."

She winced as I said it. "You're her. But I don't look anything like you."

"What do you mean?"

"He acted like I was you. He kept calling me by your name." She shook her head and shivered.

"Are you sure?"

Her fists clenched. "You think I made this up?"

"No, no, of course not. I'm just shocked. What did he say?"

"I don't speak Spanish," she whispered. "All I recognized was some curse words and your name. I read your stories. He said your name every time he hurt me."

A chill that left gooseflesh in its wake rippled up and down my arms.

I glanced up at Harry, who remained impassive. She had obviously told him all this.

"Be careful," she said, teeth chattering. "He really hates you, you know."

"She's cold," I said to Harry. "Do you have a jacket or a blanket?"

Another detective muttered something in his ear. "Send him up," Harry said.

"Your fiancé, Ben, is here," he told her.

Tears welled in her eyes, and she stared at the floor.

"If there is anything I can do for you, please call me," I said, putting my card in her hands. The long graceful fingers were cut and bruised, the nails broken.

"Put my name in the paper," she said, her voice rising. "Tell everybody what he did to me. I was just trying to do my job. They were supposed to protect me. Everybody knew about the rapist. Why didn't they have better security?" Her voice broke into a sob.

"We don't normally identify rape victims," I said, "unless they agree to be quoted and have their names used."

"Do it," she said. "I want you to put my name in the paper. Tell them what he did."

"Think about it first," I said softly, as a pale young man came rushing in, his face taut.

"Oh, my God, Marianne," he said, taking her in his arms. After a moment he noticed me.

"Who are you?"

I told him.

"Good God! You're not going to put this in the newspaper, are you?" He stared at me in disgust. "Please have enough decency to show us some privacy."

Harry caught up with me in the hallway and walked me down to the lobby. "Watch yourself, Britt," he said.

It was the second time I'd received that warning in less than twenty-four hours.

10

Sinister shadows haunted the streets as I walked through the soft, moist air to my parked car, my footsteps echoing in the dark. I locked the doors and drove out of the police station parking lot, headlights piercing the night. I have nothing to fear from the rapist, I assured myself. Criminals are cowards who prey on the helpless. They abhor publicity and avoid people whose bosses buy ink by the barrel.

As I sat waiting at a red light west of the Boulevard, without another vehicle in sight, a figure loomed at the mouth of an alley, emerging from the shadows like a wraith. My spine tingled. My fingers tightened on the wheel. The man lurched my way and I tapped the gas pedal, rolling through the red light, heart pounding. Why don't they set these signals on flasher at night? I thought angrily. The dark form stood alone in the deserted street staring after my taillights.

The rapist did not know me or how to find me among the fifteen hundred or so people who passed through the huge *News* building each day. That is one advantage of print as opposed to TV, where a reporter's face is as well known to viewers as those of their own family.

I circled my block before parking, eyes checking the rearview mirror and scanning the quiet street, the parked cars, the hibiscus hedges, all potential hiding places for an intruder. It is not Miami, or the night, that is frightening, I told myself. It is the man who is loose in it. A man who has not been stopped by publicity or intense police presence.

Stepping quickly from the car, house keys in hand, I strode purposefully to my apartment, glad I had left a light on inside. I closed the door behind me, sighing with relief, secure at home with good locks, a vigilant landlady, and a dog with police experience.

I brushed my teeth, turned out the lights, and retired for the second time that night. Even I was surprised when I got out of bed in the dark to double-check the front door lock, then took the gun from beneath my mattress and slipped it under the pillow next to me.

I awoke early next morning, skipped breakfast, and went straight to the office to write the story of the new attack. Feeling strangely alert despite my lack of sleep or appetite, I looked up the number for Dr. Stone Simmons, the police shrink, whom I had met only in passing before. What the story needed, and I wanted to know, was more about the rapist and his behavior. The doctor answered his own phone but did not seem thrilled to hear from me.

"This is not authorized procedure," he said. "You know I am unable to discuss a case under investigation without the approval of the detectives or Lieutenant Riley."

"Doctor, I'm not asking for specifics about evidentiary material that may be withheld by the investigators. I'm just seeking your opinion about state of mind. Why would the man mention my name? What motivates the anger the most recent victim saw in him, his change in MO, the escalation of violence?"

I heard small sounds like lips smacking, Simmons puffing on his ever-present pipe. A lean middle-aged man with a salt-and-pepper beard and a gray sweater vest no matter how steamy the weather, he had a disconcerting way of scrutinizing those around him as though studying them like insects from some more lofty plane of knowledge and understanding.

"Interesting questions," he commented.

"What do you think?"

"I would expect that the man you refer to as the Downtown Rapist has a fair amount of intellect, given the fact that he is reading the newspaper—which is obvious," he added, "since he knows your name. Rapists are not all stupid lowlifes, half-wits, or morons."

"And he's been smart enough to elude capture so far."

"Correct," he said, as though I were a slow learner who had surprisingly come up with a right answer.

"Do you think he changed his MO because too many people are aware of it now?"

"Not exactly. He's angry, and what do rapists do to express themselves when they are angry?"

"They rape."

"Correct again. Generally speaking, someone with his proclivities would seek to make his presence felt to the person he is most angry with, which in this case is you, judging from what this victim has said." He went back to sucking on his pipe.

"Why would he be so angry at me? Everybody in town has been reporting this story."

"Ah, but you were the first, weren't you? And therefore responsible in his eyes for everything, all the coverage that followed. And of course you have written about him in greater detail than anyone else. Maybe it was something you said."

He seemed to consider that amusing. I wasn't laughing.

"And, of course, you are a woman. It is important for him to have power over women. I noted that in your weekend story you used a quote from the psychological profile prepared for the investigators, stating that he commits these rapes to tell himself he is in fact a man, and sexually adequate, which he of course is not. He may very well take that personally."

"But what made him change his MO?"

"When was the last story you wrote about him?"

"Sunday. Monday in our Spanish-language edition."

"And the rape followed by two days." He paused, ruminating. "Of course, we don't know exactly when he saw the story."

"You're saying that the rape may have been a result of the story?"

"It might be reasonable to believe that he was attempting to send a message, the message being that this could happen to you. Or that the victim in his eyes was a substitute. He had no access to you, so he raped her."

"Dr. Simmons." My voice sounded strained and felt tight. "I resent being made to feel responsible." I thought of Marianne Rhodes's slashed face and haunted eyes. "This man was out there raping women long before my first story. The police were trying to keep it quiet, and there were several attacks before word one ever appeared in the newspaper. Women had to be warned, the public had to be made aware, they had to become outraged and aroused enough to help apprehend him."

"But they haven't thus far, have they? Methinks you protest too much, Ms. Montero. I understand your point of view, but it seems clear that this time, in this most recent assault, he took his rage against you out on another woman."

Unconsciously my hand went to my cheek, fingers trailing the path of the stitches I had seen on Marianne Rhodes's face. I imagined the bruises on her body and closed my eyes for a moment.

"Are you suggesting that he might come after me?"

There was silence as he puffed. "Could be. It's impossible to predict exactly what a person like this will or will not do. But it would not surprise me if he attempted to communicate with you."

I swallowed.

"Is your phone number and address listed in the telephone directory, Ms. Montero?"

"First initial only," I said, trying to sound jaunty. "And there are a lot of Monteros in Miami."

"I don't mean to pry into your personal life, but are you married or do you live with someone?"

"No," I said crisply. "I like living alone."

"Do you reside in an isolated area?"

"My apartment is the farthest one from the street, but I have a dog, and my landlady and her husband live nearby."

"Very reassuring. And you have not been the recipient of any unusual calls or messages?"

"Are you kidding? Every weirdo, obsessed wacko, paranoid schizo, and lonely senior citizen in Miami tries to communicate with me. Dr. Simmons, you would have a field day with my calls and letters. It's routine in this business. I have one pen pal who swears he's radioactive and has traveled to distant planets—without a space ship. Another guy sends me grungy letters with some kind of dusting powder on them. There's a former mental patient who complains that he's constantly followed by a stranger who looks like Sylvester Stallone in *Nighthawks*. Another one accuses his neighbors of causing his headaches by aiming laser beams into his apartment, and a lady insists that if we watch some old *Kojak* or *Perry Mason* show we can solve the case." I realized I was babbling. Why do psychiatrists always make me nervous?

There was a long pause. "All very interesting. What do you do with all this correspondence?"

"I've been thinking of papering my bathroom with it."

He chuckled. "Do you plan to continue writing about the Downtown Rapist?"

"Of course. I'm working on a story now. You're not suggesting a press blackout because it might make him mad?"

"Far be it from me to interfere with the fourth estate. I was simply curious if you yourself plan to continue, rather than passing the torch on to a colleague."

"It's my story," I said simply. "Anything you want to say about him?"

"Only the obvious: that the violent nature of his attacks is escalating and the danger to future victims could be considerable."

"Do you think he might commit murder?"

"Anything is possible."

"What would your advice be to any woman who might find herself in an encounter with him?"

"I would advise any woman in such an unfortunate position to try not to make him any angrier than he already is."

Not much of a choice, I thought.

After saying goodbye, I sat thinking about the questions he had asked. Simmons probably thought he was being funny. That SOB is trying to scare me, I thought, though the telephone book does list my address. I do live alone. My dog weighs only six pounds. And my vigilant landlords are elderly and unable to hear anything through the thick walls of our old building.

I thought about calling Marianne Rhodes, but before I could, she called me. "You *are* writing the story, aren't you?" she said, her voice unsteady.

"Yes, I'm working on it now."

"I wondered why you hadn't called me." She sounded as though she had not slept and repeated her demand that I publish her name, though I could hear her dissenting fiancé in the background.

"Well," I said cautiously. "With the man still at large, it might not be advisable."

"It doesn't matter," she insisted, her voice rising. "He knows who I am. He took my purse, my driver's license, my ID. This should be my choice. It's time rape victims came out of the closet. I want everybody to know what happened. Send someone to come take my picture, so they can see what he did to me!"

By that time her fiancé and she were quarreling, and at one point he tried to hang up the phone. "Stay out of this, Ben!" she shrieked.

I cringed at their pain and assured her I would discuss with my editors whether or not she would be identified in our story.

I brought it up when Fred Douglas asked me to fill him in on my story before the news meeting.

His eyes were troubled. "What do you think, Britt?"

"No way. She's not responsible, not in her right mind at the moment. She'd regret it later."

"Sounds like the right call to me."

I also mentioned that Dr. Simmons thought our stories had angered the rapist into action. "That's ridiculous." He snorted.

I wondered why his denial did not comfort me. "That's what I thought," I told him, adding that the doctor felt that the rapist might attempt to communicate with us.

Fred chewed his lower lip, scrutinizing me thoughtfully. "Britt, would you feel more comfortable handing the story off to Ryan?"

"Not on your life." I spoke with more vigor than I felt.

Backing off on an unpleasant story would play right into the hands of those in the newsroom who still believe no woman belongs on the police beat.

"Atta girl," Fred said. "I guess I should alert Maddie, in case he writes an angry letter to the editor." Maddie Elliott is the proper sixtyish secretary who handles the Letters column on the editorial page.

"Have her get his return address."

He grinned and hurried off to his meeting as I went over my story.

Marianne Rhodes had provided no new information about the rapist, and his change in MO was disconcerting, I thought, pushing open the wooden door marked LADIES. I walked down the narrow corridor to another door that opens into a lounge and locker room with two showers. In an adjoining room are six stalls and six sinks. Both rooms appeared empty. The only sound was water dripping slowly in one of the shower rooms. He could be anywhere, I thought. Even here.

When I returned from the cafeteria later, with a cup of coffee, one of the messages on my desk instantly caught my eye.

Call Lt. McDonald at his office, ASAP. That was it. Not exactly ardent and romantic enough to sizzle my socks and curl my toes. Perversely, I shuffled it to the bottom of the stack.

Phone tucked under my chin, I began returning calls and opening mail simultaneously. One message was from Dan, and I returned it immediately.

"Where have you been?" I scolded. "You're never home. I was ready to file a missing-persons report. I tried twice to call you."

"Didn't know I was supposed to wait for your call. Been busy." His words were brusque. "Got a TV there?"

"Sure." Three small sets sit in front of the city-desk clerk who monitors the TV news, listing the stories and their play, to ensure that we haven't missed anything.

"Something you should see on the noon news, Channel Seven. I'll hold."

Gloria, the city-desk clerk, was on the phone. I stood at her side watching the screen. The face was familiar. Marianne Rhodes. "Oh, no," I whispered.

When the blond anchorwoman with the big hair and silly smirk asked, "How does it feel to be the seventh victim of the man known as the Downtown Rapist?" I swore softly and went back to my phone.

"Thought you'd be interested," he said. "I'm surprised they didn't protect her identity and show her only in silhouette. They used her name and everything. The promo said they'll have more at six."

"I know, I know," I mourned. "They're vultures. They took advantage of her. I'm sure she'll be sorry she did this."

"You gonna use her name?"

"Not if I can help it, but she sure blew it by being on TV."

"What were you trying to call me about?"

I filled him in on Fielding.

"Wish I coulda seen his face," he gloated. "That son of a bitch."

"He definitely didn't go away happy," I said.

"What's new on the rapist?"

"Nothing, really, except that he's mad as hell and has changed his MO," I said. "Hey, Dan, did you hear about the guy they arrested for impersonating a cop?"

"No." He was dead serious.

"He was asleep at three A.M. in a donut shop."

"Not funny. Did you ask the Rhodes woman if she knows any of the other victims?" he demanded, his tone businesslike. No one would ever believe this man had retired, I thought.

"No. I guess I just assumed that if she did, she would have brought it up."

"Never assume anything. What you really ought to do," he suggested, "is find out what, if anything, they have in common. Maybe they've attended the same parties, the same aerobics class; maybe they buy their gas at the same service station."

"But I thought these victims were random," I said, frowning, "in the wrong place at the wrong time. He lurks in a ladies' room and attacks the next woman who walks in."

"But what if they aren't? A lot of older women work in these buildings, but did you notice that all his victims have been attractive and between the ages of twenty-one and thirty-five? Maybe it's not so random. Somehow he's able to come and go without being noticed. What if he's selecting and stalking these women? There might be a thread linking them together, like shopping in the same supermarket, eating lunch in the same restaurant, or going to the same beach."

"What makes you so smart about rape investigations? You always worked homicide."

Gloria had caught my eye, gesturing and mouthing a message. "Lieutenant McDonald on the other line. Says he has to talk to you."

There was a time when I would have hung up on God to talk to that man. I put my palm over the mouthpiece. "Tell him I'll call him back," I said breezily.

"Same stuff applies to serial killers as it does to serial rapists," Dan was saying. "And you forget that up until ten years ago, homicide detectives also investigated sex crimes. I put my share of rapists away."

He sounded like the old Dan. "Let me take some of these questions down," I said. "I'll have to ask Harry, because I don't have all the victims' names."

"Good, maybe it'll light a fire under 'im. Also check and see if the victims had any contact with the police or fire departments in the month before they were attacked."

"You think the rapist could be a cop or a fireman?"

"Some cops are capable of anything," he said quietly.

"But we think he's Cuban, probably Marielito."

"Could be anybody. We have our share on the city payroll."

"What's your gut feeling, Dan? Do you have a hunch?"

I picked a letter from the stack of mail. The handwriting looked familiar. I tore it open, then looked up at Gloria. She stood at my desk, her face solemn.

"Lieutenant Riley is on one line for you and Detective Harry Arroyo on another. They both want to talk to you right away."

My heart lurched. Maybe they had caught the rapist.

"Okay," I said, excited. "Give me the lieutenant and ask Harry to hold." I bid Dan a hasty goodbye and picked up the line on the first ring.

K. C. Riley was in her usual form.

"Goddammit, Britt. What the hell's the matter with you?"

"Good afternoon to you too, lieutenant."

"Don't get smart-ass with me. Communication is a two-way street. Why the hell didn't you pass your information along to us?"

"On the Downtown Rapist?"

"Don't play dumb."

"I don't have any information," I said, tiring of the conversation fast. I should have taken Harry's call first to find out what was going on.

"We want those damn letters and we want them now!"

"What letters?"

"The ones with the fucking powder on them!"

"How'd you know about that?"

"We have information that you got them days ago." Her voice was poisonous.

"I threw them out," I said, my stomach suddenly cramping.

I held the phone and the stream of invective it spewed six inches away from my ear.

"But don't worry." My voice was tense, and my right eyelid had begun to twitch uncontrollably. "I just got another one."

"What? Today?"

"Just now. I just opened it."

"I'm sending somebody over to pick it up; you better come along. Don't let anybody touch it!"

I jerked my hand off the envelope as though it were red hot, rubbing my fingertips together.

I hung up and took the call on hold. "Harry?"

"Jesus, Britt, where you been, how come you—oh, Christ."

I heard the lieutenant's voice in the background as she bore down on him.

"See ya," he said, and hung up.

The phone rang again immediately. On my feet, about to tell the city desk what had just happened, I snatched it up impatiently. "Britt Montero."

"Britt?" The voice that used to make my knees weak. At the moment I was too preoccupied.

"McDonald."

"Yeah. Have you talked to the rape squad yet?"

"Not exactly, but I've been cussed out by Lieutenant Riley and hung up on by Arroyo."

"You should have returned my call." He sounded like he was itching for an argument himself.

What the hell was going on here? What did he have to be annoyed about? My eyes were glued in fascination to the letter. I had torn the envelope open but the folded paper inside was only half out. Should I or shouldn't I?

I studied the grimy legal-size white envelope addressed in red pen to:

MISS BRITT MONTERO
MIAMI DAILY NEWS
MIAMI, FLA.

The writer was heavy-handed on his downstrokes, like somebody in a hurry or mad as hell. The y had a chopped-off tail, and the i's were dotted with hard little circles that had the centers filled in solid. No street address. Not even a zip code. And no return address.

Had the envelope contained a sweepstakes check or a marriage proposal from a long-lost love who would save me from all this, it would have been diverted directly to the dead letter office. But let a rapist drop a line, and the postal workers perform like champions. What makes the cops even think this guy is the rapist? I wondered.

"This is a serious matter," barked the long-lost love on the other end of my telephone line.

Suddenly I caught on. "Dr. Simmons. The shrink notified the rape squad about the letters, didn't he?"

He paused a beat, as though weighing the pros and cons of lying, then owned up. "Right."

"McDonald, this is a gross overreaction. I casually mentioned a crank letter in a conversation. I get tons of them. We all do. This is embarrassing. These letters are powdery and I know the rapist uses surgical gloves, the ones with talc. But the powder on these letters is much heavier and sweeter-smelling than that."

"Right. But you don't know everything, Britt. This is serious."

I detected a genuine note of concern, prompting me to ask, "What's wrong? Why were you so uptight when they hauled that car out of the drink the other day? When I was talking to Captain Norske?"

"Captain?" I heard the sneer. "You mean that cracker in the ice-cream suit? I thought he was selling you a Popsicle."

Damn, I thought, smiling. He *is* jealous. "What do you mean I don't know everything?"

He resumed his officious tone. "The Downtown Rapist case isn't mine to talk about. It came up at a staff meeting, but it's Lieutenant Riley's investigation. I'm sure the rape squad will fill you in, but watch your step, Britt. The guy is still at large. He's dangerous. I know you never listen, but don't go pulling any stunts to get a story."

I thanked him for the advice, hung up, and beelined for Fred Douglas's office.

The news that the cops were on the way seemed to elate him. "Let's get Mark Seybold in on this," he said, punching numbers into his phone. "Think it's the real thing, Britt?" he said, before Mark, the *News'* lawyer, picked up.

"I didn't think so, but they *are* withholding information about the suspect, details I don't know, and something about this letter has them really excited—without seeing it, of course."

He conferred briefly with Mark, who said he'd come right up from his second-floor office.

"Where is it?" Fred said, bounding out his door into the newsroom.

"On my desk," I said reluctantly, feeling a slight sense of anxiety, "but we shouldn't touch it."

"Did you open it?"

"Just the envelope, I didn't even read it before I got the call from the rape squad lieutenant."

"Call photo," he said on the way to my desk. "We need somebody to shoot pictures of it now." He turned to me. "Sometimes getting things back from the police proves to be a problem. Technically, that letter is the property of this newspaper and you as its representative. We have to strike a deal with them." He rubbed his hands together like King Midas might have done right after something he touched turned to gold.

"Fred, I think we should just give it to them without a hassle. I mean, if it really is from the guy, we don't want the cops to waste any time if this could help identify him."

"This it?" He bent over my desk, his nose practically touching the envelope.

"Don't touch it," I warned, beginning to feel jittery.

"Did you call a photographer?"

I dialed photo and asked Antonio, who works in the darkroom, to come out and shoot pictures of the letter.

"What's going on, Britt?" Now Ryan stood next to Fred. The elevator pinged as Mark Seybold stepped off and joined us.

"This it?" he asked, squinting through his glasses as a crowd began to gather.

"Don't touch it," I said.

Fred and Mark conferred.

"We have to strike a deal with the cops that puts us on the inside of the investigation," Fred declared.

Mark nodded. "An information trade. We should lock them into giving us the inside info. Part of the agreement should be that they can't discuss any of this with the competition. They get the letter only with the proviso that we"—he nodded at me—"Britt, gets to see the crime lab results."

Oh, man, I thought, shaking my head, the cops are not gonna like this. "It would probably be better for our relationship with the police to just cooperate and give it to them," I said. "In the interests of justice."

"I'll call security," Mark said, ignoring me, "and have the cops detained in the lobby until we get the go-ahead from their supervisor. What's his number, Britt?"

"It's Lieutenant K. C. Riley," I said, reluctantly removing the card with the rape squad numbers from my Rolodex.

"I'll call him right now," Mark said, heading for the privacy of Fred's glass-enclosed office.

"Her, not him," I called after him.

"Take your nameplate off your desk, Britt, so if they get into the newsroom before we're ready they won't know which desk is yours." Fred's eyes glittered, and he rubbed his hands together again. "It'll make it tougher for them if they go for a search warrant." He glanced at me. "What's wrong with your eye?"

"Nothing," I mumbled, trying to hold the lid still. "Lack of potassium." They were acting like we expected a SWAT team invasion. I reluctantly tossed my nameplate into my desk drawer and stuffed the rumpled printouts of old stories in on top of it. I felt furtive. *News* security told to detain Miami cops in the lobby? This was out of hand.

Antonio showed up with a 35-millimeter Canon with a 50-macro lens. "*¿Qué pasa?* Where ees it?" Cuban born but raised in Miami, he spoke perfect English when he joined the *News* two decades ago, I was told. But with the Cubanization of Miami and of the newspaper, Antonio had steadily regressed until now he scarcely spoke English.

"Don't touch it!" I said.

He climbed up on my chair, balancing one foot on the desk and shooting straight down at the envelope. Then he jumped down and, ignoring my admonitions, pushed at the envelope and its torn flap with a pencil.

"They're taking it to the crime lab," I protested. "Don't touch it, Antonio."

"I'm only rearranging, *para la composición*," he said, standing back and scrutinizing my desktop with the narrowed eye of an artist. He frowned and shoved the envelope again, this time with his thumb.

"*¡No lo toques!*" I said, pushing at his hand.

"What is going on, Britt?" Ryan persisted.

"The cops think that letter is from the Downtown Rapist." Ryan reached for the envelope. "Don't touch it!"

Mark, on the phone in the glassed-in office, had obviously reached Lieutenant Riley. His face looked lobster red and contorted, as though he were strangling or suffering a stroke.

"There's a detective and a crime-lab man in the lobby. They want to come up and see Britt," Gloria called breathlessly from her desk in the center of the newsroom.

"Tell security to hold them there until Mark clarifies the situation with the police department," Fred ordered, a general issuing battle plans.

"Fred," I protested, "how can I go over there every day to press them for information when we refuse to cooperate when *they* want something?"

"It's not the same thing, Britt. They're public officials, we're not."

Gloria, still on the phone, waved her hand excitedly and reported a shoving match in progress down at security. Gretchen joined the cluster around my desk, frowning as though the skirmish was all my fault. I was betting on the cops. The detective downstairs was most likely in radio contact with his boss. Chances were she had just instructed him to get the letter, and he was going over the top like a Marine. Probably Harry, I thought.

"If we refuse to relinquish it," Fred pondered aloud, "someone may have to go to jail for obstructing justice—"

All heads swiveled toward me. Oh, no, I thought.

"Just until Mark can take it in front of a judge," Fred said, patting my shoulder in what he considered comforting fashion. I disliked the whole turn of events and the look in his eyes. "Brief the editorial board," he muttered, in an aside to Gretchen. She hurried to a telephone, grinning.

Sure. They'd write rousing editorials while the martyr languished in jail. I would be a good soldier and go to jail if necessary to protect a source, but I wasn't even on our side in this skirmish.

"They're on the way up," Gloria sang out from her desk.

"What'd they do, shoot security?" I asked.

"Everybody away from Britt's desk," Fred shouted. "Now!"

They all scattered as I threw myself into Ryan's empty chair and tried to look innocent. "Britt!" he objected. "I don't want them searching my desk."

Reluctantly, I gave up the chair, glaring at him. I considered ducking into the ladies' room, but with my luck the rapist would be lurking.

The elevator pinged. Harry and a crime-scene technician named Warren Forester stepped out, adjusting their jackets, as Mark Seybold burst out of the glass cage. They all looked red-faced and angry.

"Okay," the lawyer said. "I just spoke to the chief, who agreed that Britt can stay on top of the investigation of this document as long as we promise not to prematurely publish anything that might compromise the investigation.

"That Riley woman is impossible," he said to me in a lower voice. "What a mouth! Do you deal with her often?"

I nodded, pleased that somebody in management finally understood the tightrope that is my beat. Yet for some reason I felt compelled to defend K. C. Riley. "All she cares about," I explained, "is catching the rapist." This entire escapade would not endear me to her small hard heart, I knew.

Harry, still flushed, looked uncertain, wary, and out of his element in the newsroom. A good street cop, he had no experience in dealing with the hostile editors of Florida's largest newspaper and its lawyer. He had to be relieved to see me. "Britt?" he said gruffly.

"Here it is," I said, indicating the envelope and smiling in what I hoped he would perceive as a friendly manner. Antonio had changed to a wide-angle lens and was now shooting my entire desk and the people milling around it. "But what's this all about? I had a couple of others like it and threw them away."

"We can discuss it later," Harry said, scanning the expectant faces around him. I nodded. Crowds at crime scenes always make me uncomfortable—and we were now surrounded by some of Miami's most aggressively curious people, my colleagues.

Warren, the crime-lab tech, put his case, which looked like a fishing tackle box, on my chair and opened it, revealing four meticulously arranged rows of compartments. From one he removed a pair of tweezers. Gingerly, he lifted the envelope off my desk by one corner and dropped it into a semi-opaque glassine envelope.

Warren's job is to collect and preserve evidence, establishing the chain of custody for future courtroom presentation. We had crossed paths at many crime scenes. Next, he took out what looked like a pad of plain white paper with thin but rigid pages and tore off the top two sheets. With one he carefully scraped the minute residue from the top of my desk onto the other, which he held like a dustpan. Then he folded it into a mini-envelope, enclosing the collection of particles, and placed it in another glassine bag.

Harry and Warren Forester invited me to ride along to headquarters with them. I was tempted by the chance to pry loose some answers along the way but felt more comfortable in my T-Bird. If things went sour with the lieutenant, at least I'd have a getaway car.

We met at the rape squad office, where Harry ushered me in to see Lieutenant Riley. His manner was strangely formal and somewhat distant, apparently influenced by the intervention of the *News'* lawyer and his chief.

"What the hell was that all about?" Riley demanded.

"Hey," I said, hoping to exonerate myself at the start. "I'm only one of the troops. I had to tell 'em somebody was coming over to pick up the letter. You know what a pain in the ass editors can be."

She nodded grimly as if she really did know. Harry sat gingerly on the edge of the only other available chair. He was boasting for his boss's benefit how he had been poised to effect mass arrests at the *News* when, to his utter dismay, he was called off. I could tell his heart wasn't in it. Not totally anyway.

"If there is something obvious about this letter and the first two like it, I wish you had told me," I said ruefully. "Then I would have been informed enough to recognize it and give you a call." No response, so I forged on. "Everybody at the paper with a byline or a name on the masthead receives crank letters. This is probably just another fruitcake."

"That remains to be seen," Riley snapped, then blossomed into a wide, radiant smile. For a moment I was dazzled, then realized it was not intended for me.

Lieutenant Kendall McDonald had just stuck his head in the door. He nodded in my direction. "Everything okay, Kathy?"

She could not have looked more pleased. "Thank you much, Ken."

Kathy? This smiling woman coyly batting her lashes and suddenly tossing her hair was once poised to smash both my kneecaps if I so much as breathed her given name.

McDonald closed the door behind him, and her eyes dropped to me, smile fading. I attempted to concentrate on the subject at hand. "Why," I asked, leaning forward, "do you suspect that the rapist wrote this letter?"

She stood up, staring pensively out her window, lean and trim-looking in man-tailored navy slacks, her blouse unadorned except for a gold sharpshooter's badge strategically placed over one breast. "The deal is that you print no new information until we say it's okay?"

"No new info that I get from you guys." I thought it best to clarify the ground rules.

She sat down again at her desk, looking restless, eyes thoughtful, tapping a pencil on the firing pin of her hand grenade. "We've analyzed powder left on the victims' skin."

I looked up. "Talcum from the gloves?"

"No. I'm surprised you haven't been told. My detectives seem to leak everything else to you."

Harry squirmed beside me. I refrained from glancing his way and tried to appear innocent. He probably looked guilty as hell. Cops are not good at concealing their own transgressions.

Her expression was sardonic. I wondered if McDonald found her attractive. I bet he did. They'd have lots to talk about—multiple murders, serial rapes—secrets and shoptalk he would never share with me.

"After the rapes," she said, "he likes to powder his victims' skin, their faces, their bodies."

I cringed at the sick vision. "What kind of powder?" My voice was hushed.

"Cheap white dusting powder, perfumed, called Midnight Jasmine, comes in round hot-pink boxes with big fluffy powder puffs. A brand you can find in almost any discount drugstore, Kmart, the five-and-dime."

"Why does he do it?"

"Why does he do anything? Maybe he's living out a fantasy. Remember the scumbag who liked rubbing Wesson Oil on his victims? Maybe he likes the smell or the feel." She shrugged. "We'll ask when we nail him."

"Any other details you're withholding?"

"Always, but nothing we're ready to discuss."

I sighed. "Where did my letter go?"

"Warren took it to the lab," Harry said.

"Can I watch?"

Her eyes narrowed.

"That's the deal," I said.

"You take her, Harry." The lieutenant picked up her phone as she waved us out. I saw her punch in a four-digit number, an inside extension. From the softened line of her cheek, I would have bet a stone-crab dinner that Kathy was calling Ken.

11

I'd been to the department's state-of-the-art crime lab only once before, on an official media tour when the new station opened. Ceilings are high, lights bright. A shiny counter that borders both walls is broken into little islands for chemists, criminalists, and technicians. Each work station has a window with a view; on one side of the building a training field, on the other a parking lot.

Another floor up, on the roof, is a ventilated drying room for wet evidence. That's where they store the smelly stuff, the blood-soaked garments or other items found on decomposing bodies. Technicians snip samples to test for blood types, chemicals, and powder burns, then lock the rest up on the roof.

Warren greeted us. He was a small man with light curly hair, glasses, and a neat mustache. Like most crime techs, he relished the job, I knew, because he was able to perform his police work without enduring the petty politics of the department and without dealing with the public. The crew in the lab was keen on puzzle solving, piecing clues together and decoding riddles from the dark side. They played on the A-team with the homicide cops, major crimes prosecutors, medical examiners, and high level courts, all the varsity stars from the legal, medical, and law enforcement professions.

"I already briefed the latent fingerprint expert, the document expert, the trace analyst, and a serologist," he told Harry.

"Serologist?" I asked.

He nodded, looking pleased. "We can do a DNA profile if he licked the envelope. See if it matches up with the semen samples taken from the victims."

Terrific, I thought. If one body fluid doesn't give him away, another will. "How long will that take?"

"Quick DNA procedures will tell us in two or three days if the sample is consistent with our guy. The complete profile takes four to six weeks."

Warren plugged in a small canister-type vacuum cleaner and hit the switch. It began to hum. Carefully he vacuumed the envelope, then withdrew the folded letter with tweezers and vacuumed it as well.

"So that's what those machines are for," I joked. He didn't smile. "I always wanted to meet a man who could vacuum. You do windows?"

"The sophisticated feature is the uniquely designed trap on the end of the canister," he told me, obviously in love with his gadgetry. "That's where we capture the particles."

"Let's see what he wrote," I said impatiently. Painstakingly, he opened the letter and spread the paper out flat. Drifts of powder had collected in the folds, and he sucked them up neatly with the vacuum.

"Hummmm," said Warren, as Harry and I peered over his shoulder.

The writer had pressed so hard that his red pen had torn the paper in several places. Not a good sign, I thought.

Say Britt Montero,
You don't listen. You have offended me.

Signed with the same symbol, which seemed to be a bow with three arrows.

Short and to the point, but not terribly original. I tried to picture the writer and how his mind worked. Was it my description of him as diseased and dysfunctional that had him ticked? Would he be as offended if a man had written the same stories?

"I've see that before," Harry said, studying the signature symbol. "Tattoos on some of the Marielitos."

"Yeah," I said, looking at it again. "I think it's a Santería symbol for one of the gods." I know who can tell me more, I thought.

Warren selected a handbook from his desk and began leafing through police training papers detailing the myriad religions whose practitioners have set up housekeeping in Miami during the past two decades. Voodoo from Haiti, Obeah from Jamaica, Yahwehs who call themselves black Hebrew Israelites: you name it, we've got it.

Santería, I knew, was the worshiping of saints, a mingling of Catholicism and an African religion brought to Cuba by slaves from Nigeria, imported to work in Cuba's sugarcane fields two hundred years ago. Forced into Catholicism, the tribesmen clung to their old religions, tricking their captors by substituting the image of Catholic saints for their African deities and continuing their former practices, which included animal sacrifice.

"Here we go," Warren said, thumbing through the section on Santería.

In between the black iron cauldron, symbol of the god Oggun, who is the patron of war, employment, iron, and steel, and the double-headed stone ax of the god Chango was the same drawing of a bow and arrows.

" 'Symbol of the god Ochosi,' " Warren read, " 'the patron of hunters, owner of the birds and animals. Likes offerings of roosters and rum. When angry he can cause problems with the law.' "

"If the rapist is really practicing this stuff, he probably thinks he's invincible," I said.

"Let's hope he keeps on thinking that," Harry said grimly.

Warren took pictures before other tests could disturb the handwriting or lettering. He laid the letter flat on a stainless steel tabletop using a sophisticated Polaroid and a 35-millimeter Minolta. The letter next went to criminalist Andy Eckberg.

Andy had wavy salt-and-pepper hair, horn-rimmed glasses, a toothy smile, and degrees in biology and chemistry. When he retired from the FBI lab after twenty years, he moved to Florida for the sun and a job with the Miami police lab.

I learned all this when Warren introduced us and we shook hands. His grip was pleasantly firm, though his hand was callus-free and as soft as that of a woman.

Andy illuminated the letter and envelope with an oblique light to reveal the shadows of any prior tracings on the paper. It would have been nice to discern the imprint of a previously written note, preferably bearing a name and home address, but no such luck.

The envelope, paper, and ink were common and inexpensive. He dusted metal filings across them to bring up fingerprints. No prints on the letter, but a really good right thumbprint on the envelope.

Before announcing cause for jubilation, Andy brought out an ink pad and a cardboard fingerprint chart, then firmly rolled my fingers one by one onto the designated squares. I hated being printed, but it was necessary for elimination purposes. The little loops and whorls were a perfect match. The print on the envelope was mine.

"He was probably wearing those surgical gloves," I said, rubbing my ink-stained fingers with a soapy gel. I rinsed them in the stainless steel sink and dried them on a paper towel. "How come this guy wears them but not a condom?"

"Why would a rapist wear a condom?" Harry sniffed, as though it was a dumb question.

"Why would he wear gloves?"

"Sounds like somebody unclear on the concept," Warren said, gathering his gear to go out to another crime scene.

A stereo microscope that magnifies up to a hundred times confirmed that the powder on the letter was an inorganic compound with added fragrances.

"Let's take it to the polarizing microscope and see if we can match it up to the other powder," Andy said. "The basic component of talc is just a mineral extracted from the ground and processed. The identifying characteristics in a commercial product are absorbents, fragrances, and brighteners added to give it a more silky appearance and texture. The polarizing microscope shows us the crystalline content. And the FTIR, Fourier Transfer Infrared, will tell us the chemical analysis."

"How'd you ever identify the manufacturer?" I asked.

"Fragrance and cosmetic manufacturers all have associations. They can identify their own product and tell us if it's exclusively theirs."

"The same way you can identify the paint and the tire specs on cars?"

He nodded. "We have the standards on Dupont,

Pittsburgh, and Glidden in our computer library."

It turned out that Andy had worked a homicide case I had covered, a whodunit in which the only clue was a partial tire impression left at the desolate site where the body was dumped. The tire trade association revealed, based on the impression and the track width, that Goodyear had manufactured the tire in 1989.

The auto manufacturers' association spec list was intended as a resource for the engineers and architects who determine such things as turning radius when developing parking garages. In this case it provided the information that the tire that left the impression at the murder scene fit only a Checker or a special-model Cadillac, both relatively rare vehicles.

Only one person in the victim's circle of acquaintances drove such a car—the Caddy. Detectives zeroed in, built a case, and won a conviction. Andy knew what he was doing.

I began visualizing a story on the unsung heroes in the crime lab. It would be fun to write, and maybe I'd develop some sources in the lab for future reference. The Scientific Detectives, their high-tech investigations and their most fascinating cases, I thought. Perfect for *Outlook*, our Sunday magazine section. Once this rape case was closed I would propose the story to Pete Sanchez, the *Outlook* editor.

Andy came up with only one possible clue. Mingled with the powder vacuumed from the letter was a single microscopic particle. "It could have fallen from somewhere in his environment, or off his skin, or out of his hair as he wrote the note."

The mass spectrometer identified it as a minute trace of paint. "Lead-based," Andy said.

"Where would you find that?"

"Few occupations use lead-based paint anymore," he said. "You find it in marine products, in shipyards where they scrape the bottom of boats."

"Not much help in a city surrounded by water, marinas, boatyards, and a Coast Guard base," Harry grumbled, turning to me. "Maybe you should lay off, Britt, and have some other reporter write about the rapist in the future."

"Are you crazy?"

"Just thought I'd make the suggestion. Makes sense."

Not to me. He shrugged and turned away from my withering gaze.

From home, I called my Aunt Odalys. Happy to hear from me, as always, she asked about my eating habits, my love life, and my job. I asked about Ochosi.

"*Sí,*" she whispered, her voice silky. "Saint Norberto. What is it, Britt, that you wish to know?"

"Tell me about him."

"He is the hunter. The god of hunting and traps, the protector of those who seek to avoid confinement. His symbols are the bow and arrow, the antlers of the deer, and beads of green and brown. An Aguan can be prepared to honor him with Eleggua the trickster, Oggun, the owner of the knife, and Oshun, protector of private parts."

"Oshun? Is that the one . . . ?"

"A chalice filled with beads and powders and, on top, a rooster's head."

My own head began to ache. I wondered if I had any aspirin.

"For the Aguan, you must have meat and honey,

rice, fruit, and eggs—and animals, for the blood."

I thanked my aunt and promised to see her soon.

The hunter, I thought, and shuddered as I put down the phone.

12

The next day started with a bang, leaving me little time to think about either the rapist or the Mary Beth Rafferty case. A Chevy van caught fire, bursting into flames on the expressway at the height of rush hour. The driver managed to extricate himself, leaving behind two cases of .44 Magnum bullets. In the heat from the blaze the ammunition began to explode, and firefighters and motorists who had stopped to help ran for their lives, dodging stray bullets. The bursts sounded like sporadic machine-gun fire. Both sides of the highway were closed to traffic, and cops and firemen took cover in a ditch until it was over. Each time the gunfire died down and it seemed that all the bullets had been expended, a new barrage began, exploding in clusters like popcorn in a microwave. It sounded as if war had been declared at 8 A.M. as the horns of irate commuters blared in the distance.

Lottie was happy for the opportunity to wear the flak jacket she kept with the other extensive and essential gear in the trunk of her Chrysler.

We were too busy at the scene to talk, but we met later in the *News* cafeteria for a fast cup of coffee. "You get good art of the van?" I asked, tearing open a sugar packet and dumping half into my cup.

"Yeah, did you see it?"

"Haven't seen anything so bullet riddled since

Mauricio Miranda's business partners opened fire on him in a clear case of overkill."

"He that Colombian coke dealer shot more than fifty times in his car?" She peered into a tiny mirror and daintily applied coral-colored lipstick.

"Yep." I glanced at the big round clock hanging high over the tables, a not-so-subtle hint to employees inclined to tarry.

"Anything new from your pen pal?"

"The rapist? Nope. But I haven't checked today's mail yet. Lottie?" I stirred my coffee with the wooden stick provided instead of spoons. "I'm worried."

"I'd be too if a rapist was writing to me."

"It's something else," I said morosely, then told her my suspicions about Kendall McDonald and K. C. Riley.

"The lieutenants from hell. Maybe it's not what it appears to be." She sipped her coffee. "It's hard to compete with somebody the man works with," she mused, "somebody he sees all the time." She patted my hand. "If it *is* so, could be they deserve each other. She sounds like a real ass-kicker. What you need is some R and R." She looked coy. "Talked to Captain Curt lately?"

I shook my head.

"Call him, take his little cruise. See what develops."

"Hey, girls." Ryan was carrying a Styrofoam coffee cup that was too full in one hand, a giant oatmeal cookie in the other. "Gretchen has been trying to reach you, Britt."

Shoot. I checked the beeper clipped to my purse. "Hell, I forgot to reset it after I got paged this morning."

"Forgot?" Ryan said knowingly.

Lottie grinned. "Yeah, you knew Gretchen was in the slot today, didn't you, Britt?"

I pushed my chair back and headed for the newsroom, where I picked cautiously through my mail. No powder, nothing weird or suspicious, at least nothing more weird and suspicious than usual. One message seemed to be addressed in orange crayon. Another was on an ancient, yellowed postcard that looked like it had been in somebody's bureau drawer for the past twenty-five years; it was covered with tiny spidery handwriting that continued up and around the margins. A fat letter with a prison postmark began, *Dear Sir or Ms., whichever the case may be. I AM INNOCENT!*

"Where have you been?" Gretchen demanded.

"Running up and down the expressway where bullets were exploding and traffic was backed up for miles."

"Don't spend a great deal of time on that story," she said. "Keep it brief, we've got a tight paper. There are mishaps in rush-hour traffic every morning," she said airily.

"Not like this one," I said. "One firefighter was grazed, and a bullet knocked the dome light off a trooper's car." I glanced down at my notebook for confirmation. "And we had two heart attacks and one stroke among the commuters. Thousands were late for work. Plus we have good art. Lottie was out there."

Gretchen displayed no enthusiasm.

"All the TV stations and the print competition were out there too," I said. "I think TV's making it their lead story. And I heard that one of the networks is taking a feed on it."

That caught her attention. The managing editor

monitors all three networks as well as the affili-
ates. If a network plays a South Florida story that
the *News* missed or gave short shrift, there is hell to
pay.

"Well," she said, pretending that did not influence
her decision. "Write it for what you think it's worth
and we'll see."

Actually I had not spoken to any TV people out at
the scene, as most were hovering overhead in heli-
copters. But somewhere at that very moment I knew
some TV reporter was making the same sales pitch to
a reluctant editor, saying, "Well, I heard the *News* is
front-paging it."

The rush hour from hell was one of those stories
that the Chamber of Commerce and the tourist bureau
would hate—but everybody would read.

I was wrapping it up when Bobby Tubbs, one of
the assistant city editors, appeared at my desk.

"We just got a call on a construction accident you
might be interested in," he said.

"Construction accident?"

"Yeah, the contractor, the guy who owned the company, apparently got buried in wet cement. Sounds
like your kind of story." He dropped the address onto
my desk.

The site was that of yet another new shopping mall
under construction in west Dade, invading what was
once subtropical wilderness, the home of migratory
wading birds and lush foliage. Apartments and a new
expressway exit were all under construction nearby,
and I had to maneuver the T-Bird past trucks and large
equipment. The breeze from the high-speed expressway driving had been pleasant, but as soon as I slowed
down my hair began to curl damply along my forehead and at the nape of my neck. Damn, I thought,

I had to stop procrastinating and have the air conditioner repaired.

I parked in the shade of a sapodilla tree and left the windows rolled down so the car wouldn't get too hot.

Detectives from the county were busy, conferring with the owner, the architect, and the concrete foreman, but the superintendent in charge of construction filled me in. Al Benjamin, sturdy and sun-bronzed, shirt straining over a slight paunch, wore an orange hard hat bearing the company logo and his name. His crew had been temporarily idled by the investigation, and I began to get the impression that he was more agitated about the delay than the contractor's tragic demise.

"It's the liquidated damage clause in the contract," Benjamin explained, lighting up a cigar. The mall center was targeted for springtime opening, and the building project was on a tight schedule with a $10,000 bonus for each day early it was brought in and a $10,000-a-day penalty if late. Meeting or beating the completion date also appeared to be a matter of professional pride. "My projects have always come in on time and on budget," Benjamin said. "These men are all paid by the hour, and we can't afford to lose even half a day."

He scowled, took the cigar from his mouth, and called to one of his men, "Here comes the roach coach!" A small truck with aluminum siding, a rolling canteen that peddled sandwiches, coffee, and snacks, pulled up sounding its melodious horn—the first few bars of "La Cucaracha"—and was mobbed by the construction workers.

We resumed our conversation. After hearing what happened, I wasn't surprised that everybody needed coffee. Personally, I wanted something stronger.

Twenty-five concrete columns had been poured for the shopping mall's vertical garage. Positioned in each were four steel reinforcing rods, bound together by metal straps. Three-quarter-inch plywood forms had been erected in the shape of a pillar around each group of rods two days ago.

Then, at dawn yesterday, the first six of thirty trucks were in line, each ready to unload eight to ten yards of ready-mix concrete. The contractor, Sam Farrington, age fifty-five, was not there, though his big black Mercedes-Benz was parked in its usual spot next to the construction trailer. Farrington was a pugnacious boss who tended to tightly oversee and interfere with the sub-contractors, according to Benjamin, and I sensed that the crew was not bereft by his absence. This was a major pour and, due to the nature of wet concrete, timing was paramount. Delays were costly. The subcontractor waited twenty minutes, then gave the foreman the order to proceed with the scheduled pour.

The foreman maintained constant radio contact with the drivers, and as each empty truck left the site, another was on the way. As concrete flowed into each form, a worker on a wooden catwalk lowered a vibrator linked by a long hose to a gasoline-powered generator. The vibrating action prevented the concrete from honeycombing, ensuring the integrity of the pillar. The crew finished the pour, and the concrete was left to set up for twenty-four hours. Today they had returned to strip away the plywood forms with crowbars, exposing the brand-new pillars.

Farrington was still absent, his Mercedes in the same spot.

Where he had vanished became obvious when a

worker peeled the plywood away from the fourth pillar.

"Come on, I'll show you," Benjamin said grimly, turning on his heel.

We walked around a new concrete column in what would soon be the northwest quadrant of the shopping mall's parking garage. Though I knew what to expect, I could not help but gasp. "That's him," Benjamin said flatly. "First time I seen anything like this, and I grew up in this business."

The missing contractor was standing, the only position possible inside the pillar. A tuft of hair, his nose, fabric-clad kneecaps, and the toes of his shoes protruded slightly through the hardened concrete. They had obviously been pressed against the inside of the plywood form when wet cement gushed over him.

He looked like the victim of an ancient volcanic eruption, overtaken by lava and frozen forever in stone.

The owner's representative, the architect, Benjamin, his assistant, and a county inspector had been attending a job progress meeting in the construction trailer when the concrete foreman shouted the news over Benjamin's walkie-talkie. Somebody dialed 911, thinking the mishap had just occurred, but this was no emergency. It would take dynamite to move this body before the cops arrived.

In fact, that was my first question. "How will they get him to the medical examiner's office?"

"That's what they're discussing now," Benjamin said, frowning at the workmen, who were straggling off in various directions with their food and coffee.

Police said the entire twenty-five-foot pillar had to come down. Seemed reasonable to me. The concrete foreman, a lanky man wearing boots, seemed pleased at the difficulty his men encountered as they tackled the job with jackhammers. "We build 'em to last," he said, nodding.

A homicide detective named Orestes Diaz was in charge from Metro-Dade, the police department with jurisdiction in the unincorporated area of Dade County.

"How do you think he got in there?" I said, shouting over the sound of the jackhammers. Diaz was sweating, and flying flecks of concrete had lodged in his shaggy mustache and hair.

"Don't know," he yelled back, as the Mercedes was hooked up to a wrecker, to be towed off for scrutiny by the crime lab.

"Are you thinking accident or foul play?"

"We're not ruling nothing out," he said. Farrington was last seen at the site on Wednesday, after the forms had been readied for the Thursday morning pour. "The crew said he normally didn't hang around after the end of the day." Diaz scratched his head and snorted. Irritating dust from the jackhammers hung in the hot, still air around us, sticking to damp skin. "I tell ya, Britt. If he hadn't been right up against that plywood form, he'da never been found. You know how they say Jimmy Hoffa got paved over in the end zone at the Giants' stadium? If this is a homicide, this guy wasn't supposed to be found either. He wudda been holding up this shopping center for the next hundred years."

When the pillar was reduced to a height of about fifteen feet, workers used welding irons to cut the reinforcing rods and straps, freeing the block in which the body was encased. A crane hoisted Farrington's concrete coffin, a section about twelve feet long, onto a flatbed trunk. The men covered it with a tarp for the drive to the medical examiner's office.

"Think they'll be able to determine a cause of death?" I asked.

"Probably, but it's gonna take a lotta work first, getting him outa there."

I piled back into the T-Bird to go back to the office and file a brief account for the early edition. On the way I stopped in a little roadside store for a cold drink. Concrete dust packed my sinuses, and my head was beginning to ache.

I used the rest room, splashed water on my face and arms, browsed the cooler, picked out a Yoo Hoo chocolate drink, and took it to the cash register. I didn't spend more than seven or eight minutes in the store, a small family operation that would probably be forced out of business once the shopping center opened. The T-Bird was parked at the side of the building, where spaces were marked off for half a dozen cars. Mine was the only one there. I backed out, sipping from the bottle as I drove.

When I finished, I reached for a litter bag on the back seat. Good citizen that I am, I would never dream of pitching an empty soda bottle out the window. I was navigating traffic on the east-west expressway, eyes glued to the road, left hand on the wheel, the right groping blindly on the back seat for the bag, when my fingers blundered into something sticky and slimy. I jerked my hand back, taking my eyes off the road. Blood!

Horns blared as my car veered all over three lanes. The driver of a van gave me the finger and other motorists cursed and scowled, but I managed to regain control, using one hand. Shuddering convulsively, I was loath to touch the steering wheel with bloodstained fingers. My legs too shaky to stomp the accelerator or the brake, I swung onto the shoulder and coasted to a dead stop.

Whimpering, I resisted the urge to jump out of the car and run. I rested my forehead on the steering wheel for a moment, then steeled myself to look at what was in the back seat.

I opened the door, slid out, and pulled the front seat forward for a closer inspection. My first instinct was to hurl it away from my car and drive off, but that would be stupid. Queasy and trembling, I got back in and started the car. At first I intended to drive straight to police headquarters, but then I considered taking it to my Aunt Odalys. This was more her bailiwick. I tried to think clearly. I could not swear it had not been in my car when I left the construction site. But if not, then it was placed there during the few minutes I was in the store.

I had a pretty good idea who was responsible, and that scared me. I regretted that my gun was at home and not in the glove compartment. Finally I stopped at a roadside telephone booth and called the city crime lab, while nervously scanning passing traffic. He was out there, somewhere, watching. Of that I was sure.

Thankfully, Warren was in. "Hi, Britt, ready to do that story about the scientific detectives? You should see the case I'm working on now—"

"Warren, can you meet me in ten minutes, in the parking lot behind the station? It's important. Bring rubber gloves."

He sounded doubtful but agreed. I got there in five. He was waiting.

"It's Santería," I said.

"Yeah," he agreed. "Looks like somebody's little magic spell, and I'm betting it's not intended to help you win the lottery." He gingerly removed it from the car with both gloved hands, a red ribbon trailing. The bloodied item, tied with ribbon, was the severed tongue of a cow. Now I saw that it had been slit open and the two halves pierced by a metal nail. Something was sandwiched in between. The inserts, skewered by the nail, were messy but recognizable. A story with my byline, clipped from the newspaper, and a small photograph. The story, of course, was about the manhunt for the Downtown Rapist. The photograph was me, the one that had been on my old police-issued press ID card. I had never liked it. The smart-aleck police photographer had snapped the picture when my mouth was open and my eyes half closed, then refused to shoot another. The cards are only valid for a year, and I had been happy when it expired and a new one, with a more presentable photo, was issued.

"Where'd he get it?" Warren said, scrutinizing me from behind the lenses of his glasses.

I racked my brain. I didn't know where I had seen the card last. I might have tossed it into the trash at the office or at home, which chilled my bones even more. My mind raced. Could it have been in my unlocked glove compartment or in the all-purpose drawer in my kitchen? Could it have been taken from my apartment?

I shivered in the hot sun, my skin as cold as ice.

"Was your car broken into?"

"No, I've been leaving the windows down because the air conditioner doesn't work."

His expression said I was not the smartest person in the world. I already knew that. "Look," I said, "I'm on deadline with another story. I've got to get back to the office."

"This didn't happen in our jurisdiction," he said.

"It's the county's, but it may relate to our case. We have to make a report, Britt, and notify the county."

"I don't want a fuss."

"You know we have to make a report. We'll process this, and I have to call Harry."

"Well, okay," I snapped. "Do what you have to do, but I have to get back."

"He'll want to talk to you."

"He knows where to find me," I said. I got back in the car and slammed the door.

"Britt, if the guy did this, he knows what you look like, he knows your car—maybe he even knows where you live. Talk to Harry."

"Later," I said, and turned the key in the ignition.

13

The message was clear. The rapist was into Santería, which meant I was now the recipient, thank you very much, of some evil hex he had cooked up with his Santero. Swell.

The specter of animal sacrifice and Santería worship stirred vague and shadowy memories of a dark night in my childhood. No time to think about that, I told myself, hurrying into the newsroom. I had a story to write. Deadlines leave no time for panic and have preserved my sanity more than once. I willed myself to focus only on the Sam Farrington story. There would be more stories, more deadlines later. What a blessing that newspapers are published seven days a week.

I called Onnie in the library, requesting anything we had on Farrington. "There may be business side stories. He was a contractor."

"What's the matter?" she said. "You don't sound right."

"Nothing. Well, it is something, but I'm on deadline and I'll tell you later. See what you can find on this guy."

I dialed the number for the medical examiner and caught the chief in his office.

Farrington had arrived, he said, and was still aboard

the flatbed truck in the receiving area. He would remain there for the time being.

"You haven't weighed him yet?"

"Not unless they stopped at a truck weighing station along the way," the chief said.

A pathologist was supervising an investigator and an attendant, who were wielding hand-held chisels and two- and three-pound hammers to free the body. The receiving area was the perfect location for the job; it is a huge space like an enclosed hangar, where even plane wreckage can be brought intact from crash scenes. Wrecked vans or cars occupied by murder victims can be processed under bright lights, in comfortable air-conditioning, sheltered from the weather, and out of the sight of gaping or unruly crowds.

"I guess you've never had a body encased in cement before," I said with certainty.

"Just once," he said quietly.

"When was that?" Funny, I didn't remember one. But the chief has been in charge for almost as long as I have been alive.

"Eighteen years ago," he said, his voice placid. "The victim was a young woman apparently murdered by her husband, who disposed of her body by cementing it into a stairwell that he built himself." He paused. "She was this gentleman's wife, in fact."

"He killed her? Farrington killed his wife?"

"That's right."

"Did he go to jail?" I felt shocked by a sudden elusive thought I could not quite fathom. "Whose case was it?"

"He was never convicted—never tried, in fact—a fluke in the law," he said, responding first to my initial question. "Statute of limitations. I believe it was investigated by the city. The file's been pulled, but I haven't reviewed it yet."

"There is no statute of limitations on murder," I argued, never knowing the chief to be mistaken but wanting to protest, trying to grasp the reason for my sense of apprehension.

"There was a statute of limitations in this case. A fluke in the law. Check your newspaper's old stories. As I recall, the case received a lot of coverage."

I hung up the phone, heart pounding, as Onnie appeared at my shoulder and dropped a fat blue number-eleven envelope on my desk.

"Jackpot," she said with a smile. "A whole file full of stories on this guy. You know he killed his wife?"

"I just heard," I murmured, focused on the neatly folded clippings in the envelope.

She waited a moment, then retreated. "I know what you're like on deadline. Call me later," she sang out and returned to the library.

I didn't answer. I was scanning the clips. They were arranged by date and began more than twenty years ago with small, short items from the business section. His young company had been involved in several modest building projects. He had started out building single-family homes.

Then a missing persons story. His estranged wife had disappeared during a bitter divorce battle. Both had moved out of their home, which was to be sold and the proceeds divided. The wife had the keys, and she and her husband were to meet a real estate agent at the house at four o'clock one long-ago afternoon.

The agent arrived on time. Mrs. Farrington's car stood in the drive, but no one answered the doorbell. The agent persisted, rapping on the back door as well and peering in windows. The house appeared empty and she eventually left.

Alice Farrington remained missing for seven years.

Immediately after she vanished, her mother and friends had insisted that her estranged husband was responsible. He had abused and terrified her, they said. He denied it, saying he had also arrived for the appointment, either shortly before or after the agent, had seen no one, and left. Since his wife was not present to object, he moved back into the house and made a number of improvements.

When the woman's frantic family insisted that police search the premises, Farrington allowed them access. They found no evidence of foul play but did note a newly poured cement staircase, landing, and stairwell.

Fearing the worst, her family begged police to go in and knock it down. But, as the police pointed out, they could not just begin demolishing a house without proof a crime had been committed. And no one had proof. Farrington even claimed to receive occasional taunting phone calls from his wife. He said she refused to say where she was.

A highly publicized fluke in the law occurred at this time. The Florida legislature abolished capital punishment. Six months later it was restored, by popular demand.

But the wording of the original order had abolished "capital" offenses in Florida during those six months, and the law clearly stated that all felonies, except capital crimes, were subject to a statute of limitations. Since, technically, there was no such thing as a capital crime for six months, first-degree murders committed during that period were no longer considered such and therefore became subject to the statute of limitations. Once the clock ran out, killers could shout confessions from the courthouse steps with no fear of prosecution. There were a dozen such cases in Dade County. Free murders, on the house. Those who got away with it for seven years got away with it forever and could thumb their noses at the system.

Farrington held on to his house for seven years, then sold it to buy a luxurious Bay Point home more in keeping with his enhanced status as a successful contractor. He had maintained the old house well, probably never dreaming that the new owners would remodel. They found Alice Farrington in the stairwell where she had been all along, but it was too late for her husband to be charged with her murder.

Farrington had won, but he was no longer thumbing his nose at the system. He was dead.

Dan called as I was finishing the story.

"Remember Sam Farrington?" I asked.

"A pillar of the community, I hear."

"That's not funny."

"I always try to make you smile. You look pretty when you smile, and life's too short not to."

"How did you know what happened?" I blurted. "They haven't released his name, not till they confirm ID and notify next of kin."

"Ken McDonald knew it was my old case. Couldn't have happened to a nicer guy."

"I thought you'd feel that way." I remembered the scene at the construction site and what followed.

"What's the matter, Britt? You sound edgy."

"I am." The friendly note in his voice caught me off guard and my eyes flooded. "I had a problem today."

"Gimme his name and I'll pay him a visit."

"The Downtown Rapist, and if you can find him,

a lot of people will be very grateful, especially me."

I told him about the cow's tongue.

"Jesus Christ, Britt. Is the city taking this seriously? Are they giving you any protection?"

"I can take care of myself," I muttered.

"Listen, nobody's better at surveillance than an old cop. I can come sit on your place tonight."

"No, thanks, Dan. It just bothers the hell out of me that he knows me and my car. I thought I was pretty alert, but I never even saw the son of a bitch. Just like no one's ever seen him roaming the office buildings where he's hit. I swear the man's invisible."

"You've got a gun, don't ya?"

"Yeah," I said, realizing that my voice sounded doubtful.

"Where is it?"

"Home, in my bedroom."

"A helluva lotta good it's gonna do you there. This guy ain't never hit anybody at home that we know of."

"I know."

"Keep it loaded, keep it with you, and, Britt, don't leave it in the car and don't hesitate to use it if the SOB makes a move on you. If you have to shoot 'im, don't just fire once. Empty it. That's what I always told the rookies. You have to shoot somebody, you wanna make sure you kill 'em. Then there's only one tale to tell, and that's yours."

"That's right, Dan," I said, running my hand through my hair. "Make me so nervous I wind up blowing away the UPS man."

"First thing ya gotta do is get the hell outa that apartment. Take somebody with you, pack up a few things, and check into a hotel, or better yet crash with a friend. Hey, you can stay here. I got plenty of room." His voice softened. "You can use my daughter's room. I'm not the world's greatest housekeeper, but you're welcome aboard for as long as you like."

I shook my head. "I don't need you to fuss over me," I said, then began to think it might not be such a bad idea. Dan could fend off the rapist while I snooped in his stuff and kept an eye on him.

I laughed hysterically and shook my head, as if to clear it of the craziness that seemed to be spinning and multiplying. This entire day had left me punchy.

"It ain't funny, Britt."

"I know, I know. If I didn't laugh, I'd cry."

I begged off and promised to check in with him later.

"Make sure you show no set pattern coming and going," he growled. "You should probably switch to another car, and don't go home if you think you're being followed." He lowered his voice, but it became more passionate. "Remember, Britt, I don't have to tell you. It's us against them. Use the gun."

I shook my head. Dan made it sound like we were draftees in all-out war, as though we should barricade the doors and practice our fast draws. He has got to get out more, I thought, and mingle with ordinary people, not just cops. But somehow I couldn't imagine him playing cards or bingo at the local retirement center.

I finished the Farrington story, then took a cup of water, some soap, and paper towels out to the parking lot to scrub the back seat of the T-Bird. Then I stopped and asked security to try to keep an eye on the car.

Ron Sadler, the *News* political writer, drifted over to my desk as I sat down. "Hear you might be leaving us, Britt." His voice was low and confidential.

"What?" I stared at him. A trim and studious-looking man in his thirties, Ron has an uncanny insight into politics on all levels and has covered both state and nationwide campaigns.

His intelligent brown eyes looked cagey behind the owlish glasses. "You can level with me. I won't say anything."

"I don't know what you're talking about," I snapped. "And if this is a joke, forget it. I'm in no mood for games right now."

He leaned over the desk. "The Fielding campaign is asking questions about you." His voice was a near whisper.

He mistook the concern in my face. "Don't worry, don't worry." He smiled reassuringly. "I told them nothing but good. How thorough and tenacious you are, and how persistent, how you never give up on anything."

"Ron," I protested with a growing sense of dismay, "I don't have the slightest idea what you're talking about."

He looked puzzled, tugging at his lower lip with a thumb and an index finger. "I assumed you're under consideration for a job in Fielding's administration. Seems he's a shoo-in for governor and is already putting together his staff. You say you haven't applied for anything?"

"I would never work for a politician, particularly Fielding," I said.

"Well, you should expect an offer. They're really interested in you, Britt, hot to know all about you."

"Such as?" I asked, fighting feelings of dread.

"Oh, everything, your reputation, style, habits, where you live."

"Goddammit!" I said. What the hell was this? The

only retaliation I had feared from my confrontational elevator encounter with the candidate was a possible complaint to *News* management.

He stepped back. "I told them everything I could, Britt. I thought I was helping you."

"Ron, if I needed your help I'd have asked for it. How could you give out information about me without asking first? You know the paper never gives out personal information about reporters."

"I'm sorry. But you weren't here and I thought it was important to you. They were being very discreet, and this wasn't some loony citizen with a beef asking about you, it was the next governor, or at least somebody in his camp." Ron looked perturbed, but not as perturbed as I felt. What was going on?

"I know you didn't realize," I grimly acknowledged. "Who precisely was asking?"

"Martin Mowry, Fielding's security chief." Ron looked uncomfortable. "He's ex-military, the big guy you always see in the background, escorting the candidate."

"Oh, swell," I said.

"What's going on? You don't think they're going to offer you a job?"

"No. Don't say anything about this, okay, Ron? I'll explain later, when I have more time."

I called Fielding's local campaign office and left a message for Mowry to call me. It didn't sound like the woman who took the call recognized my name, but I couldn't be sure. By now, I told myself, I probably am paranoid.

Then I called the library and asked Onnie to meet Lottie and me back in photo. We sat around an empty desk as Lottie plugged in her electric kettle to boil water for tea.

I swore them to secrecy, then unloaded, telling them about what I'd found in my car. "No problem," I quickly assured them, trying to sound confident. "People who actually mean to do you harm never call or write warnings first."

"Unless they're your deranged ex-husband or lover," Onnie commented.

"Yeah, then all bets are off," Lottie said.

They were right. Restraining orders and warnings from police are minor inconveniences to former loved ones in hot pursuit of uncool things—like murder and revenge. We'd seen enough of them to know that when your ass is on the line, don't rely on the cops to save it. The truth is that we are all responsible for rescuing ourselves and maybe our helpless neighbors. The cavalry arrives just in the nick of time only in old movies. John Wayne is dead. The world can be mean, especially as seen from the police beat.

"That's not all," I told them.

"What else?" demanded Lottie, sipping her herbal tea.

"You won't believe this," I said.

Onnie's chin was in her hand and she was frowning. Lottie's eyes were bright and alert.

I told them about Ron Sadler thinking I was about to go to work for Fielding.

Lottie gave a low whistle. "Hell-all-Friday, Britt. Congratulations! You're as popular these days as crotch rot in July."

I nodded miserably. "It's like everything's coming down at once."

"If Fielding's bodyguard don't get you," Onnie said, "the Downtown Rapist will."

"Maybe they'll get each other by mistake," Lottie said.

Naturally she urged me to come crash with her for a while. Onnie said the same thing, adding that Darryl, her little boy, would love it. I wanted to see him, too, but declined. No way would I risk leading the rapist to my friends. There was one other important reason.

"Nobody is going to make me leave my place," I told them. Admittedly, it's not much, just a rented one-bedroom apartment with a refrigerator that groans in the night and a neighbor who believes he can play the bagpipes when he's drunk, but it is mine. "I refuse to let some piece of scum force me out of my home!"

"Why should you be different, Britt?" Lottie hooted. "Hundreds of thousands of other Cubans let themselves be forced from their homes by a piece of scum with a beard and dirty fatigues."

I stuck out my lower lip and put on a determined face. "Maybe that's one reason I'm determined not to let it happen to me." Then I remembered the rapist's penicillin-resistant gonorrhea and pondered packing a bag.

We set up a system where I would check in with one or the other at specified times. If I failed and they couldn't reach me, they would come running.

I returned to my desk feeling somewhat better. Wariness comes easy to me because of my job and the intimate knowledge it brings of all the bad things that can happen. Most people, especially newcomers and senior citizens, are seduced by South Florida's warmth and beauty, tempted to relax and daydream in the sun's sultry embrace—a sometimes fatal mistake. I warn them to watch their step and keep in mind that Miami is like a jungle full of dangerous and wild animals that may attack at any time. I try to follow my own advice and remain reasonably alert and aware. Knowledge is power. The more I know, the better.

I called Aunt Odalys to ask if I could drop by. Delighted, she immediately forgot the telenovela she was watching on Univision and poised to start cooking. I don't need food, I told her, I need your expertise. She was thrilled.

Her small well-kept house in Little Havana radiated the heavenly scent of *pollo asado*: pot-roasted chicken with garlic, Spanish olive oil, onions, lime juice, white wine, and oregano. Beautiful pink and red hibiscus, huge blossoms with innocent wide-open faces and golden centers, bloomed outside her front door. A not-so-innocent face stood just inside. The crude clay image wore a grimace, with cowrie-shell eyes, nose, and mouth. Eleggua: the trickster god who controls doors, crossroads, and gateways and funnels communication between Santería priests and the Orishas, the deities. He guards the door, keeping away the unwanted. During raids on the homes of criminals, cops have found their own pictures or business cards tucked beneath an image of Eleggua. Under this one I would not have been surprised to find a picture of my mother.

My Aunt Odalys was dressed simply, all in white, as usual. Slightly shorter than I, she is about five feet three but carries herself with a graceful dignity that makes her seem taller. My father's younger sister is still beautiful in her fifties, olive-skinned and green-eyed with high cheekbones that give her face a faintly feline look. She hugged me warmly, murmuring words of endearment and kissing my cheek, huge eyes glowing with affection. At one time after my father's death, this aunt wanted to raise me.

One night when I was five and staying with Aunt Odalys, I remember being taken from my bed, dressed in white, and carried to another place. First I was curious, then frightened. I remember drums beating, bells, chanting, and the cries of dying animals, strangers surrounding me, a headless red rooster fluttering in a corner, perfumed water, herbs and something else warm and sticky smeared on my forehead, and a necklace of red and white beads draped around my neck.

After I innocently reported the whole business to my mother she decided, much to my relief, that there would be no more sleep-overs with my Cuban relatives. She and my Aunt Odalys still do not speak. I am the sole link between their worlds and am never completely at home in either. Aunt Odalys, I suspect, is my only Cuban relative deeply involved in Santería. I love her dearly but do not believe in angry gods or evil spells. All those ceremonies inspire in me is an animal lover's outrage.

But I was always close to my aunt, who loved telling me stories about my father's youthful escapades. Later, when I became a reporter and covered my first Santería-related homicide, her knowledge came in handy.

The killer, apparently advised by his Santero, covered himself with oil, chicken feathers, and glitter, the same sparkly stuff we sprinkled on art projects and greeting cards in elementary school. I learned from Aunt Odalys that he had probably been promised that this combination would make him invisible to his enemies, or at least invincible. At any rate, he had marched solemnly off to shoot the rival he believed had placed a hex on him. The trail of glitter and chicken feathers led cops directly from the murder scene to the killer's apartment in the same neighborhood. They found him still full of glitter, with chicken feathers in his underwear.

"Big Bird, you're under arrest!" cracked an Anglo cop. I think that was when I began to have serious reservations about Santería and its practitioners.

I related none of this to my aunt now as we sat in her living room and sipped strong Cuban coffee from tiny china cups. I avoided looking at the Nganga, a large iron cauldron dominating one corner of the otherwise cozy room. Ngangas are packed with a variety of objects: railroad spikes, feathers, knives, beads, stones, machetes, prayers, dried leaves, and mirrors mounted on animal horns used to see the future. Certain ceremonies call upon the spirits of the dead to come live in the cauldron.

Ngangas also contain blood and animal and sometimes human remains. Mostly skulls and long bones. Miami police academy classes teach rookies how to recognize skulls used in Santería rituals. Among the telltale clues are candle wax drippings, a packing of dried leaves, and stains from animal blood and rust from the cauldron.

Many of the skulls are purchased from local botánicas and prove to be of African or West Indian origin, intended as anatomical specimens for educational and medical purposes.

But some who practice Santería insist on skulls still containing brains, in order to make the spirits smarter. That creates potential problems. The demand leads to grave robbing, a practice definitely against the law.

Differentiating between Santería-motivated grave robberies and simple cemetery desecrations is simple: Look for the symbolism. Santería beliefs are dominated by the seven African powers. The victim in the first grave robbery that I covered for the *News* had died at age seventy-seven in 1947. Her grave was the seventh from the cemetery gate. Something to keep in mind when shopping for a cemetery plot.

"I have a problem," I told my Aunt Odalys.

"A man," she said, placing her beautifully manicured hand over her heart.

"Sort of," I began uncertainly.

"His name?"

"I don't know. The police are looking for him." Her arched eyebrows lifted dramatically and frown lines marred her perfect brow. I told her about the rapist. She knew about him via Spanish-language radio. I told her about the letters, and the thing I found in my car, and why I had asked about Ochosi.

"*Ay, Dios mío. ¡Qué horror! ¡Chica!* We must do a divination," she said gravely, and got to her feet.

I began to feel silly. What was I doing here? Yet this had seemed right; my aunt would know how the man was thinking if he relied on Santería.

We sat opposite each other at her highly polished dining room table. The cowrie shells rattled as she threw them like dice. The shells are asked yes-and-no questions, but only in Spanish, and her muttered Spanish was too fast for me.

She calculated how the cowries fell, open sides up or hidden. Murmuring, she gathered them up and threw them again and again.

"The saints say you are too trusting," she said, her tone accusing. That didn't sound like me at all. I wondered if the saints had mixed me up with somebody else but kept my mouth shut. She threw the shells again. They tumbled from her slim, graceful hands gleaming and innocent, the way the surf must have tossed them up onto some sunny beach.

"Danger, mortal danger, *muerte*," she whispered,

lifting frightened eyes. The shells scattered again, across the table. "This confirms what you say. It is here. Danger from someone you have never met."

Oy, I thought. At times my landlady, Mrs. Goldstein, is a greater influence on me than my aunt.

"We have to perform a *despojo*," my Aunt Odalys said firmly, "to seek the intervention of the deities and the dead."

"No way," I said flatly. "No animals, not even a chicken."

"But I am your *madrina*, Britt," she said persuasively, her expression hurt. "I can call on the father of the spirits who live in the cauldron to help you."

"You'd help me best by telling me what you can about the rapist."

Based on what I said, my aunt concluded that he had evidently taken his problems with me and my stories to his religious adviser, an apparent practitioner of Palo Mayombe, the most malevolent magic. Obviously a *brujería*, connected with evil sorcery, had been performed. The ritual with the cow's tongue, a high-ticket item, probably cost him upwards of $500.

With all that magic in his corner, he probably considered himself powerful and omnipotent.

"Britt," Aunt Odalys said. "You must let me help you."

After increasingly shrill negotiations, we settled for a minor ritual of cleansing. She insisted on rubbing some herbs in my hair and made me promise not to wash it for three days.

This day cannot become any more weird, I told myself as she rubbed pungent leaves into my scalp. I wondered what reporters in other major American cities were doing at the same moment.

"You need protection," my aunt said. "A *resguardo*, a talisman."

"No animals involved?"

I got as close to a dirty look as she has ever given me. She moved to a sideboard and proceeded to fill a tiny cloth pouch with pinches of various herbs, a coin, and a bullet.

"Where'd you get that?" It looked like a .38, a hollow-point.

She pursed her lips, regarding me from beneath lowered lashes, as a doctor would a reluctant patient.

"It will protect you."

"Only if there is a trigger on that little bag," I said.

"A stranger out there will try to do you harm," she said, eyes serious. "You must wear this, you must never take it off."

I sighed. I hate people telling me what I must do.

She closed the pouch and jabbed a safety pin through it. "Do not carry it in your purse. You could lose it. Wear it inside your clothes. Pin it to your *pantalones*," she said. "Now."

At this point, I wasn't going to argue. I needed all the help I could get. I did as she said, lifting my skirt and pinning it to the elastic at the top of my underpants. What a surprise for Curt, I thought, if he should ever succeed in getting them off.

Aunt Odalys had disappeared into another room, and that worried me. "One more thing," she said, returning with a necklace of small red and white beads. She placed them over my head, arranging them around my neck.

I was so relieved that she hadn't come back leading a goat, I did not demur.

"You are a daughter of Chango," she whispered,

"the warrior who controls thunder and lightning. Wear these." Last time I had a necklace like that, I was five years old and it was confiscated by my mother, who threw it away.

I declined to stay for supper, but hinted I would not be adverse to a Care package. Aunt Odalys filled some Tupperware containers with her wonderful food: the pot-roasted chicken, *calabaza* fritters reeking of nutmeg and cinnamon, and mango flan.

She hugged me at the door as I peered up and down the darkening street like a thief. Then, hair smelling like an herb garden, I dashed out, unlocked the T-Bird, and piled in with my booty. The aromas mingled and filled the car.

"Britt." I jumped, startled. She had followed me out and stood next to my window. Worry creased her face. "Stop at a botánica and buy seven red candles. Burn them for twenty-four hours around a statue of Santa Barbara. Then make an offering of fruit—"

"Eh, if I have time," I lied. I blew a kiss and escaped. In the rearview mirror I saw her still at the curb, like an apparition in her white dress.

I was not about to start shopping at a botánica. Stores that service Santería practitioners have existed in Miami for decades but have proliferated since the Mariel boatlift. There now seems to be one on every Little Havana street corner, selling potions, herbs, candles, mystical charms, beads, special soaps, statues of the saints and gods, and other mystical paraphernalia.

They are small, dark, and mysterious and accept all major credit cards.

I drove home feeling better, buttressed by food, herbs, and magic. Even so, I checked the rearview mirror frequently and cautiously held my breath as

I entered my apartment. Bitsy excitedly danced and wagged her tail; Billy Boots was curled up on a chair. He opened his eyes, stood up, and stretched, motivated not by my arrival but the scent of food. Everything, including my gun, seemed to be as I had left it.

I hadn't realized how hungry I was. After checking the apartment, I sat down and ate ravenously without even rewarming the food. Then I took Bitsy out but only as far as the street, watching for strangers as I tossed my hair, trying to shake out the herbs. On the way back I saw lights on in the Goldsteins' apartment and stopped to warn them. I didn't want to alarm them but I did want them aware, especially since Mrs. Goldstein unlocked my door to take Bitsy out a couple of times a day. I suggested that perhaps we should discontinue the practice for the time being but she would have none of it, insisting that Bitsy needed the exercise. Secretly I was relieved.

I went back inside and called both Lottie and Onnie to let them know I was home. Each had been waiting for my call.

Then I sat down to eat more mango flan and figure out what to do next. The flan was so silky smooth and went down so easily that, as usual when I am nervous, I ate more than I had intended. If a sinister stranger showed up to do me harm, at least I was well fed.

Deciding my next move was easy. I would keep following the Downtown Rapist story. I hoped the next major break would be an arrest but, realistically, that might never happen. All I could do was watch my back and keep doing my job. But I could take action when it came to the Fielding camp. I would confront Martin Mowry directly.

As I got ready for bed, the doorbell rang, jangling

my nerves. Throwing on a bathrobe, I carried the gun to my door.

"Sorry to startle you, Britt. I should have called first."

I quickly slipped the gun behind a sofa cushion and opened the door.

Mr. Goldstein stood on the threshold, carrying his toolbox and looking shy. "The wife thought I should put this up for you." He shrugged and cocked his head. "It's not such a bad idea."

I grinned as he went to work efficiently, drilling small holes, inserting screws, and mounting a mezuzah on my front doorframe.

I kissed his wrinkled cheek as he left, then checked the doors and the windows. I touched the mezuzah, pinned my *resguardo* to my nightgown, tucked my beads and my gun beneath my pillow, and stared at the dark.

14

My dreams that night included spectacular chase scenes in which I seemed to alternate between being the prey and the pursuer. The cast changed constantly, tormenting my subconscious as though trying to tell me something that I could not quite hear in the dense darkness around me.

I woke up feeling like hell and knew what I had to do. I called Curt Norske and invited myself on a sightseeing cruise. Like Lottie had said, I needed a break. I hadn't felt so beaten up and shell-shocked since the last riot.

This is always my favorite time of year, when temperatures soar and heavy rains fall. Late each afternoon black clouds roil over the peninsula, sweep across the Everglades from the Gulf of Mexico, and drench the city. You can hear the grass grow. During the night huge ripe, rosy mangoes fall from the trees outside my bedroom window, dropping to the ground with soft thuds.

I gather them in the morning, selecting one of the biggest and best to devour with my newspaper, cereal, and Cuban coffee. The rest I deposit at the door of Mrs. Goldstein, who believes in sharing the bounty.

I went through the usual motions but lacked appetite and my usual sense of contentment. All I hungered for was answers.

My first task at the office was to track down Martin Mowry. He was upstate with the candidate, according to the local Fielding for Governor campaign headquarters. I missed him at the hotel where the entourage was staying but caught up with him by phone in LaBelle, where Fielding was about to participate in the annual Swamp Cabbage Festival. His speech at the Veterans of Foreign Wars post would follow the parade and precede the gospel sing.

I didn't say it was the press calling, simply announced it was long distance for Mowry. After several minutes, he barked, "Mowry here," into the phone.

"Good morning," I said cheerfully. "This is Britt Montero from the *Miami News*. I understand you've been asking questions about me. Is there anything I can fill you in on?"

There was a pause. "Britt Montero," he repeated. His deep, distinctive voice had the crisp quality of a man accustomed to dispatching and following orders.

"Yes," I said, "and I'd like to know the reason for your inquiries."

"You damn well know the reason," he said. "That pack of lies and accusations you raked up."

"They were questions, Mr. Mowry. Questions," I said. "I'm a reporter; that's what I do. I ask questions, and most still haven't been answered."

"Don't get your panties in a bunch," he said arrogantly. "Let me tell you something. You may be unaware that Eric Fielding has been your publisher's personal lawyer for years. They went through Harvard together and each was the best man at the other's wedding."

"I didn't know that," I said respectfully. "But that has no bearing on anything we do in the newsroom."

Or does it? I wondered. Christ! Was that why Fred Douglas told me to back off? Was I jeopardizing my job?

"You're not doing yourself or your career any good," Mowry warned. "You don't seem to realize that you're about as important to your newspaper as a pimple on an elephant's ass."

I swallowed. "But I still want to know—"

He had hung up.

That bastard, I thought, directing my anger at Fielding. Mowry was probably just following orders to try to intimidate me.

If only there was a way, I thought, to get back into the Mary Beth Rafferty story before the election. We had never published the name of the witness, the little boy, Mary Beth's playmate. Perhaps I could locate him. Or possibly someone involved would go public and demand that Fielding undergo a polygraph. Too bad Mary Beth's father is dead, I thought. I bet he'd do it in a minute.

Meanwhile, it was my job to keep the Downtown Rapist story alive until his arrest. I wrote a follow-up piece about Marianne Rhodes for the early edition.

Despite her TV debut, Fred Douglas had stuck by our decision not to publish her name. I identified her only as "the dark-haired junior executive." Bitterly, she told me she had retained an attorney to file a civil suit for damages against her employer for failing to maintain a safe workplace. Sounded right to me. Too much litigation clogs our courts now, but if this was what it took to keep women safe on the job, I was for it.

Deliberately, I again used the line that Dr. Simmons indicated probably infuriated the rapist most, that the crimes were attempts to prove to himself that he was sexually adequate, which he obviously was not.

I finished the story and took off, leaving a note that I had gone to investigate the crime lab clue found on the letter, the particle of what could be marine paint. I drove to Bayside and parked the T-Bird, leaving my pager locked in the glove box.

The *Sea Dancer* is white and immaculate, a sixty-four-footer with double decks and stainless steel fittings. The captain welcomed me aboard personally, his gold-flecked eyes as warm as I remembered. I wore white cotton slacks with a peach-colored blouse and sat up near the captain, the wheel, and the public address system.

Biscayne Bay is a live work of art, constantly changing. Today it was smooth and flat, bridges and skyscrapers reflected in its brilliant blue-green surface.

Whether I hit it off with Curt Norske or not, this would be a welcome treat, I thought, settling expectantly into my seat among laughing, chattering tourists. I love to see Miami, and one of the best ways is from the water. The sight always fills me with fantasies about what it had to be like long ago, before the original city skyline gave way to the modern metropolis.

The boat was about three quarters full of noisy summer visitors in shorts and bright cottons, the smart ones protected by hats and sunglasses and swabbing on sunscreen. Some kids sported mouse ears acquired at Disney World during their trip south.

I dreamily scanned the bay's shimmering surface, its beauty driving away the dark images that had shadowed my thoughts. Waterfront has always been in demand. Tequesta Indians camped on these shores three thousand years ago, and archaeological digs in the South Biscayne Bay area had unearthed ten-thousand-year-old traces of humanity. Ponce de Leon sailed into this bay. Spanish galleons swept by, loaded with treasure, as Seminoles paddled dugout canoes. These waters were home to pirates, pioneers, runaway slaves, and battle-scarred Civil War veterans. What would they think of it today, the busiest cruise-ship port in the world? Today's news stories, trials, and turmoil, I thought: will any of it matter in a hundred years?

Taking a deep breath, I began to regain perspective, realizing how much I needed this respite. Then I began to wonder if I really should have included that line about the rapist's virility in my story. I looked around. There had to be a phone aboard this boat, I thought. No. I forced thoughts of the newsroom from my mind, focusing on Miami's chameleon colors, shifting shades of aquamarine, silver, and grass green.

We rumbled away from the dock, and the Dupont Plaza hotel drifted by to the south, near the mouth of the Miami River, which was crystal clear and clean enough to drink from until 1896, not coincidentally the year the city was born. The Dupont site was always inhabited. Slaves, settlers, soldiers, and Seminoles were early residents, but not the first. Builders paved over a massive Tequesta burial mound for hotel parking. The hotel opened in 1957, and my mother attended fashion shows, luncheons, and afternoon tea dances there. Miamians of every generation have had their own personal memories of the Dupont Plaza or the historic ground on which it was built.

My memories are unfortunate. Whenever I see the hotel, a wedding comes to mind. I was neither invited nor a participant. I was dispatched to cover it after gunfire broke out. I remember the beautifully appointed buffet table and its centerpiece, a magnificent multi-tiered wedding cake. Hors d'oeuvres platters, fresh shrimp nestled on shaved ice, and lavish flowers. Two rows of just-filled champagne glasses remained undisturbed. Ideal images for the caterer's advertising brochure, except for two men in evening clothes sprawled dead across the table next to the cake. One had been best man, the other a guest. The shooter, an old acquaintance of the bride, had not been invited, obviously for good reason.

We cruised past the causeways, the cruise ships, and the rich red rooftops of Fisher Island, where homes and condos, accessible only by boat, sell for millions; past waterfront property commandeered by an increasing army of homeless people who hang their tatty belongings from the fences intended to keep them out.

His resonant voice rich and professional, Curt was giving his spiel, pointing out the seaplane terminal on Watson Island, the Freedom Tower, and the big *News* building on the bay.

I listened demurely as our handsome captain show-boated as though for me alone, smiling and boldly winking until I couldn't help flushing and smiled back. He was telling a story about the hermit who lived in 1925 on a small sandy spoil island which is now the Dodge Island seaport. I knew this snippet of history. The hermit had refused to evacuate his tiny island as the savage hurricane of 1926 stormed toward the coast, and he was never seen again.

"Except," our captain intoned, "on moonless evenings, when port employees, crewmen, and tourists have reported sightings of a mysterious bearded man. They are especially prevalent whenever storms threaten: the ghost of the Dodge Island hermit, stalking his former home."

The tourists shivered with delight as I looked questioningly at our captain. I never heard that the hermit was haunting Dodge Island. Curt continued, adding that the summer storm season produced so many eerie sightings that some workers had quit their jobs while others refused to remain at the port after dark. I frowned, wanting to talk to people who had seen the apparition.

The landmark Palm Island home where mobster Al Capone died in 1947 was now in view. Tourists snapped pictures as our captain described how Capone masterminded his vast criminal empire from poolside at his waterfront mansion and how machine-gun fire had cut down Capone henchmen on that very strip of causeway in a deadly territorial dispute with Florida mobsters. Wait just one minute, I thought, sitting up straight in my seat. Gotcha! That one never happened. Our captain was telling them tall! One perk of being on the *News* payroll was access to the library, where I love to pore over old original news accounts. Scarface came to Miami to escape Chicago's cold winters and brutal violence and pretty much minded his manners. By the end he was too brain-damaged from venereal disease to run any criminal enterprise.

If the captain saw my skeptical squint as he steered us into the sun, he showed no sign. We chugged north, under the drawbridge where he had spotted Eldridge's submerged car. A network of pilings outlined the watery rectangle once intended to be Pelican Island.

"Starboard, to your right," broadcast our captain, "you can see the pilings that form the framework of Pelican Island, once planned as a romantic honeymoon Garden of Eden for a lovestruck millionaire in the twenties." His eyes lingered fondly on me. "The man-made tropical island was to be his wedding gift to a beautiful Ziegfeld Follies showgirl. But his sweetheart died tragically on her way to join him in Miami. Heartbroken, he abandoned construction and died soon after." The captain's voice was low as he related the tragedy, his eyes solemn. He paused for dramatic effect. The tourists were rapt. "Some called it suicide," he said, his voice regaining its brisk pace, "but I call it a broken heart. The island was never completed and the pilings remain, half a century later, a monument to love."

A beautiful story, well told. Truly impressed, I cut my eyes at Captain Norske as the tourists gazed mournfully at the lonely pilings and mouthed the words, "You're full of crap." He did a double take, then winked before continuing his talk, standing strong at the helm, overlooking his watery domain like a prince of the sea.

Not a word was true. The Venetian Islands, strewn east-west across the bay, were built in the twenties. Pelican Island, slightly to the north, was to follow, next in the newly emerging island chain, but the developers went broke in the bust that followed the 1926 hurricane.

Late-afternoon sun streaked the water crimson as we pulled back into the berth. The tourists scattered, and the captain and I strolled to an outdoor café serving up big strawberry and banana frozen daiquiris along with music from a steel-drum band.

He looked relaxed and happy. I couldn't stand it. "Where did you get that Pelican Island story?"

"Like it?" He flashed his megawatt smile. He was pleased.

I jabbed at my icy drink with a plastic straw. "None of it's true, you know. The millionaire and the showgirl, it sounds like some old B-movie."

He looked wounded, brushing back his shock of blond hair. "It's original," he said. "I made it up myself."

"Right. The truth is that the developers went broke and stopped construction."

"Think tourists want to hear that? It's a yawn. Doesn't have the right mystique."

"The city has enough authentic mystique." I couldn't help smiling. "I love Miami, but sometimes I swear Rod Serling must be the mayor. You don't need to make up stories."

"You don't understand these summer tourists," he said seriously. "They're not the rich and famous, they're not historians researching books. They're people who worked all year for this vacation. Think they wanna hear how some developer went broke? They want adventure, romance, chills, and thrills."

"Such as the ghost of Dodge Island?"

He grinned. "Like that one?" The top two buttons of his uniform shirt were undone and golden hairs peeked through, glistening in the waning sunlight.

"I don't believe it. Nobody's ever really seen him. Right?"

The stress of interrogation apparently caused him to gulp his daiquiri too fast, and he winced in pain as it froze his sinuses.

"Don't you think you have an obligation to the truth?" I demanded, as he gasped and massaged the spot between his eyebrows. "Don't you feel guilty about misleading your passengers?"

"No and no," he said, and leaned toward me across the small table. "You know better than most of us that the truth can be too mean. Think these people spending their last buck for some fun and good memories want to hear about the rapist you're writing about? Or grim, depressing facts? Nah. They get that on the news every night back home. Money's tight, they want to play. Give 'em a break. Let 'em take home a few good stories. You're the one with the obligation to be absolutely accurate, the five W's or whatever," he said, gesturing broadly. "Not me. I'm entertainment. These people are blowing big bucks on a vacation. My job is to make it memorable. That's my obligation." His righteous smile melted my disapproval. Or maybe it was the daiquiri. I knew what he meant about cold, hard truth. That's why I was here. I wanted a vacation from the truth myself. But what he did was still unethical, I thought.

"You work this hard at making everything memorable?"

His piercing eyes met mine. "Character flaw. I'm a unrepentant perfectionist. What about you, Britt?"

I knew he was coming on to me, but I felt a tightness in my chest and a tingle below the waist. I sucked my upper lip and gazed into my glass to suppress a silly grin.

"You probably deserve the Academy Award," I admitted grudgingly. "The Pelican Island story is excellent. Of course, you know there was no Capone shootout in Miami?"

He nodded. "Sure, but what's a Capone story without machine guns?"

We rode south in his convertible, top down, my hair streaming in the wind, the night soft and steamy around us. We ate dinner at a seafood restaurant in north Largo. We danced to island music with a throbbing drumbeat. Curt was built like an athlete, with narrow hips and the natural grace of a man comfortable in his own body. He had a lot more warmth and rhythm than one would expect from a Scandinavian sailor type. He held me close as we slow-danced, and I closed my eyes, blocking out every troubling thought about my job, every disturbing vision, every fear. Except for one embarrassing moment when he buried his face in my hair. "What is that?" he asked, sniffing. "Some kind of conditioner? Smells like salad dressing."

Later he took me to my car parked back at Bayside and we necked and petted like teenagers in the vast darkness of the nearly empty parking garage. He was very warm and sexy—as far as it went. And I wanted it to go further but was suddenly startled in his embrace, certain I heard a sly footfall in the shadows around us. "What was that?" I said fearfully, eyes straining. "Somebody's out there."

He blinked, gazing around sleepily. "Nothing," he murmured in my ear. "You always this jumpy?" Maybe the sound was my subconscious stepping on the brakes, I thought. Caution and common sense prevailed, as I pried my body loose from his and insisted on going home. Before I did, Curt insisted that I agree to an unscheduled night cruise aboard the *Dancer*, as his only passenger. "Nothing like it," he promised. "We can anchor out there alone in the middle of the bay, under a full moon. Wait till you see how it looks on the water."

Sounded dangerous to me: bad, mad, and damn good.

I promised to think about it. He said he'd check to see when the next full moon was due and let me know.

I drove home as though in a drugged stupor, yearning for sleep, even if it was alone. As I dropped my clothes and slid into bed, my thoughts, strangely enough, centered around Kendall McDonald and the comfort we had found in each other's arms until our careers tore us apart.

15

My mini-vacation faded fast the next morning. My phone messages, some computerized and printed out, others handwritten by a city-desk clerk, were waiting. The initial flood of calls on the rapist was down to a trickle. The last pink message slip bore a cryptic note. *Caller says "Maybe a blonde next time."* That was it, no name or number. I squinted at the words a second time as chills rippled up and down my arms. No, I thought hopefully. It can't be.

I showed it to Gloria, the city-desk clerk. "Did you take this one?"

"No." She looked up at me, her black eyes curious.

"Who did?" Day and time had been left blank, as was the space the message taker should have initialed.

Gloria studied it. "If it came in today, it could be the new intern who sat in while I took a break, or anybody on the city desk."

"This could be important," I said urgently. Gloria's eyes fell again to the words on the slip of paper. I realized that the content certainly didn't make it appear important. But Gloria is a champ. She takes me at my word.

"That could be Gretchen's printing," she said finally.

"Oh, no," I moaned.

Gretchen peered at the message slip as though I was proffering a doggie turd. "I wouldn't know, Britt."

"It could be important. Surely if you took such an unusual message you'd remember." The more I sputtered toward meltdown, the more vague she became.

Her blue eyes were bland. "Maybe I did. . . ."

"You remember what the caller sounded like? What time of the day or night it came in? Did it come in on my line or the city desk? Did the caller say anything else?"

"Britt, I have a great many responsibilities, and message taking is not one of them." Gretchen used the tone of an exasperated parent addressing an unruly child. "If I happened to pick up the phone and take a message, as a favor to you—"

"It was a man, right?"

"Yes."

"Did he say anything else?"

"Not that I recall." Her voice grew impatient.

"When did it come in?"

"Britt." She looked amused and slightly annoyed. "I am much too busy for this."

"Gretchen, who do you think this was?"

She blinked and shrugged. "Some friend of yours."

"No, Gretchen. The Downtown Rapist."

She reacted with a slight start, but her voice was patronizing. "Why ever would you think that, Britt?"

I inhaled a deep breath, fighting frustration. "He has written to us, remember? And you do recall our last story? On his most recent victim?" Still no comprehension. "The *dark-haired* computer expert?"

Gretchen scrutinized the message again. I read it aloud. *"Maybe a blonde next time."* I watched the light bulb flick on. "That's right, Gretchen. You're a blonde, I'm a blonde."

I took it to Fred's office. "Think we should report this to the police?" he asked, perplexed.

"I don't know. What do we tell them? If Gretchen had at least bothered to note the exact date and time of the call," I said sullenly, "or if she could remember anything distinctive about him or his voice. But this," I said, displaying the note, "gives them nothing more to go on, nothing new. It could be anybody trying to be funny or playing a sick joke. Wish I'd been here when the call came in, then we'd know. Somebody should teach that woman how to take a proper message."

Fred waved off my pout. "That's not her job. More important, Britt, do you think it could be a personal threat against you?"

"Probably not." There in the light of day beneath fluorescent bulbs, high on the fifth floor in the busy newsroom with headline writers to the left, sports department jocks to the right, and security manning the lobby, this anonymous message was nothing more sinister than a scrap of paper. Although some still, small voice inside me wondered how I would feel about it when I was home alone at midnight.

But I had some pride and certainly didn't want to acquire a crybaby reputation. I still remembered the jokes and derision directed at a reporter for the Spanish edition after he received what he thought was a telephoned threat. He had insisted that the paper send him to lie low in Puerto Rico for a few weeks and demanded Wackenhut bodyguards for a month after his return.

I still stuck to the theory that people who call are only trying to scare you. Succumb, and you have played into their hands. There are still people at the *News* who swear it's a mistake to put a woman on the police beat. No point playing into their hands either.

"No big deal," I said jauntily, and turned back toward the newsroom.

"Well, watch yourself."

"For sure," I said, and smiled reassuringly. But who, I wondered, is watching the rapist?

I called Harry, who had news from the crime lab. No surprise, the preliminary DNA tests on the envelope indicated that the rapist wrote the letter. Harry wasn't enthusiastic about Marianne Rhodes going public either. "But it's her choice," he said grimly.

For a moment, I felt tempted to tell him about the telephone message Gretchen took, but to what point? If the same man called again and convinced me he was the rapist and not simply a crank, then I would report it.

Ryan went to the cafeteria for a snack, and I persuaded him to bring me back coffee. When he leaned over to place it on my desk, he stopped and sniffed loudly. Then he did it again.

"What's that in your hair, Britt?"

"Never mind."

"You been out on a raid with the cops again?"

I turned to look at him. "No, why?"

"Smells like marijuana," he said softly, closing his eyes, leaning into my hair, and inhaling deeply.

"Oh, Ryan," I snapped, pushing him away.

"No offense." He smiled, backing off. "I like it."

I drank my coffee and dialed Detective Orestes Diaz at the county for the results of Farrington's postmortem. After whacking concrete with little hammers for hours, doctors had found that, like his wife eighteen years earlier, Farrington was shot in the head before being encased in cement. His death had been ruled a homicide.

The body slid down between the pillar's steel reinforcing rods after he fell or was pushed from the catwalk. He would have remained dead center, at the heart of the column, but the rush and weight of flowing concrete had forced him between the rods and up against the inside edge of the plywood form. The detective had been right. Farrington might easily have remained missing forever.

"Sure it wasn't suicide?"

"No gun, and believe me we looked. And he was popped in the back of the skull, just like his wife. I got a copy of the old file from the city. Detective over there did a helluva job back then. Sketches, diagrams, everything. This case was a carbon copy."

"Think it was a coincidence, that maybe the killer wasn't even aware of the first murder?"

"There are no coincidences in homicide cases."

"Then you think it's retaliation, some kind of street justice? You looking at the dead woman's family? But why would they wait so long to take revenge? And then make it so obvious? They could have shot him on the street and made it look like a robbery." I was puzzled, thinking aloud.

"You forget, Britt, he wasn't supposed to be found. Only Farrington and his killer were supposed to know."

"What caliber was the bullet?"

"We want to withhold that information," Diaz said.

"Why?" I said impatiently.

"Because if the killer reads it in the newspaper he might dispose of the gun, and we want to catch him with it."

I sighed. Made no sense to me. Killers all watch television, and they all know about ballistics. If the murderer intended to dispose of the weapon he had already done so. Other criminals develop an attachment for certain guns and will keep them no matter what. But we had fought this argument before, in other cases, and Diaz remained adamant.

"Did he have any other injuries? What was in his pockets? Was he robbed? Had he been drinking? Think they might have met in a bar? Did you check the construction crew to see if somebody who worked with him might—"

"Britt, you're getting way ahead of me and I got to go," Diaz said impatiently. "He still had his wallet and ID, some cash, was wearing a Rolex. Other injuries were minor, probably from when he went from the catwalk down into the form. That's all I can tell you now. Later." And he hung up.

I went to the library for the Farrington file, which I had returned after the initial story. Onnie was relieved to see me. She looked perky in a smart sand-color slack set, her dusky makeup flawless, small gold hoops in her ears.

She was humming and seemed happy. I found her cheerfulness annoying but kept it to myself. The Farrington clips had been refiled, and she used a stepstool to reach up into the *F*'s. As she stepped down in the close quarters between the shelves and handed me the envelope, she sniffed several times and looked puzzled. "What kind of shampoo you using, Britt?"

"It's not shampoo," I said. Hell, it was only thirty-six hours, still thirty-six to go.

"Hairspray?"

"Don't ask. It's a long story."

"Smells like salad or soup seasoning." She shrugged and hummed some upbeat Tina Turner song. I wondered why I don't confide more in friends. The only person I spill everything to is Lottie, and that is only because she either guesses without my telling or torments me until I do. I wondered how Onnie would react if I told her about the herbs in my hair or the *resguardo* dangling from my underwear at that very moment.

I wrote the Farrington follow-up, focusing on the eerie resemblance between his death and the murder police had accused him of eighteen years earlier.

I transmitted the story, printed out a hard copy for my own files, and stuffed it into the bottom drawer of my desk where I keep my printouts and notes. My system is simple. When the drawer is too full to close, I sort and file the contents in a squat two-drawer cabinet file next to my desk.

Tired and edgy, I had slept little the night before and wanted only to escape the office before somebody out there somewhere started shooting at something or somebody and I wound up working all night.

The phone rang and I snatched it up with a feeling of foreboding. The strange voice was male and angry.

"This is Ronald DeAngelo."

It took a moment to compute that he was the man now married to Mary Beth's mother. The man who operated the fluorescent bulb factory in Hialeah. "Yes, Mr. DeAngelo."

"I have just become aware that you have been out here harassing my wife."

I closed my eyes and sighed. "I don't think harassment is the word, Mr. DeAngelo."

"It's also been brought to my attention that you are attempting to discredit our candidate for governor, Mr. Fielding, an old friend of the family."

"I'm afraid you have the wrong impression—"

"I'm putting you on notice that I consider this a threat to the safety and well-being of my family. My attorney has advised me that this is a gross invasion of privacy." His voice grew more heated.

"It involves an unsolved murder," I said calmly.

"To bring up painful history and use it against innocent people is an invasion of our privacy. I warn you, I will take any steps necessary to protect my family."

I wanted to ask if his wife had remembered the name of the only witness, Mary Beth's playmate, but this did not seem like the right moment. It was too late anyway; he had hung up.

I reached for the phone to call him back, to assure him that the last thing I intended to do was to cause his family pain, and then remembered that the number was unlisted.

As I stood to leave, the night city-desk clerk handed me a message that had come in while I was on the phone. Marianne Rhodes had left word that it was urgent.

I sighed and dialed the number. Three times, it was busy. On the fourth try she answered immediately, her words loud and slurred.

"Do you know anything, Britt? The police aren't telling me a thing," she pleaded. "Detective Arroyo isn't even returning my calls."

"He's probably out in the field," I said gently. "I'm sure he'll let you know right away if there are any developments."

"Those bastards aren't doing anything! They've botched the investigation. They're going to let him get away with it." She sounded fragile, about to shatter.

"They've got lots of manpower on it," I assured her. "They're working the case really hard."

"Not from what I hear! And you, you didn't even have a story today." Her voice was accusatory.

"Because there were no new developments. Have you had any rest?"

"Can't sleep," she muttered.

"Did the doctor give you anything?"

"I hate taking pills. A friend of mine heard that one of the other victims has been on all kinds of medication since it happened and is walking around like a zombie."

"You have to get some sleep," I told her, thinking I could use some myself.

"I've been drinking too much," she acknowledged remorsefully. "It's the only thing that helps."

"You have to go on, get on with your life."

"What life? What life?" The words were a sob of anguish. "I can't go back to my job, which was the best one I ever had. I drove away the only man who ever loved me." I heard ice tinkling as she paused to gulp from a glass.

"Ben? Your fiancé?"

"That's right, that son of a bitch. He couldn't take it. Who could? I have to keep going back for exams of my throat and my private parts to see if he gave me VD."

I winced. "Do your parents live here?"

"Yeah, Cutler Ridge."

"Why don't you stay with them for a while?"

"I can't stand being around them. All they do is look at me and cry."

"Look," I said, sounding upbeat and sensible, though I wanted to cry myself. "You've got to get yourself some help. You've got to stay together so when they catch this guy you can help convict him." God forbid if he isn't caught, I thought.

"I don't want him convicted!" she screamed. "I want him dead for what he did to me!"

"I know," I said bleakly.

"He's after you, you know."

"You'll get over this," I said quietly. "You and Ben should see a counselor together."

"Would you call him for me?"

"Ben? I think it's better if you call. The last person he wants to hear from is a reporter."

"But I threw his things out in the street. I told him I never want to see him again. Why don't you put this in a story?" she sobbed. There was a crash as she dropped the phone.

"Marianne? Are you all right?"

She did not pick it up again, but I could hear her weeping and muttering.

After several minutes I hung up, called the rape squad, and left a message for Harry, asking him to call her, that she needed help.

I have had better days at the office, I thought, staring at my telephone as though it were the enemy. I left alone, cautiously scanning the parking lot, glad to see a security guard. I waved to her, unlocked the car, checked the interior, and watched to make sure I wasn't followed as I drove out of the lot, toward home.

16

The world sparkled in the morning, washed by an overnight storm. Alamandas bloomed on their white wooden trellis, a brilliant pink against a sky so blue and grass so green they hurt my eyes. I showered, shampooed my hair with great delight, then went to the office. A surprise waited on my desk, a large manila envelope. Inside, a glossy eight-by-ten of a handsome, smiling Captain Curt Norske, shot aboard the *Sea Dancer*. He leaned against the railing, skyline behind him, relaxed and laughing, probably at something the photographer had said. Lottie must have dug back in her old negatives to find it. Attached was a note in her distinctive left-hand scrawl: *Don't miss the boat!*

Even frozen on film, his engaging grin made me smile in return. I slid the photo back into its envelope and dialed Lottie's extension.

"Thanks for making it up for me, Lottie. What a neat way to start the day."

"Did you see it?" she asked.

"It was on my desk."

"The editorial." Her voice sounded flat.

"What?" Though I had glanced through the morning paper over orange juice and coffee, I hadn't read the editorial page. I rarely do. It's usually boring, sometimes embarrassing.

"We endorsed Fielding today."

I went to the city desk and picked up a copy. The editorial writer extolled Fielding's sterling qualities, enthusiastically recommending him as best choice for governor. I wondered if Dan had seen it yet and suddenly decided what I wanted to do today if I could avoid being captured by some other story.

I bustled out of the newsroom as though headed out on my beat. The Center for Forensic Pathology is a block-long structure that will accommodate as many as 350 corpses at a time. It is not listed among the Chamber of Commerce attractions designed to draw tourists, but Miami does have the world's best morgue.

I stated my business to a disembodied voice piped from somewhere inside the imposing edifice, and the security gate opened. I parked between a shiny black hearse and an unmarked homicide car and skirted the building to the front entrance, guarded by an ancient bronze cannon salvaged from a shipwrecked Spanish galleon.

The *Santa Margarita* sank with all aboard during a hurricane off the Florida coast three hundred and seventy years ago. The chief medical examiner selected the cannon when given the option of choosing the art for his new $12 million complex. The politically appointed committee on art in public places was appalled. Members argued that a big gun, even a big gun crafted by fifteenth-century artisans, is no work of art. They prefer incomprehensible abstracts created by expensive modern artists. One critic denounced the cannon as a militaristic symbol of death.

The barrel is leveled at the inner city, where the last riots broke out. I think it's appropriate.

The chief investigator was at his desk. Records here

date back to 1955 and are never disposed of. Common
practice is to withhold the files on unsolved murders,
assumed to be still under investigation, from the press.
Reporters are referred to the police detective on the
case. But a twenty-two-year-old homicide is a cold
case, and I anticipated no problem unless someone
was aware of the link to Fielding. Then it might
be considered a political hot potato. I was glad the
chief medical examiner was lecturing to students and
unaware of my presence.

The investigator, a tough and savvy former police
detective, was agreeable, and I tagged along to one of
the storage rooms where he dug through several cardboard cartons for the file on Mary Beth Rafferty.

"Just let me know when you're through with it," he
said, and returned to his office.

I settled down at a conference table. The pictures
were attached, with color slides in a separate envelope.

In the scene pictures, Mary Beth looked like a broken and discarded doll. No wonder the case haunts
Dan, I thought. I closed my eyes and pushed them
aside to read the autopsy report, noting that the chief
had done the cut himself.

*The body is that of a well developed, well nour-
ished female measuring 49½ inches and weighing
55 pounds. The appearance of the deceased is consistent with the stated age of eight years.*

*The hair is brown, wavy, and shoulder length, the
irides are brown, and the pupils each measure .5
centimeter. Numerous petechiae are present over the
conjunctiva.*

Petechiae are little broken blood vessels in the eyes,
and I knew enough to understand that their appearance
indicates some choking or smothering.

The dentition is in good repair.

Her teeth were good.

The frenulum is torn, lacerated, and contused.

The little tag of skin between her lip and gums was torn and bruised.

Examination of the neck reveals multiple linear to regular partially confluent abrasions with scattered contusions.

Scrapes and bruises on her neck.

I imagined Fielding posing for television in a classroom full of eager children and shivered.

The next line set my heart to thumping. *On the left shoulder there is a bite mark measuring 3.5 by 2.5 centimeters in cross dimension. The abrasions caused by the teeth marks are red and dried. There are underlying subcutaneous purple-red contusions of the soft tissue.*

The redness and bruising under the skin indicated that the bite was inflicted before she died, that her heart was still pumping and blood vessels were crushed. If the bite had occurred after death the underlying tissue would have been bloodless.

What interested me was the bite mark itself. I reached for the pictures and shuffled through them.

Some graphically revealed what the reporters meant when they wrote that Mary Beth was "sexually molested" and "sexually mutilated."

She had been raped with a tree branch.

Revolted, I tried not to look at those, searching quickly for what I wanted. Taken in the morgue, the naked child, pitifully small on the autopsy table. The close-up of the bite marks. Yes, I thought.

The chief always documented pattern injuries meticulously, even before the science of forensic odontology came afield. There were several close-ups, shot from various angles. In each, the marks on Mary Beth's shoulder were placed in perspective by an L-shaped millimeter ruler.

The copy I made of the best photo on the office Xerox was not as clear as I would have liked, even though I fiddled with the contrast controls, making it first lighter, then darker. I folded it into my notebook and walked out with it.

Dr. Everett Wyatt's office is at my favorite old historic downtown address. The Ingraham Building is not all neon, smoke and mirrors, or clever Architectonica, it is one of Miami's jewels, a neo-renaissance revival building finished in 1927. In those days ten stories was ambitious. The lobby ceiling is gold-plated, with one-of-a-kind bronze chandeliers, and the elegant bronze elevator doors are engraved with early Florida wildlife scenes.

The building was named for Miami pioneer James Ingraham, who arranged the historic meeting between Henry Flagler and Julia Tuttle, the mother of Miami, in 1895. The railroad came south as a result, a watershed event that changed the face of Miami forever.

The lobby, with its high ceilings and all that marble, has the kind of echoing acoustics that make me want to yodel.

I sat waiting in a comfortable leather chair in Wyatt's private office, looking west out the windows behind his desk, over a city and expressways undreamed of when the building was new.

An ebullient fast-talking man with an intense curiosity and quick intelligence, Dr. Wyatt has a thriving practice among both living patients and the dead. He expanded his interests into forensic dentistry about a dozen years ago, using his expertise to identify the dead through dental charts. It takes a special kind of dentist to work with skeletons and decomposed, burned, or disfigured bodies. He then expanded into bite-mark analysis.

His expert testimony has been responsible for numerous murder convictions, two of which ended in the electric chair. Bite-mark comparison can be more damning than fingerprint evidence. A suspect might be able to explain his fingerprints found at a crime scene, but it is pretty damn hard to convince a jury that he innocently left his tooth marks in a murder victim.

A room full of patients, most probably unaware of his second specialty, waited. The fact that Wyatt is also my personal dentist won me almost instant access. He remembers me because we always discuss cases, and when in his chair I constantly beseech him to remember, "I'm alive! I'm alive!"

He entered the room with his usual speed, wiry and intense, with brilliant blue eyes. "What's up, Britt? You say it's important?" He glanced at my file, which his receptionist had placed on his desk, and frowned. "When's the last time you had your teeth cleaned?"

"Dr. Wyatt, could you still match the bite mark left on a murder victim twenty-two years ago with the teeth of the man who left it?"

"Twenty-two years!" His bright eyes sparkled with enthusiasm at the idea. "I'll be testifying soon in the case of Archie Greene."

Greene is a laborer believed to have killed a dozen prostitutes over a number of years.

"He bit one in 1984 and we got his impressions in 1992 and were able to match it up. But never a case twenty-two years old. The killer would have to have some kind of unusual—"

I whipped out the copy of the picture from the medical examiner's file. He took it and frowned. "I'd need to see the original, of course, and have it enhanced."

"Enhanced?"

"Computer enhancement. Is this from the medical examiner's file?"

I nodded.

"Good, that means we'll have a slide. We'll print the slide and get the computer to bring it up. Amazing what they can do to enhance it."

He squinted at the copy.

"A classic bite ring," he exclaimed cheerfully, turning the copy sideways. "Look here, even on this lousy copy you can see marks on the skin from sharp uppers, looks like the drag pattern of an eyetooth.

"The killer would have to have some kind of unusual arrangement of the teeth, a gap or a space that would remain for twenty-two years." He pondered, thinking aloud. "Any unusual individual characteristics of the teeth themselves would be worn away by now."

I tried not to betray my growing excitement.

"What would rule out a comparison, extensive dental work?"

"If he had braces, or had his teeth capped or pulled out, forget it."

"Capped," I echoed with concern, picturing Fielding's perfect politician's smile.

"Right, capped teeth are man-made."

"Barring any of that, you think it can be done?"

"I would go after it with enthusiasm," he said.

"What would you need for the comparison?"

"Ideally, an impression of the suspect's mouth. But we've done it many times from something else the individual has bitten. I just made a match with the tooth marks a guy left when he bit into a moon pie.

The best is bologna or cheese, or a candy bar, though those tend to melt. An apple or a cookie would be good."

He leaned back in his chair.

"Remember when they were trying to get impressions from Bundy in prison? They kept giving him fruit, apples, but he was smart; he knew what they were up to and he ate them right down to the core. They sent me a chewed-up apple core once. Nothing left to get impressions from; he ate it up completely."

Mind racing, I half listened to Wyatt's Bundy story. Finding Fielding's dentist should be no problem, and though the same bond of confidentiality exists between dentist and patient as with a doctor, lawyer, or member of the clergy, there had to be a way. Maybe justice could be won for Mary Beth Rafferty after all.

"Too bad this didn't happen today," Wyatt was saying. "Now they swab bite marks for saliva samples that can reveal alpha amylase and the presence of antigens that could help identify the biter through blood grouping."

I wrote down the case number, and he promised he would pull the file and examine the photos at the ME office by the end the week.

Dr. Wyatt returned to his patients and I asked his receptionist for the rest-room key on the way out. If this works, I thought, it could nail Fielding. What a hell of a story! These are the ones you look for after writing about the same events time after time: the drug murder, the love triangle, the jealous rage, the holiday tragedy. They happen over and over on my beat. But this story was different.

My skin felt flushed and my body quick and light,

buoyed by the intensity that throbs through every reporter hot on the trail of a big one. Rarely had I felt so alive, so full of purpose.

The old-fashioned rest room was small compared to those in newer buildings, but immaculate and well kept, with the original black and white tiles. There were four stalls, two sinks on pedestals, and a mirrored wall. My entrance startled a woman standing at one of the sinks in front of the mirror, digging into her large bag. I caught sight of my reflection in the mirror and smiled at my own face, animated and flooded with color above the string of red and white beads.

It was not quite time to tell my editors, I thought. I had to be sure. Despite Fred's warning and Mowry's intimidation, there would be no resistance from my bosses if I could produce this story. It was still only a possibility, but the prospect electrified me.

In the mirror something about the woman just a few feet away caught my eye. She was tall and slim, with tanned bare legs in sandals, a wraparound skirt, long-sleeved shirt, and dark hair, long and shiny. Beads. Had to be her beads. Similar to mine, but multicolored and longer, worn under one armpit and across her chest like a bandoleer. She must know my Aunt Odalys, I thought, slightly giddy. Our eyes met in the glass. I looked away quickly and entered a stall.

I sighed as I went about my business. I had to be the only woman in the world who excreted more fluid than she took in. Did I really drink that much tea and coffee?

Something cascaded soundlessly to the tiled floor outside the stall, just within my range of vision. It spread out in billows on impact. A wig. Dark hair, long and shiny.

I froze, holding my breath. No sound came from outside except for a slight rustling. A garment landed on the floor: the wraparound skirt the woman had been wearing. This room has no windows, I thought, stomach tightening in panic. Buttons on the long-sleeved blouse clicked against the tiles as it too was discarded. I cursed my carelessness. Horrified, I stood up, hands shaking as I adjusted my clothes. As I reached for the gun inside my purse, hanging from the door hook, my feet were suddenly jerked out from under me.

I fell, striking my shoulder blade painfully on the toilet seat. Strong hands gripped my ankles, dragging me under the door. I heard myself screaming. Two realizations flashed clearly through my mind in that moment of terror: what had troubled me about the woman was the Adam's apple, and I had to pee again.

I clung desperately to the door with both hands, struggling and thrashing.

He scrambled up my body, tearing my right hand loose from its grip on the bottom of the door. He was smiling. My attacker was the woman I had seen. But now she was a naked man, wearing only tattoos. They covered his chest and forearms.

He grabbed my hair and yanked hard as he leaned back. "*Chupen*," he whispered, smile widening into a triumphant grin. "*Chupen*." His tattoos were a dull, almost turquoise, hue. A crude dragon extended across his right shoulder from his back. A woman's face with the body of a snake stared from over his left breast. Words on his left shoulder. Arrows everywhere.

"No! Let me go!" I screamed, struggling. The knife had to be somewhere. The thought terrified me.

We grappled and he reached behind him—for the knife, I thought. No, a roll of duct tape. Clutching it in his left hand, he reached for my wrist with his right. Wrenching out of his grasp, I scrambled on hands and knees. I embraced the wire wastepaper basket in the corner, thrusting it between us, glimpsing the knife and the round box of dusting powder on the sink. He reached for the knife, his eyes on me, and the powder box flew off the sink. The room exploded in a cloud of sweet-smelling white dust.

My screams bounced off the floor, walls, and ceiling as in an echo chamber, but in this solid old building I knew they would not be heard out in the hall, much less the nearby offices.

The out-of-order sign must be posted on the exterior door, I thought, trying to evade his grasp. No help was coming. I willed Dr. Wyatt's receptionist to wonder why I wasn't returning the key and come looking for me.

The choking powder cloud began to settle. On the floor, in my hair, on my eyelids. He did not seem alarmed by my screams. His eyes revealed that he enjoyed them.

He savored the chase, sidestepping and parrying like a wild creature toying with helpless prey. He wants me to struggle and then he will use the knife, I thought.

My gun. Hanging out of reach, inside a locked cubicle.

He yanked the wire basket from my grasp, hurling it to one side as I skittered backward. No way to get past him to the heavy wooden door.

Screaming and choking, I staggered back into the last stall in the row, fell into a sitting position on the toilet, and kicked out with both feet as he advanced. Naked, his sex was vulnerable, and he danced back a few steps, like the practiced ballet of a boxer in combat. I saw the knife in his hand, the words tattooed on his shoulder:

Mis amigos son los muertos. My friends are the dead.

Sweat glistened in the Brillo-like pubic hair surrounding his testicles and hooded penis.

I thought of Marianne Rhodes. The disease he carried. The son of a bitch! I leaped up, whimpering, gritting my teeth, and slammed the stall door. I threw the metal bolt to keep him out, aware, as tears stung my eyes, that it was only temporary.

My gun was three stalls away. So much for carrying the weapon with me at all times, I thought, breathing hard. Thanks for the advice, Dan.

A sound in the stall beside me. He hurtled over the top, feet first, making an ugly guttural sound. Dropping to my knees, I scrambled under the bottom, screaming. No time to keep going. He reached beneath, long arms groping, knife blade glinting, then backed out. I slammed the door, now two stalls away from the gun.

My future as a rape victim, if I had a future, crazed me with fear and revulsion. K. C. Riley, McDonald, Harry reminding that he had warned me. People at the paper.

I stared in horror at the top of the stall, expecting him to clamber over at any moment. Instead, he came sliding underneath on his back like a mechanic sliding under a car. His grin was terrible, lips curled, exposing what looked like an arrow tattooed inside his lower lip. I kicked viciously but he grabbed my right ankle in a cruel grip, mouthing obscenities. I flailed about in panic for something, anything, to use as a weapon.

Twisting, I wrenched the heavy porcelain cover off the toilet tank, raised it over my head, and brought it crashing down on his face. He reacted in time to deflect it slightly with one hand, never releasing his hold on my ankle. Blood spurted, spattering the tile and the interior walls of the stall. The porcelain split in two. Still kicking and grunting, I snatched up the larger piece and smashed it down again. It caught him just above the hairline, then shattered on the floor as he slid back out of the stall, shouting a string of imprecations and curses in Spanish.

If he found the gun now, I was dead.

All was silent for a moment. I saw his bare feet. A drop of blood splashed to the tile floor. Then a loud rapping. Rattling, a pause, then a key turning in the door. I screamed for all I was worth. If it was Wyatt's secretary or a cleaning crew, they would surely call the police.

Quick movements outside the stall. Panting, I inched back, feet up as I sat on the toilet seat, heart pounding, waiting.

The lights went out. He had hit the switch. Total darkness. My skin crawled, fear rose in my throat. I heard the door open, a sharp exclamation, then a shout and somebody running.

Was he gone? If so, we had to stop him! I did not dare open the stall. Light flooded the room. I blinked, stepped up on the toilet seat, balanced myself, and peered over the door into the startled eyes of a short, gray-haired, dark-skinned woman wearing a blue cotton smock. Behind her stood a cart containing a mop, rags, cleaning materials, and a pail. I started to cry.

She looked annoyed. "What's going on in here?" She stared in open-mouthed indignation at the powder everywhere.

I jumped down to the floor and burst from the stall

screaming, "Stop him! Stop him! It's him, the Downtown Rapist!"

She turned, did a double take, eyes widening, then started to scream.

"Get him! Get him!"

Didn't take her long to catch on.

I did not know I was capable of producing such a high volume sound. It hurt my own ears, warbling as I pounded down the hall back to Wyatt's office. I burst through the door, into a room full of dental patients, shouting, "Dial Nine-one-one! Call the police! Call the police!"

Wyatt's receptionist, who had been expecting me to return the rest-room key, looked up, blinking. "What happened to you?"

"Call the police!" I screamed. "The Downtown Rapist! He's in the building!"

She dialed the three numbers and almost threw the phone at me.

The 911 operator's professionally serene voice infuriated me as I screamed at her to hurry. "He's still in the building! Send somebody, fast!" I cursed when she made me spell my name and hung up when she asked the rapist's name. But as I stepped back out into the corridor, now teeming with people rousted from their offices by the duet of shrieks from me and the cleaning woman, I heard the approaching static of a police radio above the din of voices and questions.

It was Harry, barking into his hand-held walkie-talkie, loping down the corridor, trailed by a panting building security guard.

"Oh, my God, Britt." He stared at the powder on my clothes and in my hair.

"It's him, Harry, the rapist. Catch him!"

He put a hand on my shoulder, and I resisted the

temptation to fall limply into his arms. "Did he rape you, Britt?" He looked embarrassed.

"I'm fine." There was no time for this. "It's him! It's him!"

"Don't go crazy on me now, Britt." Harry looked me straight in the eyes and raised one hand. "What was he wearing?" His tone was urgent. I jerked my head at the cleaning woman, who now stood down the hall talking to the security guard and a patrolman who had appeared out of nowhere.

"She saw him last, when he went out the door. I was locked in a stall." I was out of breath. My voice faltered and I choked back tears. "He's still got his bag, it's brown. He could be wearing a denim wrap-around skirt, a white long-sleeved blouse, and a black wig. He was dressed like a woman, Harry! That's why nobody ever saw him. No one ever saw the rapist in downtown office buildings because he came and went as a woman!"

Harry looked like he wanted to slap his palm to his forehead, my exact reaction when I had realized the rapist's secret. He began issuing instructions and descriptions into his radio, coordinating the manhunt. I recognized in his face the same flush of excitement, the throbbing intensity of somebody hot on the trail of the big one.

It had never occurred to me that we share the same addictive exhilaration.

I watched him stride down the hall, quickly confer with the woman, who gestured animatedly, then brief more cops as they arrived. I knew he never felt more alive than at that moment.

I joined them. "He almost got me, Harry." My knees were trembling. "He must still be here somewhere!"

"I know," he said. "We've got the lobby covered, and we're gonna do a floor-by-floor. I don't think he had time to get out. But they're setting up a perimeter and we're cordoning off the block."

"How'd you get here so fast?"

"I was already here," he said, shamefaced, lowering his voice. "We had a tail on you, in case you drew him out."

"You've been following me?" I croaked indignantly, my throat raw from all that screaming.

"Yeah, ever since he left that little present in your car, we figured the best place to look for him was wherever you were."

"Where the hell were you when I was locked in the bathroom with him?"

"I wasn't sure which office you went to. Jesus, Britt, you know you're a real pain in the ass to follow. You never even stop for lunch. I did a walk-through, went back to the lobby, and called somebody to sit on your car in case you'd slipped by me. Then security started getting calls about screams on this floor, and as we were coming up, dispatch broadcast the info from your call. I think we've got him boxed in."

"You were *following* me?" I thought of where I'd been recently, happily on a trail, unaware I *was* a trail.

The cops had used me as a decoy without my knowledge. My editors would not approve. Ethically I had the right to go out and gather the news without being trailed by police, a perfect right to be raped and murdered on my own, without being subjected to police scrutiny. But it worked, I thought. That's what counts. If they get him, it's worth it.

The rapist must have been stalking me, I realized. He'd probably seen me making bathroom pit stops virtually everywhere I went. I had surprised him still in his woman's attire. The big bag was where he carried his clothes and wig—and the knife.

As the building was evacuated with each employee or visitor showing ID as they left, it began to fill with cops, police dogs, and the SWAT team. They found his bag in a stairwell between the fifth and sixth floors. Ninety minutes later they pulled him feet first out of an air-conditioning duct on the fourth floor.

The press was kept at a distance but I was on the inside, regarded not as a reporter but a victim witness who could identify the perpetrator.

Both the cleaning woman and I did exactly that. It was not difficult, since his nose was broken and bloodied and the top of his head cut by the toilet tank lid I had tried to bounce off his face. I wanted to shout insults at the man but merely trembled and said nothing. Blood-smeared, bare-chested, in his beads and skirt, he wept like a baby. His only remorse, if any, was over being caught, the weeping a result of the tear gas the cops used to force him out of the vent.

Harry wanted me to go to the rape center, despite my assurances that the only damage was the bruises the man's fingers had left on my ankle. Police photographed my injuries, and Harry continued to insist that I might want to talk to a counselor. When I said I was fine, they wanted to whisk me off to headquarters for a statement. We struck a deal: they would take the cleaning woman's statement first, and I'd be there in an hour for mine. They weren't crazy about it, but grudgingly agreed when I insisted I had to check in with my bosses. I wanted to get back to the paper and write a quick version of the story for the next edition.

I arrived at the *News* with only forty minutes left of

my hour and went right into Fred's office with several editors to tell them what had happened.

"Are you all right, Britt?" he asked. His ashen expression made me aware that despite my efforts to brush it away, powder was still visible in my hair and clinging to my clothes.

"I'm fine. But I don't have much time," I said. "I have to write for the state edition, then go make a statement to the police."

Fred rubbed the back of his neck as though it pained him, exchanging glances with Mark Seybold, the paper's lawyer, who had joined the meeting. "What about the problem of identifying you as the victim of a sex crime?"

"No problem," I said, my hand touching the red and white beads at my throat. "His intent may have been rape, but he got no farther than simple battery." The room was quiet. "He grabbed my wrist and my ankles." I realized my voice was shaking, as were my knees under the table. Hoping they would not notice, I stopped for a moment and swallowed. "The cops may charge him with attempted rape, but technically I'm not really a sex crime victim."

Their eyes made me uneasy, a feeling that these men were seeing me as a woman somebody just tried to rape rather than as a professional, a reporter.

"Britt," Fred said, "I don't know how to tell you this, but we're going to have Janowitz write the story. You're part of it now, too involved to report it."

He paused, steeled for a proprietary, outraged outburst. They know I'm possessive about my beat and my stories. But truthfully, the news was almost a relief. I had a more important story to pursue.

The rapist coverage would consume days. First the arrest, then the arraignment. Then the story about who the man was and interviews with those who knew him. Interviews with psychologists about how he got that way. Perhaps an interview with him in his cell. Janowitz was welcome to it all.

"Okay," I said. Rapists come and go, I thought. Nailing Fielding is the story I want.

Fred Douglas looked relieved at my easy acquiescence. "Why don't you fill in Janowitz and then take a couple of days off," he said kindly.

His attitude irritated me. "I've got a couple of things I'm working on." My voice was sharp. "Why should I take time off?"

I was aware of their stares.

"Whatever you like, Britt," Fred looked unsure of himself.

All I want is to be treated like a professional, I thought, like everybody else.

Being interviewed by Janowitz, who kept interrupting each time I tried to answer a question, was grim. For the first time I fully understood how victims felt when I questioned them.

Of course Eduardo and Ryan wanted me to divulge to them every last nasty detail. I suggested they read about it in the morning.

When I arrived at headquarters the cops were finding it a problem to arrange a lineup with the rapist, whose name turned out to be Hector Ugalde. It wasn't easy finding other people with broken noses to stand next to him.

I wondered if I would be accused of brutality.

Giving the statement was not unpleasant. A court reporter took down every syllable, while Harry and another detective listened and asked questions. Hell, the guys now hanging on my every word were the same people who sometimes refused to talk to me.

At the moment I was on their good side. How long it lasted would depend on my next story. McDonald was nowhere in sight, but even Lieutenant Riley dropped by. "Nice job, Britt," she said, patting my shoulder, as though I had actually done something other than save my own skin.

"Sure," I said bitterly, realizing she must have authorized the surveillance on me. "Maybe I'll make officer of the month."

When we finished, I felt oddly reluctant to leave the brightly lit office teeming with people in various stages of jubilation. The night now held one less threat, yet the darkness made me jittery and, if anything, even more cautious. Without thinking I drove toward the office, then remembered I wasn't needed there. Perhaps, I thought, I should go in anyway to assist Janowitz, but I hated being scrutinized by all the prying newsroom eyes.

Feeling more alone than I ever have in my life, I drove home like a zombie, on automatic pilot.

17

I stopped by to tell the Goldsteins that the rapist was in custody. "What is that all over you?" she worried, urging me to sit down for some of her excellent chicken soup with light fluffy matzoh balls. I wasn't hungry, but she insisted I take it with me.

Bitsy flew into my arms, then shook her head, backed off, and sneezed. I locked myself in, pulled down the shades, and fed the animals.

Dan, Curt Norske, and McDonald had left messages on my machine. McDonald. Did he expect me to ask him to come hold my hand? Or did he merely want to say "I told you so"?

I considered calling Curt, but everything was too complicated, I was too tired, and my throat hurt.

I dialed Dan's number.

"Are you all right? Why the hell didn't you call me?" he demanded. "I heard it on the news. I left half a dozen messages at your office."

"I assumed you heard my screams," I said, trying to sound breezy. It was good to hear his voice. "They were loud enough. I'm fine. I had to go to headquarters to make a statement."

"That piece of scum didn't lay a hand on you, did he?" His voice was apprehensive.

"He tried. I'm so lucky, Dan. I've got bruises,

fingermarks on my ankle, and a sore throat from screaming. That's all."

"Son of a bitch!" There was a slamming sound, as though he had kicked or pounded the wall.

"Dan? What was that?"

"I just want five minutes alone with him. You had your gun, right? Why the hell didn't you blow away that bastard's ass?"

"Dan." I worked at keeping my voice calm, but it quavered. "I tried to follow your advice. But he took me totally by surprise. Carrying a gun around in a big purse just doesn't work. In a real emergency you have to get to the bag and dig it out. We were struggling. It got locked in the stall when he dragged me out from underneath."

"Christ! That son of a bitch!"

"I was so scared he was gonna find it." The words caught in my throat. "The only way a gun is any good," I rasped, "is if you can wear it in a holster around your waist and strapped to your leg, like a Wild West gunfighter. They wouldn't have survived twenty minutes in Dodge City if they had to fumble in a purse."

Unaware I'd been under surveillance, he heartily cussed out Harry for not being there when I needed him. "How the hell could he lose you? That guy couldn't track an elephant through four feet of snow on his best day!"

"Well," I croaked, "don't be too hard on him, Dan. He couldn't exactly stand sentry outside the ladies' room. I would have spotted him right away if he'd started stepping on my heels."

"What the hell were you doing over there anyway?"

"Dr. Wyatt. I went to see him. He's gonna look at the pictures of the bite mark on Mary Beth Rafferty. There's a possibility he can make a match."

"After all this time?" Dan sounded doubtful. "I asked somebody about it years ago and it was a negative."

"The technology has advanced." I sat down and eased my shoes off. "They can use computer enhancement on the photos."

"Worth a try," he said. "You sound terrible, kid. Sure you're okay? Need anything?"

"Thanks, Danny, you're a real friend. I'm fine. Talk to you tomorrow."

I put the phone down and ran my fingers wearily through my hair. They came out with powder on them. I shuddered and suddenly felt so dirty I wanted to strip my clothes off and burn them.

I switched off the telephone so the machine would record messages without me hearing it ring, unpinned the *resguardo* from my underwear, placed it on the bathroom sink where I could see it, and locked the door. Wearing my beads into the shower, I let hot water stream over me. When it didn't seem hot enough, I kept twisting the faucet until the room filled with steam and my skin was lobster pink. As I scrubbed myself with a stiff bath brush, I saw the imprint of the man's fingers on my right ankle and cried out. Whimpering and cursing, I tried in vain to scrub them away until my ankle was raw. For the first time I realized I *wasn't* fine. Dizzy and weak from the steam, I slipped into a sitting position, drew my knees up to my chest, and wept.

Eventually the hot water ran out. The shower cooled, then turned to cold. I could not stop crying. My teeth began to chatter as I hugged my knees, and then I heard it. Pounding. Somebody trying to break in my front door. Fearfully, gasping for breath, I struggled unsteadily to my feet, turned off the water, and listened. The pounding was louder and the doorbell, which I couldn't hear in the shower, was ringing. The gun! It was still in my purse, returned by the cops, but I couldn't remember where I left it when I came in.

Too weary and frightened to search for a robe, I wrapped a bath towel around me and, still crying, walked barefoot across the floor streaming water.

"For God's sake, Britt, open the door!"

McDonald. Without thinking, I unlatched the safety chain, released the deadbolt, turned the knob, and was in his arms.

"Why the hell didn't you open the door?" he murmured into my ear. "I was so worried." He stroked my hair. "You're all wet and cold." He picked me up and carried me to my favorite armchair, next to the telephone.

"I went crazy when you didn't answer your phone." His voice was gentle. I was still crying.

He left the room for a moment, then returned with my terry-cloth robe, awkwardly placing it around me.

"What are you doing here?" I said, sniffling and struggling to insert my arms into the sleeves.

He crowded into the overstuffed chair next to me and put his arms around me. He was so warm and I felt so cold. "I was off the air, in Broward at a tricounty conference, and didn't hear until I got back. I needed to know you were safe. I wanted to be with you."

"I thought you and K.C.—"

"Don't talk, try to relax." He went into the bedroom I had once thought of as ours and came back with the flowered comforter from my bed. As he tucked it around me, I closed my eyes like a wounded animal home safe at last. I heard him puttering around in the kitchen.

He returned with some of Mrs. Goldstein's soup, steaming in a giant mug, and I sipped it slowly. It felt good on my scratchy throat.

He pulled up another chair, lifted my feet up onto his knees, and watched me with those metallic blue-gray eyes. "Want to talk about it?"

"I was so scared, McDonald. I thought he was gonna rape me. He had a knife—" I shook my head. "I don't know what's wrong with me. I was fine. Then I just fell apart. I guess I'd been operating on an adrenaline high for hours, and when it faded so did I."

"It's a delayed reaction. You've been through a bad experience. You're entitled. What you need now is some sleep." He helped me to my feet. I leaned on him, almost too tired to stand up and go to bed.

He tucked me in. "Want to take these off?" he said, touching my beads.

"No," I said, my hand flying to my throat. I took a deep, drowsy breath and mumbled, "Don't forget to lock the door when you go."

"I'm not going anywhere," he said. He removed his jacket, unsnapped his shoulder holster, and placed it on my dresser as he had done so many times in the past. "I'll be right here. I won't leave you."

He lay down beside me, on top of the comforter. Under it, I trembled uncontrollably. He stroked my hair. "I'm right here. Close your eyes. Think about the beach and the warm sun," he whispered. "Go to sleep."

Secure and drowsy, I closed my eyes only for a moment. . . .

* * *

When I awoke, dawn was spilling around the edges of the drawn shade in my room and McDonald was dozing in the chair beside my bed. For some reason I felt no surprise at finding him there. It seemed natural. When I stirred, he opened his eyes, yawned, then climbed again onto the bed next to me. We held each other and dozed some more.

Next time I woke up, the shade was open and I could see sky and the mango tree outside and smell coffee in the kitchen.

He scrambled eggs and made toast. We ate and drank orange juice, saying little.

He brought in the newspaper and we sat in my kitchen reading like half a million other subscribers about Hector Ugalde, the Downtown Rapist. I felt removed, as though it all had happened to a stranger. There was information new to both of us. When caught, Hector was wearing his last victim's panties under his denim skirt, also a souvenir from a prior victim. Evidently, if he liked some item of apparel and it fit him, he took it. Maybe he was superstitious and thought it brought him luck, or perhaps he simply enjoyed the irony or felt uncomfortable shopping for women's attire for himself.

The charges against him included multiple counts of rape—the law calls it "involuntary sexual battery"—armed robbery, aggravated assault, stalking, lewd and lascivious behavior, battery, attempted rape, and impersonating the opposite sex. He was a Marielito, married, with an estranged wife who had once worked in a downtown office building where two of the rapes took place.

He lived in a dilapidated apartment house behind a boatyard along the Miami River, where he occasionally worked as a hand aboard a tug. His most recent regular job was selling flowers on street corners to passing motorists during rush hour.

Police said he was a Santería worshiper, adding that he appeared to be stunned and enraged at his Santero, to whom he had paid good money for rituals to protect him from arrest. Apparently he was furious at not getting what he paid for. The arrow tattoos were also designed to keep police away. I fingered the white and blood-red beads at my throat. Aunt Odalys's magic was stronger. . . .

I must be losing it, I thought, and laughed.

"You're looking better this morning," McDonald said.

He didn't. He needed a shave. But he looked wonderful in my apartment.

"Thanks. Talk to Dan lately?"

He shook his head. "Not for weeks. The man worries me, Britt, never talks about the future, or the present. He's living in the past. It's all he seems to care about."

"Maybe he feels that's all he's got left. He can be a little morose. He has to get out more among friends and good people."

"That can be arranged," he said, smiling. "If I can ever catch up with him and twist his arm."

I sipped my coffee. "You know, you might have told me I was being followed."

"It wasn't my place," he said uncomfortably. "It wasn't—"

"I know, I know," I interrupted. "It wasn't your case."

"You should have listened to Harry. This was a close one, Britt. Way too close." His eyes were serious.

"Harry said he warned you not to write any more stories about the guy until he was caught. You shouldn't
always be so stubborn. Besides, if you had known
about the tail, it probably wouldn't have worked. You
would have acted self-conscious and that would have
tipped the guy."

"You and Harry have fun discussing how stubborn
I am?" The unpleasant edge to my voice reminded me
suddenly of Marianne Rhodes.

He paused, staring at his coffee cup, and when he
spoke again his voice was softer, despairing. "Britt,
why do we always get into it this way?"

"I don't know, McDonald. I don't know," I whispered.

He reached out for my hand.

"So how is it, being a lieutenant?" I asked, squeezing his fingers.

"Good," he said vigorously. "Things are working
out. I may get to go to SPI in the spring."

"I'm impressed." I smiled, my heart sinking. Only
cops being groomed for promotion are sent to the
Southern Police Institute in Kentucky. "Every chief
we've ever had has been a graduate."

"Right." His eyes glittered. "It could be a real
break."

"What about you and K. C. Riley?"

"That has nothing to do with us, Britt."

"Oh?"

"I care about you, Britt. You will always be important to me. I'll always care, and I'll always be here for
you." He paused. "You know, I was jealous at first
when I saw you with that guy in the ice-cream suit."
His expression said he imagined I would find that hard
to believe. "But then I felt glad for you, Britt. You
deserve to be happy."

I knew what he was saying. There were so many things I wanted to tell him, so many things I wanted him to explain. But, again, our professions stood between us.

He kissed me goodbye at the door, and my apartment suddenly seemed empty.

I poured myself more coffee and reread the story about the rapist. A bond hearing was scheduled for today.

Janowitz had done a thorough job, but I would have written it differently. I noted with irritation that I was misquoted at least once. "Scared the heck out of me" sounded stupid and just wasn't something I would ever say.

The phone rang. Mrs. Goldstein had just read the story. "What a relief he's in jail," she said. "This whole thing must have been terrifying, Britt."

I scrunched down in my favorite chair, knees under my chin, the phone to my ear.

"I'm glad it's over too," I said. "That guy scared the heck out of me—"

When I heard what I said, I pressed my forehead to my knees and closed my eyes. Spend your life reporting the words of other people, and it is still a revelation when someone accurately reports yours.

"I saw your lieutenant," my landlady said slyly. "I'm glad he's back."

"He just came by to make sure I was all right," I whispered, my throat tight. "That's all."

18

I took Fred Douglas up on his offer of a day off and curled up with Bitsy and Billy Boots for another nap. I awoke again at midmorning, refreshed and glad to be alive. I returned calls from Lottie, Onnie, my mother, Aunt Odalys, and several other friends, assured them I was fine, and resisted offers of company. I just wanted to be alone today. I put the leash on Bitsy and took her out.

"You nearly had to find another owner," I told her, scooping her up and hugging her as we ended our walk.

I mourned Francie, and my heart went out to Dan. The day was so beautiful, the sky so blue. I saw it all with renewed appreciation. How can anyone bear to leave this life? I thought. It touched me that Dan, with all that he faced, had worried about me. I vowed to be a better and more caring friend.

By the time I arrived at the office the next morning I felt almost as good as new. An arrangement of snapdragons and birds of paradise adorned my desk. They were not from McDonald. *Hope you're okay*, the note said. *Don't forget the full moon. Curt.*

Janowitz was still gathering information about Hector Ugalde, who had been denied bond. The man had prior arrests on attempted rape charges in Union City,

New Jersey, where he had lived for a time. In fact, he was still wanted there for jumping bond.

His court-ordered psychiatric evaluation by a New Jersey shrink had disclosed that when Ugalde was a toddler, back in Havana, his mother, who made a living before the revolution performing in live sex shows, refused to cut his hair and often dressed him in little girl's clothes as punishment. The mother was promiscuous, the doctor had written in his report, and behaved in a seductive fashion toward her son, whose job as a small boy was to powder her naked body after she had bathed.

I am naturally dubious about psychiatrists. The doctor had to have received all that information from Ugalde himself and had no way of checking it out. But it all made sense in a sick sort of way.

That afternoon I dialed Fielding's Miami law office, asked to speak to his secretary, and lied through my teeth.

"I'm calling about Mr. Fielding's dental appointment."

"Dental appointment?" he said.

"Yes, the usual routine cleaning and checkup."

"But he just saw Dr. Wiseman ten days ago, last time he was in Miami. I don't understand. He's campaigning throughout the state, you know."

"Hummm," I said. "There must be some mistake in our records."

There was only one Dr. Wiseman in the book.

"So you're the one responsible for the candidate's beautiful smile," I gushed, after announcing that I was researching a story on Fielding, which was true. "Or did he inherit it?"

"Let's say his dentist gave him a little help in that department," Dr. Wiseman said.

Two years ago, he told me, the candidate had had his teeth capped.

Back to square one, back out on the beat, haunted by something not yet over.

I stashed the Mary Beth Rafferty clips in my desk instead of returning them to the library, intending to pore over them one more time, line by line. But Miami and my beat were hectic. Stories were becoming stranger, as they always do in our sizzling summer, the meanest of seasons.

Walking catfish were migrating across suburban roads near the water. Jellyfish that ordinarily invade South Florida in late winter were showing up by the hundred, schools of shimmery blue bubbles riding the surf. Something indefinable and troubling was in the air, as though all was not right with Mother Nature.

A hard-rock radio station promoted a treasure hunt, hiding a thousand-dollar cash jackpot in a telephone booth and tantalizing listeners with clues. The mass hunt reached its height when motorists careened into a three-car pileup near the wrong booth. A mini-riot followed a traffic jam at the right one as fistfights broke out. The most seriously injured was an innocent bystander who merely wanted to use the telephone.

The Rio Theater, a downtown movie house catering to economically deprived teenagers, made news because of its rats. Unfortunately they surfaced during a horror film. Suspense mounted as the movie unfolded. As the audience held its breath, a teenage girl relaxed her grip on her half-eaten sausage hero. As tension heightened to a horrifying climax on the big screen, a huge rat boldly grabbed the sandwich. She hung on, screeching, "It's got me! It's got me!" They engaged in a tug-of-war as five hundred screaming kids stampeded out of the dark theater into the light.

Most of the injuries were minor, but there were many.

Next morning I picked up a couple of salt bagels loaded with cream cheese, went to the office, and took them back to photo, where Lottie plugged in the kettle.

"You are a bad influence on me, Britt," she complained, biting into her bagel, then sighing in contentment. "Umm," she said. "You remembered to get the cream cheese with chives."

Since Hector Ugalde had dominated our conversation lately, I had never really filled her in on my cruise with Curt Norske. I shared with her his fanciful version of Miami history and his invitation to a moonlight cruise.

"You're gonna go, right?"

"I don't know," I said doubtfully, spooning instant coffee into a mug, then filling it with steamy water.

She rolled her eyes. "That's one I wouldn't miss. A cruise to nowhere with Captain Curt?"

I shrugged. "McDonald says he looks like an ice-cream salesman."

"What would you expect him to say? He done you dirt, he's playing kissy face with another cop, but it still spoils his day to see you happy with anybody else. Imagine, cruising the bay alone, under a full moon."

"I don't know," I said dispiritedly. "McDonald was super, just wonderful, there when I needed him. And the full moon, that's when my beat is usually the busiest."

"Britt"—she squinted into my eyes with a searching look—"are you crazy? What good is a man who only shows up when you're more dead than alive? We need to get you a blood test and see if any is getting to your brain."

A bleating sound came over the intercom from the city desk: Gretchen's voice. She was attempting to transmit a photo to the Broward bureau and needed help. Lottie sighed and stood up. "I swear that woman wouldn't know enough to pour piss out of a boot with a hole in the toe and directions on the heel! Be back in a minute." She picked up what was left of her bagel and stalked off.

I sat eating and sipping coffee, then casually reached over and pulled two catalogs from a pocket of the outsize camera bag Lottie carries instead of a purse. *Victoria's Secret of London*. I idly thumbed through the slick colorful pages of lacy lingerie and slinky fashions modeled by beautiful long-legged women.

One posed provocatively, lips apart, one hand languidly pushing back her lush mane of sun-streaked hair, the other resting on her hip. The red stretch-lace teddy she wore was whispery soft, with ribbon and faux pearl trim, according to the copy.

I stared at it for a long moment and knew what was wrong, what I'd been denying, even in my dreams. Queasy, I wiped the cream cheese with chives from my mouth and stood up.

Lottie reappeared. "I feel fat enough to kill," she gloated. "But that was s-o-o-o good." She saw my face. "What's the matter, Britt? You sick?"

"I'll be back later," I whispered, and fled to my desk. I dug through the notes and printouts in the bottom drawer of my desk until I found them: Steiner, Creech, Farrington. I read them all, a hollow place in my heart, then dug through other stories, wondering. Could it be?

What had Detective Diaz said? "There are no coincidences in homicide cases."

Half-formed fears took shape in my mind as I hurried back to Lottie. She was in the darkroom. I stepped into the circular door, grasped the side grips, and revolved onto the dark side.

Working at the far end of a row of enlargers, she was illuminated by the eerie orange glow of the safelight. Music came from her tape player, plugged in in a corner: "Mean Mistreatin' Momma," sung by funky blues guitarist Elmore James.

"Lottie, I think something terrible has happened."

"I know, I know." She turned to the bank of sinks across the center of the room. "I ate the rest of your bagel. Didn't know when you were coming back and didn't want it to go to waste."

"I'm serious." The pungent acid smell of the fixer in one of the three big trays over the sinks churned my stomach. Water ran constantly in the darkroom and the dryer was humming. I stepped closer to where she was working.

"You thinking about Ugalde? He spooking you?"

"Worse," I said. The Downtown Rapist was scary, but he was a stranger, not someone I knew and trusted. "Do you think it's possible for someone who spent a lifetime on the right side of the law to suddenly become a killer?"

"You talking about Gretchen?"

"Lottie, I'm serious!"

"I am too!" She stamped her foot for emphasis. I moved closer as images emerged on the rosin-coated papers in the tray, slices of Miami rising magically through the developer. Old men playing dominoes in the park, young Cubans at an Alfa 66 training camp in the Everglades, squatters camping in Bayfront Park.

She used tongs to transfer prints from the developer to the fixer. "Shit," she cried, stepping back and examining her turned-up shirt sleeve. "I splashed developer on my good shirt; that Dektol'll never come out."

"It's Dan," I said. "A crazy coincidence."

She turned toward me in the semidarkness.

"You know how he eats, drinks, and sleeps old cases?"

"Like an old pit bull, never turns 'em loose." She nodded, returning her attention to the prints in the tray.

"Remember Farrington, the old homicide suspect who poured concrete over his wife years ago and now somebody has poured concrete over him?"

"Right, a genuine example of poetic justice." She slid a print from the fixer into the wash.

"Exactly. Looking through your *Victoria's Secret* catalog reminded me of Creech, the guy in that sexual asphyxia death. His death was supposedly accidental. Sex-related. He was another old suspect—in the murder of his teenage niece. Sex-related.

"Dieter Steiner, Dan's old homicide suspect. Should have been electrocuted but beat it on a technicality and went home—and got electrocuted. Accidentally."

Lottie stopped what she was doing. "Hell-all-Friday," she murmured. "Lotta poetic justice going around. Any others?"

"I don't know."

"You think somebody's offing bad guys like an avenging angel?" Her voice dropped. "Dan?"

"The man's a teddy bear," I said. "I introduced him to my mom. He's kind to kids and old ladies." The room seemed cold and dank and I shivered, wishing I had a sweater. "I saw him pull over once on the expressway while he was working, to rescue a box turtle that was crossing in traffic."

"These people dying ain't innocent kids or helpless animals or old ladies, Britt. He knows they're cold-blooded killers."

"He's spent a lifetime upholding the law," I whispered.

"Look what it got him." She wiped her hands on her apron. "We know about the thin line that separates good guys from bad. Maybe he's crossed." Her face glowed in the orange light.

"Dan would never . . . though he *has* changed since he left the department." I was thinking aloud. "His health is failing, his family gone, yet recently he sounds intense, like somebody with a purpose."

"He's dying, nothing left to live for except justice, which has failed him. Maybe he's a man on a mission."

We listened to water run and the dryer hum for a few moments. Elmore James began to sing "I Got a Right to Love My Baby."

"Who better to make a murder look accidental than somebody who has investigated them for thirty years?" she said.

"It's so crazy." I fought guilt pangs brought on by my own disloyal thoughts.

"Think anybody else is on to him?"

"I doubt it. We don't even know it's true. It can't be. What the hell should I do?"

"Same thing you always do when you have a hunch or a suspicion. Investigate. Why don't you ask him? You always said he never lied to you."

"Sure." I ran my fingers through my hair. "But I never asked if he'd committed a crime. The man's heart has attacked him and he's been through hell.

He trusts me. What do I do if he tells me things I don't want to hear?"

Lottie shook her head, as though surprised by the question. "What you always do, Britt. You write the story."

"Write about Dan?"

"If it's true, somebody will. Better you than some stranger who doesn't know him. At least you care."

"We're probably wrong, you know."

"If we are, you'll find out. I've always thought your hunches were pretty good." She placed a wet print on the dryer belt. Rollers carried it slowly into the heating element and hot air was forced over it. The finished print emerged on the other side seconds later, clean and dry.

Lottie and I often debate who has the more difficult job. Now I know, I thought as I left. Photography is simpler. There are no questions. Pictures don't lie.

19

I walked out of the newsroom without saying where I was going. I wasn't sure myself. What I wanted to do was simply aim the T-Bird west, straight across the Everglades, to the Gulf of Mexico. Why did Florida's gentler coast suddenly beckon? My last trip there was with Kendall McDonald, when we escaped the escalating tensions of our jobs to flee west together for an idyllic week of white sand beaches and warm waters. That was before our relationship and the city had exploded.

I parked at a secret place where I often go to think or recharge my batteries when truth, crime, and the city overwhelm. Mine was the only car parked at this small Beach playground facing the bay and a western vista of silver water, shimmering skyline, and endless cobalt sky.

I gathered my thoughts. This would be the first time I undertook an investigative piece hoping to be wrong, hoping there was no story.

That would be best. Then Dan would never suspect the friend he trusted was investigating him like he was some money-laundering banker, corrupt public official—or cop gone bad.

I would approach Dan last. Never tip the target until all your ducks are in a row. Build your case, then confront the subject to ask for his side. Journalism 101.

With any luck, I would find nothing and it wouldn't go that far.

A battered green Buick pulled up and parked nearby. The driver was alone and glanced in my direction. He nodded. My Aunt Odalys's "spirits" had warned that I was too trusting. What a laugh, I thought. My response to the stranger was make sure my doors were locked and then turn the key in the ignition.

The truth is that I am too suspicious, excellent for a reporter, a lousy quality in a friend. Oddly, though the danger was past, I was still wearing my beads and the *resguardo*. Habit or security blanket? I wondered.

I drove back to the paper and began building a file. Luckily Tubbs was in the slot and too busy to demand a full explanation when I murmured in passing that I had a lead on something I wanted to dig into.

My first stop was the medical examiner's office. The chief was out but Dr. Duffy was in.

I sat in front of his cluttered desk. "I'm curious about the Farrington case," I told him.

He shook his head, removed his glasses, and polished the lenses, his expression expectant though slightly wary.

"So is everybody else," he said, indicating the messages stacked on his desk. "It's captured a lot of attention. But you know, Britt, I must refer you to the homicide detective in any open case."

"I've already talked to Diaz about the investigation," I said casually. "What people want to know is how the heck you freed that body. Had to be a huge job."

"True," he said. "Murder seems to run in cycles. Ever notice how sometimes we keep finding them in shallow graves? Another time it may be car trunks, or the Bay, or dumped out in the 'Glades. Hope this one doesn't start a trend."

"I guess it was impossible to find anything in there. Too bad. What if it really was a suicide and the man had a gun and a suicide note? It'll never be found."

He stood up. "Let me show you something, Britt." I followed, and we walked down the hall to a locked room in the investigative section.

Duffy deactivated the security buzzer that signals when the door is opened, stepped inside, and removed a cardboard carton from a shelf. He carried it out and placed it on the shiny counter. It contained encrusted empty pop bottles; what looked like a half-eaten sandwich; a Coke can; cigarette, cookie, and chewing gum wrappers; two empty matchbooks; nails; a cigar butt; bits of wood; a broken hammer—all wearing remnants of concrete and mixed with little pieces of rock.

"What is this stuff?"

"Workers at building sites dispose of trash by tossing it into the forms before a pour." He shrugged. "None of it will ever be seen again. At least not in most cases." He sighed. "I ruined a perfectly good bone chisel. We had to drill holes to weaken the concrete so it would break away gently when tapped with the little stainless steel hammers used in surgery."

I studied the junk in the carton. "Think any of it might belong to the killer?"

"Doubtful, but Diaz plans to take it out to the site and see how much of this stuff the crew can account for."

With the box was a clear self-locking plastic bag sealed with red evidence tape: Farrington's personal effects. "Were the contents of his pockets intact?"

"Mostly. His legs were slightly bent, so his pockets

opened a bit at the top. There was some cement, but it was mostly just wet."

"Wet?"

"The water in the concrete is what makes it flow. We have the pieces that were surrounding his head," Duffy commented. "In fact I'll be using them in a presentation at the American Academy of Forensic Sciences meeting, in Chicago next spring. It's an excellent teaching case," he said. "The back is even discolored, blood from the bullet wound."

"Was it a thirty-two?" I guessed.

"No, a thirty-eight." He seemed a bit uneasy. "You'll clear everything you use with the homicide detective first?"

"Of course," I assured him. "Look what it did to his watch."

The gold Rolex still gleamed on the inside where it had been next to Farrington's skin. The outside was cement coated. "Is it still running?" I asked.

"Nope," he said.

It was hard to recognize some of the other items in the clear plastic bag. "That's his beeper," Duffy said. "Was still clipped to his belt, along with the key ring."

There was a cigarette lighter, a slim leather billfold, a money clip, folded cash still intact, and a pill bottle. "What medication was he on?"

"Tagamet," Duffy said. "For a stomach condition."

"Was he otherwise in good health?"

"Seemed to be excellent."

I still examined the contents, shifting the sealed bag. A crumpled handkerchief—and something that made my heart catch in a painful spasm. A tiny screwtop bottle cap from a bottle of nitro pills prescribed for a heart condition. No way for a cap to tell you what's in a bottle—unless it has a small strip of bright red tape across the top.

"Where's the bottle that goes with this cap?" I asked, more stricken than I had expected to be if this moment came.

I blinked, blinded for a moment, and turned away to conceal eyes that were suddenly watery. Dan lost a daughter. I lost my dad. Now we would lose each other and he would lose everything.

"Let's see here." Dr. Duffy hadn't noticed my reaction. He was scrutinizing the inventory sheet attached to the bag. "No matching bottle was found. That cap may belong in the box with the other debris from the site, but since it was on his person, we included it here. Apparently that cap was caught in the folds of his shirt, and when the weight of the concrete shifted the body it was trapped between his chin and his shirt."

"Ever see anybody mark a pill bottle like this?" I said, touching the cap through the plastic, remembering the moment I first saw it, or one like it.

"No," Duffy said, taking the bag from my hands. "But people do all sorts of things."

He moved the carton and the plastic bag back into the lockup and returned. My face must have given me away.

"Anything wrong, Britt?"

I looked at my watch. "I'm just running late and have to make another stop before I go back to the office."

I drove to my next destination like a maniac on a rampage. This was it; it was real, not my imagination. This was now a matter of life and death. I speeded onto the narrow street, wheeled into a space, brakes squealing. Why? I thought. How could he?

She was home as I had hoped, opening the door a crack.

"Hi," I said, my voice infused with a hearty, overly familiar ring. "Mrs. Creech. Ruby. You remember me, Britt Montero. I was here the day your husband passed away. I need to talk to you."

"I have a telephone," she said coldly.

"I just need a minute of your time. It's important to both of us."

My voice sounded taut as I tried to stay calm.

"What?"

"It's about your husband's death."

"I am not discussing that," she said, her tone even chillier.

"It's not what you think. Just one minute."

The door closed, the safety chain rattled, then it reopened. She stared at me, then stepped back. "I'm probably gonna regret this," she said.

"Thanks," I said. She wore dark slacks and a T-shirt, much like the first time I had met her, but she had added a few pounds and some bright lipstick. She had had her hair done and her roots touched up. "You look good," I said, trying to go slow. "How are you doing?"

There were several packed cartons and boxes on the floor.

"You moving?"

She nodded. "Wouldn't you?"

She planned to put the house on the market, she said, and spend some time with a sister in Sarasota. I told her I heard it was wonderful there, she'd enjoy it. Good place for a fresh start, I thought.

"Why'd you come?" she said.

I took a deep breath. "Remember the old murder investigation in the death of your niece?"

She nodded, staring solemnly at the floor as she sat down at the same kitchen table where we had first talked.

"I know you hate to see that come up again." I took the seat across from her.

"What do you mean, come up again?" she said bitterly, raising her eyes. "It never went *away*. It was with us every day."

"Do you remember the detective in the case, the man who suspected your husband?"

"Detective Flood was his name. Who could forget him? I was surprised he didn't show up here like the rest of 'em, to gloat, the day I found Emerson . . . the day you were here."

"He had retired by then."

"Since when?" she said disbelievingly.

"He retired last spring."

"Retired?" she said loudly. "Retired?" Her expression was incredulous. "That old son of a bitch! Then why in hell was he tormenting us by hanging around here if he wasn't even on the goddamned police force anymore? I never knew he retired."

"You mean you'd seen him lately?" I asked, a sense of dread growing in the pit of my stomach.

She stood up, bony fists clenched. "Used to be just once a year or so, sometimes on the anniversary of the case, sometimes on holidays, Christmas or Easter. Whenever he had nothing better to do, I guess. Emerson would refuse to talk to him and Flood would say he just wanted us to know he still had the case. He always left his card and said if either of us had anything to tell him, we should call. We'd always fight for weeks every time he'd been here."

"When was the last time he came?"

"It was two days before Emerson died." She paced

the small room, three steps from the stove to the sink, three steps back. "But now he was up to something new. I went out to catch a bus that morning, got on, and as I took a seat and it started to roll, I saw him halfway down the block, parked across the street facing this direction, watching the house.

"I thought he'd come by, but he didn't. I mentioned it to my husband, and we both saw him the next day. We just ignored him, like we didn't know he was out there. Figured he was trying something new, trying to gaslight us, some psychological shit to put pressure on."

"Was that the last time you saw him?"

"No, he was there the day it happened. I went out that morning and saw him again, slouched down in his car, a dark blue Buick Riviera parked across the street. He was gone when I got back. When I found my husband I thought it had worked. I thought he was finally pushed too far and had killed himself. That was before they explained all that sex stuff." She looked sheepish. "And you say the son of a bitch was retired and was doing this on his own time? He had no right. Why?" Her voice cooled, trailing off wearily as she sat down again at the table.

"I think I know. Another thing," I said. "That lacy red teddy. It *was* yours, wasn't it?"

She smiled sadly. "Yes. Don't know why I bought it. We'd been like strangers for so long after everything that happened. It just seemed, if we were going to live out our lives together, that maybe—"

I told her to watch the paper, that I would be writing a story about Dan Flood.

"Somebody should," she said. "The man is going too far."

"You have no idea," I said sadly.

At the door I turned.

"One more thing. Do you think your husband killed Darlene?"

The light faded from her eyes and her voice was flat. "No doubt about it."

It was time to fill in an editor.

I could go on investigating for weeks, trying to unearth more evidence, but there was no time—and that was a job for the cops anyway. My job was to do what I always do, write the story, like Lottie said. It had always seemed so simple before. An interview with Dan was inevitable now. Would he hate me? Doing nothing was out of the question. He had to be stopped. I had caught on; others would too. Homicide detectives are not stupid. But it had to be before anybody else, including Dan, was hurt.

But he is a sick man, I thought, who gave most of his life to the city. Now that life could end behind bars. He could die in jail.

I swallowed hard and walked into the newsroom. When Fred was free and off the telephone I stepped into his office. "I have reason to think," I said carefully, "that a dying detective, respected and retired from city homicide, has become a vigilante seeking street justice and has murdered at least three suspects that he believes beat the system."

Fred whistled and looked impressed. "Helluva story. Can you prove it?"

No turning back. "I'm still reporting, but I have enough to write and let readers draw their own conclusions."

At the news meeting later it was agreed that if I could produce it, the story would run Sunday—after Mark vetted it, of course.

"Think he'll admit to anything, Britt?" Fred asked doubtfully.

"Despite what's he done, he's an honest man who never lied to me. I think he feels justified. The worst he might do would be to lose his temper and refuse to talk to me at all."

"Even if he denies everything, which is likely, his involvement in all those cases makes a hell of a story." Fred nodded. "Think we can arrange a picture of that bottle cap? Think anybody else has seen how he marks them?"

"Probably everybody who knows him. I'll try to interview him in the morning."

I made my last two calls from home that night.

McDonald was working late, compiling statistics to use in the new budget proposal for homicide. The best cops are promoted and don't do police work anymore, I thought. He sounded businesslike, his professional mode. "I just have one question," I said.

"Sure, Britt."

"How did Dan react when you told him about Farrington?"

"What are you talking about?" He sounded genuinely bewildered.

"Farrington, the contractor who got cemented into a pillar out at the new shopping center."

"That wasn't our case. It's the county's."

"I know, I know," I said impatiently. "But you heard about it, knew he was the suspect in Dan Flood's old case, and called to tell him, right?"

"I still don't know what the hell you're talking about, Britt. I've been meaning to call Dan but, remember, I told you: I haven't spoken to the man in weeks and definitely not about some county case."

"Oh. Guess I was mistaken. Thanks, McDonald."

Dan answered on the first ring. He sounded glad to hear from me. "I need to see you."

"Any time, Britt. Lunch on your day off?"

"No, I'd like to make an appointment to interview you, tomorrow." Did my voice reveal the guilt I felt?

He paused. "Since when do you need an appointment to see me?"

"I wanted to make sure you were available."

"Like I said, any time. What kind of interview?"

"About your old cases. Can I come to your house? Ten o'clock?"

"Okay with me." He sounded puzzled, or was it cautious? "Hope you don't shock easy."

"Why would I be shocked?" My throat felt dry.

"My pad ain't exactly *House and Garden,* you know."

"Nothing should shock us anymore. Remember, you told me that once."

"Right."

I slept poorly, anticipating our meeting. Did Dan suspect? Was he able to rest? Was Hector Ugalde enjoying his nights in jail? Finally it had to be time to get up. Dragging myself into a sitting position, I stared in disbelief at my digital clock. Four A.M. Damn, I thought, rubbing my eyes, I got more rest when the rapist was still on the prowl.

20

I dressed carefully the next morning, as though for a date. It was a date of sorts; Dan was my old friend.

I wore my favorite blue blazer. I still wore my Aunt Odalys's beads and pinned the *resguardo* to my underwear. Maybe they had become a habit. Maybe I wanted my luck to last.

I left the gun behind.

In all the years I had known Dan, I had never visited him at home. I parked in front of the pretty little house precisely at ten. It was a bit neglected perhaps, but a happy family had obviously lived there and loved it. An overhang near the front door protected an area with metal tracks on the ground to accommodate bicycles. Summer heat had decimated once-well-kept flower beds. The hedges looked overgrown. A huge ficus was spreading its branches dangerously close to the roof, and an avocado tree needed pruning.

His car, the Buick, was in the drive.

I stared morosely at it for a moment, then rang the doorbell.

He opened the door, blinking in the sunlight. The belt of his sports slacks looked loose, and he wore house slippers. His eyes looked puffy, and when we hugged, his body felt frail and breakable in my arms, so different from the strapping bear of a man he had been.

"Knew you'd be right on time," he said, smiling broadly. "Reporters always show up on time, one of the things I learned from you."

He stepped back, hands on my shoulders, peering into my eyes, then touched his grizzled fist gently to my chin.

"You look okay, kid. You had me worried there, with that freak running around."

The living room was comfortable with natural-colored furniture, bookcases, and now-empty planters. An overflow of old newspapers rose from a chair, but otherwise everything looked neat.

"Take off your jacket and stay awhile. Can I get you anything?" He looked like the anxious host. "Coffee?"

"No, thanks, unless you're having some."

"Sure thing, we can sit here." He indicated the dining room table and slowly padded into the kitchen. He saw me notice his floppy slippers and looked embarrassed.

"My ankles and my feet were swollen this morning, can't even get my shoes on. How do ya like that? Must be my medication."

I nodded. "So how is retirement?"

He set a brimming mug in front of me and another in front of his chair. "I shoulda picked up some donuts or something."

"No, thanks, I had breakfast."

"So," he said. "Didn't know which cases you were interested in so I got out the old scrapbooks." Half a dozen were stacked on a footstool next to a chair. "The wife and daughter kept 'em," he said, looking sheepish. "Clipped out every newspaper story that mentioned my name and some that didn't. All the old cases. The last one's not quite up to date. My last year on the job." He sat down heavily and gazed fondly at me. I felt ashamed and devious. This was horrible, but I had to go through with it.

I placed my tiny tape recorder next to the sugar bowl and pressed the record button. "Do you mind?"

He shook his head, eyes searching mine. "Where were we?"

"Retirement," I said brightly, and sipped my coffee.

"Well," he said, without hesitation, "it's like cutting an umbilical cord. All of a sudden you're on your own, not a part of mother city anymore. Never occurred to me all those years, but it was a cozy feeling to be with the department, with insurance, retirement, everything taken care of for you. Like a spoiled kid who leaves home, you have to sink or swim on your own. You feel a little apprehensive about leaving the family that took care of you for thirty years." He grinned. "That's not for publication. I wouldn't admit that to anybody but you."

Reaching behind him for an ashtray, he took a pack of cigarettes from his pocket and shook one loose. "You mind?"

"Only on your account."

"Speaking of retirement: you know, Irene and me, we had it all planned out." He lit up, his hand shaky, and took the first puff, exhaling a thin stream of smoke through his nostrils. "We were thinking ahead. Bought a piece of property up in the mountains, in Carolina. Were gonna build the year before I retired. The plans are still around here someplace. It was gonna have a separate bedroom and bath for the kid when she came to visit." He sniffed and drank his coffee. "Things never turn out the way you plan."

"Seems that way," I said softly.

"Gotta tell ya, I miss the job. Catching bad guys, arresting people, catching couples making love at three A.M. in the woods, seeing all this flesh jumping around in a car in the dark."

He grinned wickedly.

"It was a good run. We closed a lotta good cases. Remember that Jane Doe that went unidentified for six months, we finally made her and nailed the boyfriend up in Georgia?"

"The one where you finally matched the dead woman's fingerprint to one on an employment application?"

"That's it!" His eyes lit up. "He'd told her family she'd met some guy and run off on him in Miami."

"Great case. He still in jail?"

"Should be. He got the twenty-five-year mandatory minimum. That one's in there with the others." He gestured toward the scrapbooks as memory kicked in. "You know, it always bugged me that we never solved the Susan Stratford case. That one happened around the same time."

"The one where the girl's car was abandoned in the shopping center parking lot and she was found miles away, stabbed to death in a woods?"

"Right. Had to be a chance encounter, somebody she ran into shopping that day. Remember, she bought a shirt for her dad?"

"His birthday."

"Your memory is as good as mine." He sighed regretfully and shook his head. "Always thought we could have solved that one. Had to be something we missed. It disturbed me a lot, Britt." He massaged the loose folds of skin on one side of his face with his fingers. "I often felt I let those victims down. I was supposed to do my thing. Maybe I should have done it better. I did what I could, but a lot of times the courts or the circumstances just weren't there." He looked wistful.

"You gave it your best shot. Nobody worked harder than you," I said. "You're not responsible for the system. It leaves a lot to be desired, but it's all we've got."

His eyes hinted at thoughts unspoken. "The more I look back on the injustice, the wounds and the scars, the more hung up I get about the system, the department, things left undone."

"Sometimes you just have to leave it to God."

He scoffed, his smile bitter. "I didn't vote for God. If that freaking Marielito or anybody else did something terrible to you or someone else I cared about now, I would want to kill him. I wouldn't want to see the victim run through that meat grinder they call the system. The fairest way is to kill him and spare the victim all that crap."

He watched, waiting, as I stirred my coffee.

"I never thought I'd hear you advocate street justice."

"Yeah, I've arrested people myself for taking the law into their own hands. I got personally caught up in cases when I carried a badge, but I never thought about killing the bad guys. Not once. Never even thought about it. But now, at this stage of life—"

He shrugged.

"What exactly are you working on, Britt?" He raised his coffee mug.

"A story about what you've been doing in retirement."

He put the cup down.

"You've been keeping busy." I stated it as a flat fact, not an accusation.

"Yeah." His eyes held mine without wavering.

"I talked to Ruby Creech last night."

Dan shifted his gaze to a point somewhere over my left shoulder, the muscles in his jaw working. "She covered up for that son of a bitch all those years," he said finally.

"She was surprised to hear you'd retired, seeing as how you'd been sitting on their place around the time he died."

His expression went from bitter to bleak.

"Farrington, who wasn't supposed to be found, was shot with a thirty-eight similar to a detective special. The person who did it dropped something at the scene. Amazing, how in all that cement they found it."

He took a deep breath.

"McDonald didn't tell you he was dead, though you knew all about it when I called."

Dan stood up abruptly, startling me. Without a word, he shambled into the kitchen. I heard the refrigerator door open and close. He came back carrying a can of Budweiser and sat down again.

"I'm the last one you're interviewing, right?" He popped open the beer.

I nodded, a lump in my throat.

"See," he said, staring at the label on the can. "I know how you operate. I've watched you long enough. I ever tell ya, I always thought you shoulda been a cop? Would have made a great partner."

"If you had spaced them out more, I might never have caught on," I said quietly.

"I would've, but I didn't have the luxury of time." He leaned forward as though it was important for me to believe him. "You know I always cared about the job—"

"About justice."

"But in the end I realized there is no justice in the system."

"But why? How could you?"

"How could I not?" His voice became intense. "There is only one type of permanent rehabilitation for creeps like them, and that's death." The little wheels turned in the tape recorder. He stared at them and repeated the thought as if to be sure the machine got it right. "Death is the only known sure rehabilitation. This was preventive: proactive police work instead of reactive."

"But why you?" I said, anguish in my voice.

"I have nothing to lose."

"What about your reputation, the commendations?"

"That's right, I did good. And this was the last good thing I could do in my career. I always tried to stay in touch with victims and their families, to let 'em know somebody still remembered. This was the last thing I could do for them."

He took a pull on his beer, then licked his pale lips. "Sometimes life boils down to law and order versus justice. And some of it was probably spite on my part."

"How so?"

"I'd see some son of a bitch who should be sitting on Death Row and think, 'No way is that bastard gonna outlive me.' I wanted to read their obituaries before they read mine, okay? The best revenge is outliving the scum."

Perspiring, he winced, right hand to his chest, as though in pain.

"Are you okay?"

"As okay as I'm ever gonna be." His voice was a gasp.

"Can I get you something?"

"A glass of water." Fumbling with the pills in his pocket, he withdrew a small brown bottle with the telltale lid.

I went into the kitchen, ran a cool glass of water, and brought it back. He put two tiny white pills under his tongue and closed his eyes.

I sat and waited while they dissolved, absorbing through the mucous membranes under his tongue. After several moments he opened his eyes, with a shaky sigh.

"Feel better?"

"In a minute. The nitro works pretty fast." His pale face slowly reddened to a flush.

"They're for chest pain," he explained. "I've got it all, nitro, digitalis, diltiazem, aspirin, digoxin, Lasix, Capoten, Maalox. I'm a walking, talking drugstore."

"Maybe your medication is what caused you to—"

His gaze was scornful. "You know how I hate that. People blaming what they did on broken homes, bad childhoods, booze, drugs. It's all bullshit. We do things because we want to. No excuses."

"But in your condition, how were you able to physically—"

"The gun. I was a cop, so they never really thought I'd do it. Thought I was hassling 'em.

"Creech was pissed as hell, but he finally agreed to put on his old lady's lingerie, at gunpoint. I'd seen two of those cases over the years, so it wasn't hard to set up. I'd seen her leave, I'd been surveilling them and knew their habits. Knew how much time I had."

I sat stunned, unable to speak.

"Same with Farrington. He climbed up on that catwalk, bitching and moaning, swearing to file a complaint with IA in the morning. Didn't compre why we were going up there. Made him jump and shot him as he fell.

"Had some chest pains, the angina. Had to take a couple of nitro pills. I got shaky and fumbled the bottle, lost the top. It rolled off and I didn't see where it went. They found it, huh?"

"Yeah."

"They know who it belongs to?"

"Not yet."

"You're probably the only person who woulda recognized it."

"What about Steiner? How'd you rig the wires?"

He did a double take, raising his eyebrows. "You think I did him?" His voice was full of wonder, his expression incredulous.

"You didn't?"

He shook his head, with a snort that came close to a laugh.

"You know I don't lie to you, Britt. Closest I ever came was to hint that Ken had tipped me about Farrington, but, if you remember, I didn't actually say it." He aimed his index finger at me like a gun. "I didn't do Steiner. The dumb son of a bitch did himself. It was so appropriate." He smiled like a church deacon, inspired by a sermon. "That's what gave me the idea. So you thought I did him!" He gloated. His expression said I wasn't so smart after all.

He saw me check the recorder, then licked his lips. "When you gonna run this story?"

"It has to be lawyered first."

He gave a short, ironic bark. "Why? I'm gonna sue you? Did you forget? We're friends."

"The paper has to have the lawyer go over a sensitive story like this. It'll probably run Sunday."

"This week?" He looked startled.

I nodded.

"That soon?" He seemed lost in thought.

He put both elbows on the table after a moment and leaned toward me.

"Look, Britt, I've been absolutely straight with you. Like always. I couldn't care more for you if you were my own kid. I know you have to do what you have to do. If our positions were reversed it would be the same thing. Do me one favor?"

"If I can."

"Give me a week. Sit on it for one week. It won't be any less of a story." His hands were clasped, eyes pleading.

I swallowed hard, eyes watery. "Can't do it, Daniel."

He reached over and pushed the recorder's STOP button, eyes grim. "Say you've got more reporting to do. Tell your editors it'll take you longer than you thought to write. One last favor for an old friend. We go back a long time. Trust me, Britt. I'm just asking for a week."

"I can't. My editors already know about it."

"Son of a bitch," he muttered. "You know all hell is gonna break loose when it hits the street. You always were stubborn. Always had to do things your way."

"I'm sorry." I held back the tears.

"You're just doing your job," he said wanly. "That's something I always liked about you, kid. You were always pushing, looking for the truth, reaching for the light." Slowly, he got to his feet. "More coffee?"

"No, thanks."

He took my empty mug anyway.

He returned from the kitchen with two full mugs and set one in front of me. He lifted his to his lips. "What's the matter?" he asked, as I hesitated. "You don't trust me?"

"We've been friends too long not to trust each other," I said, raising the cup.

The coffee was strong and good.

"You still carry your gun?" I asked.

"Nope. Only when I have to use it."

"Where do you keep it?"

He turned in his chair, opened a drawer in the sideboard against the dining room wall, lifted out a worn leather shoulder holster, unsnapped it, and withdrew the weapon. He placed it gently on the table, gleaming dark-blue steel, a handsome well-polished weapon, a tool for those who dispense justice. I imagined how it had looked to Farrington and Creech.

I reached across the table, touching his hand. "Dan, can I take the gun with me?"

"No. But don't worry, I won't get rid of it. And I won't eat it if that's what you're afraid of." His smile had no humor.

"Promise you won't try to hurt yourself."

"I wouldn't do that, and I'm telling you true." His eyes were steady.

I finished my coffee and he walked me to the door.

"So the story's gonna run Sunday?"

"As far as I know," I said.

"I'll need a lawyer," he said matter of factly. "What can they do to me? The death penalty? Sentence me to life? Nobody else sees the story till then?"

"Nobody outside of me and my editors and Mark, the paper's lawyer. I may have questions as I'm writing. Is it okay to call you?"

"Any time. I'll be here, Britt."

We hugged. I caught my breath and stepped out into the scalding sunlight. He's not afraid, I thought. He knows his life is ending, and he doesn't care.

21

The news meeting took place in a conference room. Fred, several assistant city editors, the managing editor, the state editor, the photo editor, the national editor, and Mark Seybold, the paper's in-house lawyer, attended.

They were elated by Dan's staggering admissions and by the fact that the police still had no clue that two of the three deaths were murders, much less by the same man, one of their own. I didn't share their exuberance.

"Will he pose for pictures?" asked Joe Hall, the photo editor.

I hated the thought. "We have a good one taken about two years ago when he broke that murder-for-hire case," I offered. "The one where the husband hired a hit man to kill his wife through a magazine ad."

I liked that photo: Dan, strong and in charge at the microphone at a press conference, the chief standing behind him.

"But we should have something new. Especially since you say he looks so different now," Hall said.

"He looks terrible," I said. "His heart is failing." This meeting was much more difficult than I had imagined.

"Let's get art of him at home," Fred said decisively. "You can talk him into it, Britt."

"Well," I said, uncertainly. "He knows Lottie. He'd probably agree if she was the photographer."

"Any chance he'll run or kill himself before we get into print?" the managing editor asked.

"I don't think so," I said, exhausted. "He promised he wouldn't. Where would he go? He's been straight about everything else."

"What if he dies?" somebody asked.

"Then we've got a deathbed confession," Fred replied.

This whole scenario seemed unreal, in a spacious conference room, bright sky and bay dominating the picture windows, discussing Dan's life and death with strangers who didn't know him, like he was a slab of meat, simply story fodder. He would never mean more to them than a Sunday headline.

"Worse, what if he picks up the phone and confesses to his old buddies in the department? Or spills it all to some TV reporter before we run the story?" asked the news editor.

"If investigators showed up, he wouldn't lie, but he won't call them—and I'm the only reporter he talks to." My voice sounded as weary as I felt. "He doesn't like TV."

"What are the chances of his hurting anybody else?" asked Mark, eyes thoughtful behind the lenses of his wire-rimmed glasses.

"Not when he knows we know. Besides, the guy's in bad shape," Fred said. He turned to me for confirmation.

"His feet and ankles are so swollen he couldn't even put his shoes on today," I said in a hushed voice. "He had to take a couple of nitro pills while I was there."

"Think it's true he didn't kill that German guy, the first one?" The news editor's eyes were narrow and suspicious.

"Yes. He says Steiner's accident gave him the idea."

"Maybe he's been doing this for years, all along, while he was still carrying a badge," said the state editor, a man I have never liked. "Who knows how many he's killed? What about his wife? Think he killed her? What did you say she died of, Britt?"

"She collapsed and died on the street of an aneurysm. He loved her very much. He's not a monster. He was a good cop, an honest-to-God hero who worked hard all his life."

Something in my tone of voice, or in my eyes, made him glance away and shut his mouth.

"A good cop." Fred nodded. "That's what makes this such a great story."

"We should call the cops for reaction," the managing editor said.

"If we do they may move fast, to defuse the impact of the story," Fred said.

"Right. Remember how the chief scooped us and called a press conference in the Brown case?" the news editor said. "That son of a bitch."

Muttered resentment echoed around the table.

"We can't give him that chance," the news editor said.

"Let's run it in the state edition, then have Britt call him for comment before the final."

"Yeah, he can't get the jump on us once it's already in the paper," Fred said. They all made sounds of agreement.

Fred turned to me. "Start writing, Britt. See if we can get art of the victims, Steiner as well, and set up art of Dan. We need the story as early as possible so we can look at it before leaving tonight."

"It's gonna take some time," I said reluctantly. "We'll need space. I want to do a sidebar on the big homicide cases Dan has solved over the years."

"Good idea. But do the main first."

I wanted readers to know how much more there was to the man and his life than just this summer. Reporting Dan's achievements was not only fair, it was the right thing to do.

"I'll be in promptly at ten in the morning to go over the copy," Mark told me.

"What do you think will happen to Flood after it runs?" Fred said. The editors, scraping back their chairs, paused.

"He's stoic," I said quietly. "Homicide will go into high gear because of the publicity. Detectives from the city and the county will surely meet with the state attorney and the medical examiner on Monday. They'll probably bring Dan in for questioning by Tuesday, Wednesday at the latest. I guess he'll be arrested and charged with murder. . . ." My voice trailed off. Fred's sharp glance forced me to continue. "They'll book him, but they won't put him in general population because as a cop he'd be in danger. It'll probably be a single safety cell near the nurse, where he can be watched because of his health."

I felt a catch in my throat. Saying it aloud made Dan's future real and imminent. It was impossible to envision him behind bars like the criminals he had put away for years. "Maybe his doctor will get involved," I said, "and they'll put him in the hospital. If his lawyer creates enough delays he'll never stand trial because of his physical condition. His life is over either way."

The room was silent.

"That's why he did it," somebody said. "A last hurrah."

"Hell of a story," somebody else muttered.

"I'm glad it's ours," Fred said. "Nice work, Britt."

I forced a smile.

Heavyhearted, I returned to my desk and reread all the old clips on Dan, the clips on all the cases, and my own notes before beginning. A rough version of the story was in the system by 6 P.M. and the sidebar by 7:30.

I thought about calling Dan to set up his picture but put it off. Onnie found mug shots that had run when Dieter Steiner and Benjamin Farrington were arrested. She also came up with a more recent likeness of Farrington, lifted from a group shot that had appeared in the business section.

We needed one of Creech, but I couldn't reach Ruby by phone and wondered if she had already left town. Onnie pulled the picture file of Darlene Fiskus, the murdered niece, and hit pay dirt: a news photo of the victim's family, shot near the site where her body was found. The mother was weeping, face in her hands, her husband's arms around her. Uncle Dirty, wearing a plaid shirt and a baseball cap, face averted from their pain, seemed to be gazing into the distance. He looked guilty as hell in retrospect.

I would go home, I decided, get some rest, and come in early to reread the story with fresh eyes before Mark arrived at 10 A.M. Then I would call Dan to ask any final questions and set up his appointment with Lottie for about eleven. I knew he would want to shave and dress for the picture. Any photo

Lottie took would be less demeaning for later use than a police mug shot with a number under his chin.

Lottie and I talked about it back in photo, before I went home.

"Damn it to hell, Britt, you were right. A-course, they probably should pin a medal on the man. Betcha somebody starts a Dan Flood Defense Fund."

"A lot of people will feel that way," I said bitterly. "We all want to rid the world of scumbags. Why didn't he just deny everything or refuse to talk to me?"

"Time's running out on him," she said. "Instead of just sitting home and waiting to die alone, he did something he thought he had to do and he's man enough to own up to it. Now he'll be back in the system, on the other side. But at least the system is something he knows. The devil you know is better than the devil you don't know."

I sighed, wondering where it would end. "I'll call him in the morning to say you're coming over."

"Sure, long as we do it by two o'clock or so, no problem."

At home, I took Bitsy out for a while, then took a long walk alone on the boardwalk, watching the light fade. Later I busied myself with a load of laundry and mindless household chores, trying not to think.

When I finally slept, I dreamed in headlines and bad news-speak: predawn fires, shark-infested waters, steamy tropical jungles, the solid south, mean streets, and densely wooded areas, populated by the ever-present lone gunman, fiery Cuban, deranged Vietnam veteran, Panamanian strongman, fugitive financier, bearded dictator, slain civil rights leader, grieving widow, struggling quarterback, cocaine kingpin, drug lord, troubled youth, and embattled mayor totally destroyed by Miami-based, bullet-riddled, high-speed chases, uncertain futures, and deepening political crises sparked by massive blasts, brutal murders, badly decomposed, benign neglect, and blunt trauma. I woke up nursing a dull headache and swallowed two aspirins before brushing my teeth.

While dressing, I stared in the mirror and slowly removed my necklace of red and white beads. About time you grew up, I told myself, and dropped it onto my dresser, where it lay coiled like a snake. I put the *resguardo* in a drawer and slammed it shut. On second thought, I reopened it, took the talisman out, and dropped it in the garbage, enjoying a sense of power over my own destiny. The danger from strangers is over, I thought. The people who can hurt you most are the ones you care about.

The radio broadcast sinister storm warnings and a tornado watch up and down the coast as I drove to the office, but the sky over Miami was hot, muggy, and clear as a bell.

I took a Danish and Cuban coffee to my desk and scrolled through the story several times, making minor fixes. At about nine, I dialed Dan's number. He usually answered quickly, but not this time. I dialed again, letting it ring, nine, ten, eleven times. No answer. He might be in the shower or out in the yard. He could have gone out for breakfast, I thought, or to the store.

I dialed back in twenty minutes. Then again at ten o'clock. Other reporters, editors, library staffers, and the city-desk clerk were drifting into the newsroom. As I read through the sidebar, my phone rang. Lottie wanted to know if I had made the assignment yet.

"He's not answering his phone. I'm worried."

"Keep trying," she said. "Maybe he turned it off and slept in. He could have gone to his doctor. He could be anywhere."

"Yeah, like on his floor unconscious. He told me he'd be there," I said anxiously. "Maybe he—" I didn't say the words aloud.

"Don't box shadows," Lottie said. "I have to head over to the Seaquarium to shoot the new baby manatee twins. Be back in an hour."

I printed out the stories for Mark. Dan still didn't answer. I checked with the police desk reporter, who said there had been no rescue or police calls at Dan's address.

Ryan had come in and appeared to be quarreling with Gretchen up at the city desk; unusual since the two had been on such good terms lately. Striding back in a snit, he flung what looked like a press packet onto his desk. "Why me?" he said. "I hate this damn stuff!"

"What?" I casually swiveled in my chair.

"Politics. I'm not a political writer and I hate this stuff. Here I am, assigned to this stupid—"

"What?" It made me smile to see normally sweet, gentle Ryan as mad as hell.

"The campaign for governor," he said, pouting. "Eric Fielding's here on a campaign swing, and I have to cover his damn speech." He shoved a notebook into his back pocket.

I was on my feet, gripped by a feeling of dread.

"Fielding in Miami? Where?"

I snatched the packet from his hand. He misunderstood my interest.

"Want to do it, Britt? You can take it. I hate politics."

"Where is he? When?"

"Here, at the Hilton. I have to get over there right now, if I'm going." He checked his watch. "He's speaking at a luncheon, the Biscayne Bay Club."

Hands shaking, I dialed Dan's number again. No answer.

"Do you want to take it or not?" Ryan looked impatient. I shook my head and he stomped toward the elevator.

Trying to stay calm, I dialed the number again, praying, letting it ring, whispering his name, willing him to answer. When I knew he wasn't going to, I panicked.

Mark was reading the printouts in Fred's office. I stuck my head in the door. "I have to go out for a while. I'll be back."

He smiled and nodded, thumbs up, indicating that what he'd read so far was okay.

I ran down the fire stairs, berating myself for not being smarter. When he asked for another week I had assumed it was to clear up his personal affairs before all hell broke loose. What if he wanted the time to seek street justice for the murder of Mary Beth Rafferty? Hers was the open case that troubled him most over the years. How could I be so blind?

He had told me himself that he couldn't stand to see Fielding become governor.

Breathless by the time I got to my car, I burned rubber leaving the parking lot. The T-Bird ate up the miles between the *News* and Dan's house as I cursed traffic and hapless weekend drivers. Please be there, Dan, I prayed.

The Buick was gone, the driveway empty. I knocked anyway, first with my fist, then with my heavy key ring. Peering in a living room window, I saw no one, then ran around and pounded on the back door. He could be inside. A mechanic might be working on his car. Maybe someone had borrowed it. I felt along the top of the doorframe and looked beneath the mat. People who live alone often hide spare keys in case they lock themselves out.

I groped around the roots of a dying spider plant in a hanging pot next to the door. Nothing. I looked furtively around. No one watching. The man who lives here is very sick, I thought, rehearsing my story if caught. He could be unconscious on the floor. I'm justified, I thought grimly, looking for something that would break glass. On impulse I tried the door. Unlocked. I pushed it open. The hinges pleaded for oil. "Danny?" I whispered. "Please be here."

I stepped into the kitchen. "Dan?" I called. "Are you home? Dan? You in here?" The coffeepot was cold. Not a smell, not a sound. Only the second hand of the clock above the sink.

"Dan!" I walked rapidly through the living and dining rooms. Checked the master bedroom. The bed was made. What must have been his daughter's room was now occupied only by old stuffed animals, gathering dust, staring back at me blindly. Tears stinging my eyes, I walked into the Florida room. Stacked on a neat and orderly desk were the scrapbooks we had never looked at and copies of police files. Dan's old cases.

One lay open, a brown file folder neatly labeled 71-1479—Mary Beth Rafferty.

I left at a run. Then a terrible thought occurred to me and I darted back to rifle through the drawer in the sideboard next to the dining room table. Nothing but woven place mats, napkin rings, and tea towels. No gun. "Damn you, Dan! Damn it!"

The Hilton was near the airport, a fifteen-minute drive at best. I backed out the driveway too fast, bouncing the T-Bird's undercarriage off the curb. I had thought he would stop. Instead, I had made it easier for him. He didn't even have to be careful anymore, because I already knew.

Fielding would be surrounded by press aides, campaign workers, and supporters. There would be no opportunity to corner him alone. But my story was about to appear; this was Dan's last chance. He wouldn't care if the world was watching.

I saw the flower beds bordering the Hilton's circular ramp up ahead and abruptly changed lanes. Sirens overtook me from behind. Oh, God, I thought. I abandoned my car on the ramp and ran toward the lobby. A security officer and a valet parking attendant waved their arms and shouted.

"Move it!" the valet yelled. "You can't leave it there. We've got an ambulance coming in!"

I tossed him the keys and kept running. Oh, no, I prayed. Left, past the gift shop, toward the main ballroom where the luncheon was scheduled. Other people running. A woman crying. A security guard blocked the door. "The *News*," I said, flashing my press card. He hesitated for a moment, uncertain. A policeman shouted, "Nobody gets in here!" Too late. I was inside.

A sea of people parted and I caught sight of Fielding's silver-gray hair. On his feet, unharmed, face stunned, he was being maneuvered toward the door by his people. "Bring the limo up," one yelled into his walkie-talkie.

" . . . obviously deranged . . ." I heard Fielding say as they whisked him by.

"What happened?" I asked a young man in a waiter's uniform.

"Some nut tried to attack the candidate," he said, "and Fielding's bodyguard shot him."

Two paramedics appeared through another door, beelining for a small anteroom behind the raised dais where the dignitaries' tables flanked the podium. I followed to where two other medics were already huddled over somebody stretched out on the lavender carpet. I saw the baggy gray suit and untied shoes that barely fit over his swollen feet.

The medics were cutting away his bloodied shirt. I dropped to my knees beside them. "This man's a heart patient," I said urgently. "He's seriously ill."

"That's not the issue right now. He's been shot. You know him?" a medic said.

The bullet hole, oozing blood, was on the right side of Dan's pale chest. Breathing rapidly, he was gasping for breath as one of the medics placed an oxygen mask over his face.

"Yes, he's a police officer, Miami homicide, recently retired." The medics reacted. One, in contact with the hospital, radioed that the patient was a police officer. That would guarantee a top-flight reception at the hospital, I thought. If Dan made it to the hospital.

The medics pressed a gauze dressing over the bullet hole.

"Start the IV with lactacted Ringer's solution and run it wide open," one directed.

"He tried to kill Eric Fielding, our next governor!" boomed a red-faced man who hovered over us, showering us with spittle. "I saw the whole thing."

"Who shot him?" I said.

"That fellow over there," he said, pointing at Martin Mowry, who looked exactly like his pictures. "Works for Fielding. The old guy walked up to Fielding, said something, and pulled a gun, and the other guy shot 'im."

Mowry, crew-cut, husky, and in his late thirties, had just removed his weapon from a shoulder holster and handed it over to one of several police officers surrounding him. Another officer had Dan's dark blue steel revolver.

Someone from the hotel staff had taken the podium and was announcing that the unfortunate incident was under control, the candidate had departed, and luncheon would be served. Nobody paid attention.

Dan's eyelids fluttered, and I took his right hand in both of mine. His bluish skin felt cold and clammy.

"Daniel. I'm here."

A medic radioed his vital signs ahead to the hospital: "BP is eighty over fifty, pulse one-twenty, respiratory rate is forty."

They glued three silver-dollar-sized pasties to his skin, to each side of his chest and his abdomen. Each was linked by an electrode to a machine the size of a boom box.

"I've got the heart monitor hooked up," one radioed. "Looks like sinus tachycardia."

"You were supposed to stay home," I said inanely, squeezing Dan's hand, "in case I had any questions."

He rolled his eyes as if to say it was just one of those things.

Because it was a chest wound they were in a big hurry to transport him to the trauma center. I heard them request air rescue but both choppers were tied up, ferrying traffic victims from the south end of the county. They wheeled him out on a stretcher, literally running him through the dining room and the lobby past hundreds of hostile, questioning, or curious eyes.

Running with them, I glimpsed Ryan with police and hotel officials but averted my eyes to stay with Dan.

They insisted I sit beside the driver when I wanted to ride with Dan in the back of the rescue van. A young policeman did climb in next to him, to take down any statements Dan made.

The siren's wail washed over us as traffic scattered in our path. The van speeded up, veered, and turned off an expressway exit as I clung to the door handle.

Dan was dying, I realized. And the son of a bitch who murdered Mary Beth Rafferty would go on to his next campaign stop en route to the governor's mansion. Where was the justice in that? Anger coursed through my veins and bubbled over into a decision.

We rolled up in front of the four-story trauma center in minutes, though it seemed longer. It always does. I scrambled out of the front as they unloaded him with all his attachments: IV, oxygen, and heart monitors. I held on to the side of his stretcher as he was rushed through the automatic doors, where a dozen people, all medical personnel, waited.

Dan reached up and pulled off his oxygen mask and I leaned down to listen. He tried to grin, eyes cloudy. "Ain't no retired Kamikaze pilots, Britt."

He did not look scared.

"Should I say a prayer, Dan?"

"Nope," he mumbled. "If I get reborn I'll be pissed off. Once is enough." I smiled, but I wanted to cry in pain and outrage.

The oxygen mask was pushed back in place and an officious nurse ordered me away. I had to tell him first. I whispered in his ear. "I'll do it, Dan. I'm going to get Fielding for you."

He looked confused but squeezed my hand. "I'll prove he did it," I said. "I'll find the kid, the witness, I swear. No way he'll win. I promise."

His eyes closed, but I knew he heard me.

The trauma team took over.

"Get me an arterial blood gas," a nurse commanded. A technician rolled up a portable x-ray unit. A doctor used his stethoscope. "I don't hear breath sounds on the right side. He's bleeding into his right chest. Get me a setup for a chest tube."

A nurse insisted I go to the waiting room. I wondered if I would see him alive again.

I called the city desk from a pay phone outside emergency and dictated what I had. My story on Dan would now run in the early edition, topped off by the new developments.

I took a cab back to the Hilton, picked up the T-Bird, and went to police headquarters. Only a skeleton crew mans homicide on weekends.

"I need to see an old file," I brashly told the young detective, "the Mary Beth Rafferty case. It was twenty-two years ago. Lieutenant McDonald said it would be okay."

"We don't keep files that old here, they'd be on microfilm at the warehouse. Takes about a week to order them," he said.

"No, it's an unsolved case. All unsolved cases stay here."

"But the press isn't authorized to see cases still under active investigation."

"Active investigation? It's twenty-two years old! I just need to check some background for a story about cold cases."

"You sure the lieutenant authorized it?"

"Would I be here if he hadn't?"

He disappeared into a storage room and came back with a fat file half a foot wide. "You're welcome to it. It's a big one."

I thumbed swiftly through the papers, fearing that Kendall McDonald, whose name I had taken in vain, might appear at any moment and catch me. He would surely respond to the news of Dan's attempt to shoot Fielding. Would he go to the hospital or come here?

I found what I was looking for among the photos: an old eight-by-ten glossy of a small boy with grave blue eyes. His young face looked frightened. His mother, a pretty, plumpish woman, held his hand, her other arm extended as though to ward off anyone approaching him. Her mouth was contorted as though in mid-protest.

An attached report listed her name, Mildred Van de Hyde, and that of her son, Robert. Bobby Van de Hyde. Skinny, he looked younger than eleven, and frail. I remembered Dan saying that the boy had been hit by a car once and nearly killed. That he had a severe limp.

I copied the names and address off the report, studied the faces in the old picture, and slid them back into the folder.

"That's all I need," I said brightly. The detective didn't even look up. Lieutenant Kendall McDonald was pushing his way through the glass door into the lobby as I left the station.

"Britt, did you hear about Dan?" His face was grim.

"How is he?" I said.

"In intensive care. This is incredible. I don't know what the hell is going on." He ran his fingers through his hair, eyes pained. "Somebody said he pulled a gun on Fielding! I don't believe it."

"Believe it, McDonald. We have a story running in the street edition."

"Well, I'm gonna find out what the fuck is happening and why some bastard shot him," he said, and stormed into the station.

I escaped. My beeper chirped persistently for the second time, and I turned it off. I knew they wanted me to work on the attempt on the candidate's life. If I returned to the paper I'd be drafted. My priorities were different.

I checked the phone book I keep in the car. No Van de Hyde. I stopped at a roadside booth and called the paper. Thank God Onnie was in the library.

"How is he?" she said.

"Still alive. Can you get the big blue crisscross directory?"

"Will do." She came back a minute later. "Got it."

"Okay." I gave her the Van de Hydes' old address. She found it. A four-unit apartment complex, she said.

"Who lives there now?"

She rattled off the names and phone numbers as I took notes and dug quarters from the depths of my purse. One tenant never heard of Mildred or Bobby. Another did not answer. The third, an older man, remembered them well.

"Are they still in Miami?"

"They live down on Malagon just off LeJeune," he said. "Bought a little place."

"Where?" I said. "I can't find them in the phone book."

"A little house," he said. "Between Thirty-seventh and Thirty-ninth avenues, somewhere in there, a little yellow house. The son fixes appliances; he repaired a radio and a clock for me."

I called Onnie back. "The city desk is looking for you," she said.

"I know, don't mention that you heard from me. Check Malagon, between Thirty-seventh and Thirty-ninth avenues."

I listened to her breathe, murmuring names as she followed the street down the directory listings. "Got it," she said, "Mildred and Robert Van de Hyde: Thirty-seven seventy-four Malagon. Phone unlisted. They still lived there as of last February, when this directory came out."

"I love you, Onnie."

I took the airport expressway to LeJeune, drove south, and made a left on Malagon.

The house was small, square, and stucco, freshly painted a bright sunshine yellow with white trim. This was better than calling first anyway, I told myself. Why give the kid time to think about it or discuss it with his mother? He's had twenty-two years to think about it.

I parked on the street, walked up to the front door, and rang the bell. I heard a slight sound and felt myself scrutinized through the peephole in the door.

"Who is it?" a male voice asked.

I identified myself and the door inched open. The same grave blue eyes and serious look as in the old picture. The sandy hair had darkened but was still tousled. Slightly sharper features than in the childhood photo, but the face was still boyish. I would have recognized him anywhere.

"Bobby Van de Hyde," I said, smiling.

"I'm familiar with your work." He smiled back. "I read your stuff all the time." His eyes and voice were gentle.

Flattered, my heart sang. We seemed to share an almost instant rapport. Maybe, I thought, this will be easier than I dreamed.

Loose and friendly, he looked more slim now than skinny. In his blue jeans and Miami Hurricanes T-shirt, he exuded a wholesome collegiate appearance.

"I'm so glad to meet you, Bobby," I said. "I want to talk to you about what happened twenty-two years ago."

He nodded slightly, looking thoughtful. "I'd like that." Stepping back, he opened the door wide. "I wondered why nobody came sooner. Come on in."

Tense and thrilled, I followed. He still limped, favoring his right leg. Along one side of the room was a worktable on which a small radio and a toaster were disassembled. There was a soldering iron, a voltmeter, tweezers, long-nose pliers, screwdrivers, transistors, capacitors, and wires. The furniture was simple and inexpensive. I sat on the couch, placed my notebook on the coffee table in front of me, and uncapped my pen.

He sat in a brown leatherette chair across from me, his expression open and earnest, happy to see me. I scarcely knew where to start.

"Bobby, I know you still remember after all these years, and I want you to tell me about Mary Beth's murder. It's important."

"I know." He paused for a moment, then rested his head in his hands. "I didn't mean to kill her."

22

Stunned, I managed to whisper, "Well, why did you? Let's talk about it."

He raised his eyes, speaking softly, the fingers of both hands intertwined, elbows on his knees. "She kept screaming and screaming. She wouldn't stop, and this guy was coming on a bicycle. I had to keep her quiet. I didn't want anybody to know. So I did it. He went on down the bike path and never saw us."

I pried my tongue loose from the roof of my mouth. "Fielding," I said. "Fielding came back and found her body."

Bobby nodded, one hand kneading the other in his lap.

"All these years, you never told anyone?"

He looked shy. "My mom didn't want me to. She said they'd put me in jail and I'd never see her again."

"You were only a child," I said. "I'm sure that wouldn't have happened."

He wrinkled his brow, his expression curious. I looked around.

"What kind of work do you do? Do you have a job?"

He studied the floor. "Not exactly. My mom always wanted me to stay home since it happened, so I wouldn't get in any more trouble. But I fix things for people, for neighbors."

He indicated the worktable, where he had apparently been occupied before I arrived.

"It's hard to get things fixed these days," he explained. "My mom says we're a throw-away society. Nobody wants to fix anything, they just encourage customers to buy new toasters, tape recorders, radios. Everybody has small appliances that don't work, that with minor repairs would be as good as new. I have a knack for it, my mom says. I'm good at figuring out how things work. That's what I do."

"You're right," I said. "I tried to get a steam iron repaired once, and I couldn't find anybody to do it. They all said it wasn't worth it, I should buy a new one."

"Betcha I coulda fixed it," he said proudly.

I was like a duck, calm on the surface, paddling like crazy underneath.

"Bobby," I said, leaning forward, "I think it's good for you to talk about Mary Beth Rafferty. It's time. Everybody will feel better, especially you. You could finally put it behind you."

He nodded pensively, then his expression changed.

A sound or perhaps a presence startled me. Or maybe it was the look of guilt in Bobby's eyes. We were no longer alone.

A woman stood behind me, to my left, in the doorway to what I assumed was the kitchen. The other person in the picture taken twenty-two years ago. Bobby's mother was no longer pretty and plump. Heavyset now, she wore her shoulder-length hair caught in a net and pulled back. It was dyed black, each strand the same flat dark shade. She looked in her mid-fifties, though she might have been slightly older. Her slacks stretched taut across heavy thighs, and a plastic ID badge from Morningside Elementary School was pinned to her white blouse.

I wondered how much of our conversation she had overheard. The hostile look in her eyes was not promising. Mouth open, she was panting slightly as though from overexertion.

"Is this your mom?" I said, trying to project an innocent, friendly impression as I beamed, stood, and extended my hand.

"Who is she, Bobby?" She remained in the doorway, ignoring me, staring accusingly at her son. "What are you doing?" She directed her questions at Bobby, as though I weren't there.

"She wanted . . . to know about Mary Beth," he sputtered, his voice defensive. "She's from the newspaper."

Not exactly the words I would have chosen.

"What have you done?" she exploded.

"Hi," I said. "Your son and I were just chatting, Ms. Van de Hyde. I'm working on a story about Mr. Fielding, the candidate. There was a tragedy today, someone was shot—"

"How dare you sneak into my house and badger my son!" Her tone was protective, and she took an angry step forward.

"I didn't sneak in," I said evenly, trying to stand my ground and still sound reasonable. "I'd really like very much to sit down and talk to both of you."

"Why?" Her suspicious eyes measured me, taking in the notebook on the coffee table, my car keys on the sofa where I'd been sitting.

"I'm a reporter for the *News*." I dug in my pocket and offered my card.

If she throws me out, I worried, she'll probably see that nobody gets near Bobby for another twenty years.

"You have no right to come in here. We're not interested in any story," she said sharply, ignoring the card in my outstretched hand.

"I think it might be good for your son." I looked to him for support, affirming my fears. At my first exchange with his mother he had begun to rise from his chair, then froze halfway in a semicrouched position, eyes darting between us. The poor soul literally didn't know whether to sit down or stand up. So much for enlisting his aid to convince his mother that the three of us should have a cozy chat.

"I know what's good for Bobby," she said, voice suddenly resigned. "But he can do whatever he likes. I have groceries to put away." She smiled, looking almost hospitable. "Perhaps we can talk another time." She turned and disappeared into the room from which she had come.

Surprised and relieved, I returned to the sofa. Bobby had sunk back into his chair, eyes shifting nervously between me and the kitchen door.

"Bobby, it's okay." He either didn't hear or didn't believe me. The best move would be to get him the hell out of here, I thought. "Let's go out somewhere for a cup of coffee or a sandwich. Would you like that? I saw a Denny's just a couple of blocks away." I snatched up my car keys. Once in the car I wouldn't stop at the neighborhood restaurant, I'd suggest another place where there was no danger of his mother barging in on us, perhaps close to police headquarters.

I smiled at Bobby, wondering why my suggestion caused such a look of horror on his face. The flash in my peripheral vision told me it was not what I had said but something he saw behind me.

She moved amazingly fast. Pain seared my left shoulder just below the neck. The woman had a butcher knife! Had I not turned, the blade would have caught me in the spinal column at the base of the skull.

My cry was more in shock than pain. The sleeve of my cotton dress was wet. Flinging myself back, I rolled to the side in an attempt to evade the slashing blade, leaving a smear of blood on the sofa cushion.

"What are you doing?" I cried, staggering to my feet, the coffee table between us.

Breathing hard, she stood with legs apart, eyes bright with anger, the knife still clutched tightly in her hand.

"Are you crazy?" I reached with my right hand and touched my left shoulder. Blood dripped down my arm. "Bobby?" I turned to him for help.

He sat mesmerized, wide eyes on his mother.

"You're not writing a story," she hissed, spitting venom. "You think I spent my life protecting my son so you could waltz your ass in here and send him to jail?"

Fear made my knees shake. I stepped back, hands raised waist high in front of me. Still in his chair, Bobby looked agitated. "It wasn't my fault!" he cried.

Both were between me and the door. "No one would hurt you," I said weakly. "You were a child. You wouldn't go to jail."

"A hospital, Bobby, they'd put you in a hospital with crazy people. You'd never get out." Her eyes remained on me.

I turned to Bobby, whose face was flushed. "If you had talked to the police when it happened you'd be free now, you'd have a normal life."

His eyes looked wild. He opened his mouth to say something, and I broke past him for the door.

"Get her, stop her, Bobby!" she howled.

I stumbled against him, shoving him back into his chair as he rose, regained my footing, and reached the door. I turned the knob, fumbling frantically. It wouldn't open.

Bobby sprang to his feet, his mother screaming orders. We grappled at the door, and when he raised his right hand, I saw he had snatched a hammer from his worktable.

The blow glanced sideways off my forehead, buckling my knees. Darkness closed in, then receded as I fought to stay conscious. I sank to the floor, Bobby on top of me, shoving me back, straddling my body, pinning my shoulders.

I saw his mother's scuffed Nikes rapidly approach at eye level and knew she was going to kill me, plunge the knife over and over into my body.

"No!" I gasped. His knee in my midsection, fists on my shoulders, he looked up at his mother, the eyes of a child seeking approval. They focused, along with mine, on the knife in her hands.

"The carpet," she said tersely. "We don't want her to ruin the carpet. Get the tape," she said. "Hurry!"

I felt the pressure relieved as he got up, but, before I could react or inhale a full breath, a crushing weight forced the air out of my lungs with a *whoosh*.

The woman was crouched on my chest, pinning my arms at odd angles. I couldn't breathe, much less scream. My lungs cried out for air, and I felt excruciating pain where she had stabbed me. Their voices sounded distant; I couldn't make out the words. The knife flashed above me as I winced and closed my eyes expecting to feel the blade. Nothing. I opened my eyes. She was using it to slash lengths of black plastic electrical tape from a roll. She began wrapping it around me, covering my mouth. I was swimming just this side of consciousness when the weight lifted from my chest and I was rolled over. My face lay against the fuzzy fibers of the carpet.

As my ankles and wrists were bound, somebody's fingers ran lightly, exploring up my leg to my inner thigh. I wanted to scream but couldn't. I was still trying with all my being to catch my breath.

Bobby's feet emerged from a bedroom. He was carrying a pink chenille bedspread that dragged across the carpet like a flowing robe. "Here."

I heard her grunt. "Lay it flat." They spread it out on the floor as I strained to watch, trying to raise my head. I was rolled up in the spread, dragged across the floor, and shoved into the bottom of a closet. The door closed and it was dark.

My legs were bent uncomfortably under me and the lint from the spread made my eyes tear and blink. I lay there in shock, catching my breath, trying to think. Would anyone look for me? Could anyone find me? There was no way anybody heard my few brief screams. Would they kill me? My eyes burned with tears. The woman is crazy, I thought. Could she be that crazy? My shoulder ached.

Dan was wrong all along. So was I. Was he still alive? How long would I be? With bitter irony I remembered the red and white beads tossed carelessly onto my dresser, the *resguardo* cast aside.

Would anyone miss me before it was too late? Who would know where to look? Onnie had no reason to remember the address she had looked up for me, much less divulge it to the city desk. I had warned her not to say she had heard from me.

The ebb and flow of voices continued for a time outside my small dark prison. A door slammed. The house was silent. What if they were leaving town and going into hiding? How long before anybody came? Too long. Too late for me.

My left leg numbed, as though asleep, but there was no way in my cramped position to relieve the pressure. After what seemed almost an hour later I alerted to a sound. My ears strained, every nerve ending tensed. A door slammed. Footsteps. The closet door opened, then closed again.

Minutes later it opened again and I was dragged out. They will kill me, I thought, and I can do nothing. Dragged by my feet through the house, over the threshold, bounced down three steps, I whimpered into the tape covering my mouth. Then I was lifted by two people and slung unceremoniously into something. The bedspread had come loose and was tossed on top of me. Hands forced me down. A lid slammed shut. I was in the trunk of a car.

Pitch dark and cramped, it smelled of stale air and exhaust fumes. I suddenly thought about my laundry, left in the dryer. Billy Boots and Bitsy hadn't been fed since morning. Would I ever see them again?

I tried to roll into a more comfortable position and my face pressed against something with the faint aroma of suntan oil, sand, and salty sea. My beach bag. I was in the trunk of my T-Bird! Somebody slid into the driver's seat. The car rocked gently. The door slammed. I heard the rattle of keys.

The engine started and the T-Bird backed out. Where are they taking me? I wondered, as panic overwhelmed me. Only one person had climbed into the car. If it was Bobby, I could try to reason with him. But I had to get the tape off my mouth first. I've seen some agile police prisoners maneuver handcuffed wrists down under their feet and bring their hands up in front. Bracing against the spare tire's raised wheel well, I tried again and again, until I thought I had dislocated both shoulders. My shoulder ached and bled. Not enough room for the necessary contortions. I had to try something else.

I was bound and gagged with electrical tape, relatively pliable and stretchy. Free of the bedspread, I could try to work on it. The tape wound around my wrists and ankles had already loosened slightly, so that it was not cutting off circulation.

I remembered that inside the trunk lid were cutouts with relatively sharp metal edges. Rolling onto my stomach, back aching in the cramped quarters, shoulder on fire, I lifted my wrists, groping. When I found one of the cutouts, I began sawing the tape against it.

The position was so uncomfortable that I had to stop after two or three minutes. Hyperventilating, I couldn't breathe. I squirmed until my head rested on my beach towel. I visualized it to calm myself: MIAMI BEACH in big blue letters, with a huge smiling dolphin. What would my father do? Never surrender, I knew that. He had engineered an escape for himself and other political prisoners from the infamous Isle of Pines prison. If he could do it, so could I.

I went back to work, sawing my wrists against the metal, trying to create as little noise and motion as possible. A loop of tape gave way. The rest slackened and unraveled. I manipulated my wrists and it fell away. My freed hands tore at the tape covering my mouth. I gratefully inhaled gulps of air and exhaust fumes for several minutes, licking my dry lips. The tape hung limply around my throat. I wished my Aunt Odalys's beads hung there instead.

I prayed Bobby was behind the wheel.

I took a deep breath. "Bobby," I called feebly. "Bobby, help me."

No answer, but the car slowed down.

My voice grew stronger. "Listen to me, Bobby. You were a juvenile. If you had told the police what happened when Mary Beth died you might have spent a little time in custody. At worst, until you were eighteen. But you'd be free now. Free of your mother, with a life of your own."

Something slammed hard against the back seat and the car swerved sharply. The sudden movement combined with the exhaust fumes made me nauseous.

"Shut up!" Mildred Van de Hyde screamed. "Shut up!"

My blood froze, my stomach churning.

"I have a gun!" she shouted, her voice full of fury. "Shut up, bitch, or I'll pull over and empty it into the trunk."

I closed my eyes, sweat and tears flooding my face.

Godammit, I thought, I never let anybody drive my T-Bird. I was glad she had to drive without airconditioning.

She slowed to a stop, probably for a traffic light. I kicked and pounded my fists as hard as I could to attract attention, hurling myself against the trunk lid. My chances of survival if I fell into traffic would be better than at our destination.

No more stops. We were on the expressway. Traffic sounds around us. What if we had an accident? What if the car caught fire? Forcing claustrophobic thoughts from my mind I worked on freeing my ankles.

The early edition must be on the street by now. Did anyone miss me? The woman at the wheel must suspect that my hands were free. Surprise would have worked to my advantage. Still might. When she opened the trunk, it would be just the two of us. If I could burst out like gangbusters and run, she wouldn't catch me. Age and weight were against her. Did she really have a gun? Mine was at home, with my beads and *resguardo*, I thought bleakly. At least it was not in the glove compartment where she could find it and use it against me.

My ankles loose at last, I massaged my fingers and toes and found my right shoe, which had come off. I tried to stretch my muscles and prepare for what was to come. My shoulder hurt but the bleeding had stopped.

Something dug into my back. The tire iron. My fingers closed around the cool metal.

Traffic noise faded. We bounced down what must be an unpaved road. The car finally stopped, engine off. Silence, just the creaks and cooling-down sounds of the T-Bird. I held my breath, listening.

Finally, she moved about in the seat, got out, and slammed the door. I braced, gripping the tire iron, dread growing inside me. Then I heard another car, another door slamming. My heart quickened, then sank. It was Bobby.

Still two against one. He must have followed in their car. I listened hard but couldn't quite make out their words. Then the voices grew louder, coming closer.

I braced again, gritted my teeth, adrenaline pumping, the tire iron in both hands.

Another false alarm. The driver's side door crunched open, but no one got in. What was going on? The engine sprang to life and the car lurched forward, though I was sure no one was at the wheel. The car took flight and the front end dropped into space. I heard laughter. When I heard the splash I knew what they had done.

Suddenly the T-Bird was sinking in water. I remembered the remains of Paul Eldridge in his long-sunken car and panicked. I had lost the tire iron and groped for it in a frenzy. A world away, I heard car doors slam, an engine start and race away.

The T-Bird floated, nose down. I heard water rushing into the passenger compartment. Sobbing, I finally found the tire iron, reached up, and frantically pried at the catch on the trunk lid with the tool's tapered end. Water rose around me. The back end slowly began to settle and the water showered in from around the trunk seal.

I pushed with one final effort, shoulders against the lid, and the trunk sprang open, yawning wide, air and water falling across my face. For a moment I was not sure it had opened. Darkness still enveloped me like a hood. Then I saw stars twinkling in the night sky above and the moon trapped in the tangled branches of distant treetops. In water up to my armpits, I leaned forward and kicked free of the car as it descended like an elevator on the way down.

My T-Bird gurgled, bubbled, and was gone, leaving little whirlpools behind. Kicking harder, I grasped the stems of straggly growths on the bank, to avoid being sucked down with it. My right foot gained purchase on a piece of shale jutting from the gravelly bank. My shoulder burned, I was shaky and exhausted, and my wet clothes seemed to weigh a ton.

Fingers clawing at the earth and the grassy outcroppings on the steep bank, I heard whimpering and stopped to listen before realizing it was me. I choked into a fearful silence, the night heavy and hushed around me. I had to be sure they were gone. I scarcely breathed as, slowly, the night sounds disrupted by the intrusion resumed.

Hand over hand, aching all over, I dragged myself up and finally collapsed, panting, onto solid ground in a bed of weeds. Somehow I forced myself to my feet, shivering in the heat, chilled to the bone.

They were gone. They got away. Anger and indignation replaced my weariness. They think I drowned. That they're home free. I'll show them, I thought, knees shaking.

Dark woods surrounded me. I had no idea where I was. This looked like one of the state water management district canals that crisscross the Everglades. They have imaginative names like C-54 and C-115. This one could be in west Broward, through it was probably Dade County. It didn't seem that we had driven much more than twenty-five minutes, maybe less. Time moves slowly when you are afraid and in the dark.

The dirt road was barely discernible in the shadows. If I followed it, a main drag could not be far off. I tried to wring out my skirt as best I could. My feet slipped around on the slick soles of my wet sandals and made squeaky sounds as I walked.

I rubbed my shoulder, which still oozed blood. I'll need a tetanus shot, I thought, hating the idea. Soaking wet and filthy, I wondered if any motorist would help me. I would soon find out. If no one picked me up, I might be able to persuade somebody to call the police. There might be a house or even a gas station just beyond the trees, I thought hopefully.

I took one last look at the eddies still rippling the smooth surface of the canal in the moonlight. Some water management canals are thirty feet deep. My T-Bird. The best car I ever had. I turned and began to stumble down the road in the dark.

23

The wary middle-aged couple who eventually picked me up were quite relieved to drop me at a pay phone on Krome Avenue, the first vestige of civilization coming east out of the Everglades.

A patrol car arrived in minutes. I told them that Bobby and his mother got away. They told me different.

Detectives heard I was missing after the early edition hit the street. At the hospital, Dan told them I went to find Bobby. They were at the Van de Hyde house when he and his mother showed up. Once separated, Bobby couldn't confess fast enough.

I asked about Dan.

Visitors are permitted in intensive care for the first ten minutes of each hour. He opened his eyes when I touched his hand. He looked gray and absolutely helpless. I didn't look so hot myself.

He squinted. "Happened to you?" His words were as dry as leaves.

As I told him everything, some of the light came back into his eyes.

"Oh, no. Jesus," he groaned when I told him Bobby had killed Mary Beth Rafferty. "All this time, I thought—"

"The important thing is, it's solved now. There *is* justice."

A nurse wanted me to leave.

I said goodbye. My ear to his lips, Dan whispered, "I'm on the ropes. This is it, kid."

"Go for the light, Dan," I said, "go for the light."

He wanted to say one more thing. I leaned over him.

"I'm gonna beat the system," he gasped, attempting a grin.

He was right.

He slipped away four hours later at 3 A.M., before murder charges could be filed.

I've thought a lot about Daniel P. Flood since his death, mostly remembering conversations and memorable moments. How he would use the radio mike in his car like an electric razor to make me laugh, and how it never failed. How I had run into him late one night in a twenty-four-hour drugstore, big and hulking, fresh from a gang murder, poring over Mother's Day cards, actually reading the verses, before selecting the perfect endearment for his wife. How he swerved to avoid the migrating land crabs one night when I rode with him as an observer. How he had helped a young reporter on stories she never could have nailed down otherwise.

How he had spent his entire life believing in the system, deciding only at the end that it didn't work.

We have all lost something. Nobody but Dan remembered so many old murder mysteries that might still be solved one day, stories that might have endings if only someone cared and persisted long enough. He was a bridge back to another era, when Miami was another world, before the mass immigration, before the drug wars, before affirmative action. But like the dinosaur, he was doomed to extinction.

My T-Bird was recovered from the canal several days later, a total loss. Lottie was a comfort. "It ain't nothing but a thang," she said when I wept. She was right and I knew it. Seeing my car again made me realize once more how lucky I am to be alive. Life is a death-defying experience. My tears were for more than that piece of metal. My ruined car was a symbol of everything lost that summer.

Fred Douglas called me into his office when I returned to work. He looked somber, a sheaf of official-looking papers on the desk in front of him. "Britt, both the Miami and Metro-Dade police departments have filed formal protests with the managing editor about your behavior."

I rolled my eyes and opened my mouth to protest, but Fred held up his hand.

"I'm not finished."

I shifted impatiently in my chair. My shoulder ached under the bandage. As he shuffled the papers, my eyelid began to twitch.

"So has the state attorney." As I began to react, he stopped me again.

Lord, what next? I thought.

"So has Eric Fielding's office."

"Fielding!" I yelped. "He should be grateful, for God's sake. He was a suspect for more than twenty years. We proved he didn't kill that little girl. He should love us."

"He's not grateful that you did it now, during his campaign."

"So?"

"No denying he was the suspect, but it was never reported in the media and the voters didn't know it. Now he's been publicly linked to the case and the world knows he was a suspect. Even though he's cleared, he feels the connection taints him in the eyes of some voters."

"He should love us," I repeated indignantly.

"He doesn't. The police and the state attorney are mad as hell that you didn't bring all your information and suspicions to them so they could have—"

"I know, I know," I said impatiently. "Anything else?" I rubbed my eyelid, beginning to feel really irritated.

"One more thing," he said, consulting the papers in front of him. "You have a ten percent raise effective in this week's paycheck."

I stared at him. "I'm not due for my annual increase until May."

"This is a merit raise, but don't discuss it in the newsroom, for pete's sake. The consensus upstairs is that when the cops and the politicians are all furious enough to lodge complaints, we know you're out there doing the job."

I thanked him, rose to leave, and then stopped. "What did you tell them?"

"Who?"

"When they complained. What did you tell them?"

"That an editor would counsel you. Consider yourself counseled."

"Okay."

"One more thing," he said. "Take the rest of the day and tomorrow off, comp time."

"This all right with Gretchen?"

"We'll make it all right."

"You sure? She wanted me to help with the weather story. Janowitz is on vacation, and the first hurricane of the season is out there somewhere."

"Don't worry about the storm, Britt. Miami hasn't had a hurricane in thirty years."

"Okay, I can use the time, gives me a chance to car-shop."

I stepped back out into the newsroom.

Lottie was waiting, leaning on the edge of my desk, long legs crossed, arms folded. "You hear Bobby had a court appearance this morning? He's being held without bond. Hopefully they'll put him in a cell with the Downtown Rapist."

Poor Bobby, I thought. "Even behind bars he's probably freer than he's been for a long time," I said, gathering up my things.

"Where you headed?"

"I'm off," I said. "Taking a cruise."

"Hell-all-Friday, it's about time you took a vacation."

"Don't get excited. It's no big deal."

She looked puzzled.

"It's not a long cruise, just around Biscayne Bay Didn't you notice? There's a full moon tonight."

She smiled and winked. "Bon voyage, Britt."